W   Broome, H. B.

         The man who had
         enemies

DATE DUE			
DEC 13 88			
DEC 27 88			
FEB 17			
MAR 10			
NOV 15 1991			
APR 2 1992			

The Man Who Had Enemies

Also by H. B. Broome

GUNFIGHTERS
THE MEANEST MAN IN WEST TEXAS

The Man Who Had Enemies

H. B. BROOME

A Doubleday D Western Book

Doubleday

NEW YORK   LONDON   TORONTO   SYDNEY   AUCKLAND

A Doubleday D Western Book

Published by Doubleday, a division of
Bantam Doubleday Dell Publishing Group, Inc.
666 Fifth Avenue, New York, New York 10103

Doubleday D Western, Doubleday, and the portrayal of the
letters DD are trademarks of Doubleday, a division of
Bantam Doubleday Dell Publishing Group, Inc.

Library of Congress Cataloging-in-Publication Data
Broome, H. B.
The Man Who Had Enemies.

(Double D western)
I. Title.
PS3552.R6598D44   1988   813'.54   88-3749
ISBN 0-385-24170-4

OG

For Marian Broome

CHAPTER ONE

Ben Jordan stretched out for his regular-as-clockwork nap in the relative coolness of the shaded back porch. The sheriff of Tom Green County, with his headquarters in Santa Rita, had once served as the marshal who maintained law and order in this part of West Texas. He slumped on the old sprung day bed—legs spraddled, head back. In minutes his mouth hung open, as it always did when he slept, and his snores vibrated gently. Ben's widowed sister, Abigail Lester, who lived with him and took care of him, raised hell about this habit, and the people smiled while she complained, "Every dad-blamed afternoon of the world, there he is, dead to the world, slack-jawed and happy!"

Near the gully about two hundred yards away, a stranger sat on his dusty brown mare. He leaned down, first to one side, then the other, removing his spurs, and then he dropped them into one of his saddlebags. The leather creaked as he stepped off, putting all his weight in the left stirrup. As he tied his reins firmly to a mesquite tree, a small dog fidgeted across the dry ground and began to yap at his heels. The stranger turned and bent down, extending his leather-gloved left hand invitingly. The brindled mutt began to wag its tail with such energy that its whole body twisted enthusiastically. Then it wriggled forward to lick at the glove. The stranger clenched the loose skin at the back of the little mongrel's neck, jerked it from the ground and with one quick motion of his right hand slid the blade of his sharp knife across the animal's throat. The dog, kicking wildly, blood spurting, rolled down the gulley's steeply inclined bank and lay still except for its last quivering, the twitches that muscles somehow make after death.

The stranger didn't clean the blood off the blade of his knife before sliding it back into its sheath. He hurried then: untying a blanket-wrapped bundle from behind his saddle and taking a heavy green bottle from it. He walked with this across the hard, grassless earth, and silently opened the door to the porch where Ben Jordan slept. He stood there, as silent as a shadow, listening to the fluttered snores. He unscrewed the bottle's cap with extreme care, and when the top came off he jerked his head back because of the fumes. Then, holding the open container at arm's length, he tiptoed to the side of the day bed. Someone looking in would have thought he looked solicitous, taking great care not to disturb the old lawman's sleep.

The bottle spilled its steaming contents into Ben Jordan's open mouth. Some splashed across his face when the first whiplash of pain yanked his horrified eyes open.

The awful shrieks Ben made must have covered the sounds of the stranger's flight: dropping the heavy green bottle to the built-up plank floor, letting the spring on the porch door slam it shut. Abigail didn't hear these things; she didn't hear the murderous stranger's horse clatter into a headlong run as the man fled, a wild expression in his eyes.

Bursting onto the porch she saw her brother standing, clutching at his face, screaming hoarsely before he spun down and began rolling as the sulphuric acid burned its way through his face and throat and stomach. It took a full five minutes for him to stop kicking, with Abigail's frail old body spread out awkwardly upon his bulk, trying to hold him, trying to still his agony, her cries blending with his. Then he lay there quivering and jerking, just like the dog.

CHAPTER TWO

I leaned forward as my big buckskin broke into a full run, crashing through and over bushes and small mesquite trees. The animal's power surged under me, and I heard the horse's heaving breath and the clash of branches whipping closed behind my back. Mesquite thorns tore at my arms and rasped across my leather leggings and boots. Ducking instinctively to my right, I missed by inches being knocked out of the saddle by a hackberry limb. Swinging back up and forward, I pulled my rope free of the saddle strings. Holding the coiled lariat and reins in my left hand, I shook out a wide loop with my right.

Exploding into a clearing, the buckskin's muscles bunched as he jumped a narrow draw, gaining rapidly on the scrambling maverick. My loop flew in a wide-spread oval and hooked over the horns. I took three quick dallies around the saddlehorn and hauled back on the reins. The buckskin braced and took the shock, and the yearling, hitting the end of the rope, yanked sideways, feet in the air, and slammed down hard upon the ground. Before the heifer could regain her feet I spun down from my horse, tie-string clamped between my teeth, and ran along the length of the tightly strung rope, held taut by the well-trained cow pony that backed up, dragging the big calf. I reached the struggling creature and in seconds latched the tie-string around three of its kicking feet. The helpless animal twisted on its side as I turned to its head and recovered the lariat's loop.

Brush popped as the cowboys riding with me broke into the clearing and pulled up their horses.

"God a'mighty, Tom!" Pepe Moya yelled at me, "You're gonna get yourself killed riding that way."

Luis Batalla stepped down from his lather-streaked bay, grinning the way he usually does. He said to Pepe, "It'll take more than a horse to kill Tom English."

Luis built a fire of twigs and dried branches. Smoke rose as yellow flames licked around a short-handled, blackened branding iron that gradually began to turn a deep red in the center and almost white around the edges. Moments later the Lazy E brand, the one used on all but two of my ranches, sizzled as it burned through the hair and into the hide of the calf's hip.

Pepe pulled his knife from its sheath at his belt and notched our mark, two vee cuts, in the heifer's left ear. Then he pulled the tie-string free and the yearling scrambled up awkwardly, rear end first, and ran off on gangly, trembling legs, shaking its head and bawling what I guess were cow cusswords.

The Mexican cowboy, one knee on the ground, wiped his blade across a clump of buffalo grass, then finished the job by whetting its razor-sharp edge slowly back and forth across the leather chaps on his right leg.

We hunkered down on our boot heels after this, talking softly to each other. I don't know why it is, but everyone probably has experiences like the one I had then. The realization hit me all of a sudden: I'm going to remember this. I had a deep sense of peace, a knowledge of how good it is to be alive. We needed to get on with our work but we put it off, savoring the moment. Time slowed down for us, and the sun's warmth pressed through the denim shirt and across my back. It had been a long time since my splintered nerves had allowed me to enjoy something as simple as an ordinary day.

A branch cracked behind us, and I rose, hand jerking reflexively to the butt-end of my Colt. Then, to my amazement I saw my wife walking her little sorrel mare toward us. Sally leaned back, balancing her distended stomach before her. She looked very pale, and as she neared I saw her face glistening with perspiration.

"Something has happened," she said as I held my arms up to help her down.

"You're too far along to be on horseback," I said. Then, suddenly angry, I burst out, "You almost lost Rebecca, and Doc Starret warned you—"

"Tom," she broke in, putting her arm on my sleeve. "Ben Jordan is dead."

I stood there, stunned, looking into her face, unable to accept what I had heard.

Sally put her arms around my neck. "Manuelito brought the news—he nearly killed that little pony of his on the trip to the ranch from town." Her voice broke as she added, "I couldn't let anyone else tell you."

"Ben had a good life," I finally was able to say, "but I thought he had a few more years."

Tears welled in Sally's eyes and she buried her head on my chest. In a small voice she said, "Someone killed him, Tom. Someone poured acid down his throat."

The sound of horses' hooves made a muffled drumbeat on the trail. Six of us rode in a stretched-out ragged line, jolting along in that traveling trot which horses can maintain for hours. Luis rode point, about a quarter mile ahead, and Pepe ranged behind us. Every man wore a six-gun and carried his rifle in a saddle scabbard. Ever since the trouble in Montana I've lived this way, surrounded by what some call my palace guard. More like an irregular detachment of Mexican cavalry, I'd say.

Ben Jordan had insisted on it, and it may be that his advice had saved me. After being forced into more showdowns than I like to remember, I had given up the life of a gunfighter. Twice I'd tried to get away from it by traveling to places where I wasn't known, but each time I'd gone from the frying pan into the fire; which is to say, I rode into more trouble than most people can imagine. During the time while my body healed when I returned from Montana, Ben came to see me. We sat on the veranda at the Upper Ranch, which is headquarters for the Lazy E spread, and over a bottle of sour mash bourbon he impressed on me that I would have to live the rest of my life like a Scottish chieftain. I didn't understand what he meant by that, but Ben had explained himself. He said that from that time on I'd have to keep my ranches guarded as if they were fortresses, and that I should seldom leave them. But when I did I'd have to be surrounded by well-trained, well-armed men. He said with careful emphasis that I would have to ride with warriors who would be prepared to do my fighting for me —if it came down to a time of kill or be killed. The two of us agreed that it was a hell of a way to have to live—but that it beat dying. Ben said he'd help set up this arrangement if I'd go along with it. And of course I had no choice in the matter. There were too many hard cases who wanted to be known as the man who gunned down Tom English. Although we didn't talk about it, Ben and I knew that beside them there was another breed out to get me.

The truth of the matter is that I've killed thirty men. I try not to think about it, but then the images force their way into my mind. I try to make excuses for myself by reasoning that I was forced to defend myself—I didn't start the trouble. That is so except for once when I was one hell of a lot younger. As a natural result I have received firsthand—as well as secondhand—more threats than most would believe. It seems as if every man I've downed has relatives or close friends who have sworn vengeance, so there are quite a few people whose one goal in life is to see me dead. Add all the ambitious young gunslingers to that and you can see why I protect my back.

We settled into the rhythm of the ride, breathing as much dust it seemed as air, brushing past the sharp-spined branches of mesquite trees while our horses picked their way through prickly pear. The hours passed, and the only sounds I heard were unshod hooves on dry ground, creaking leather, and a ringing that built within my head. Once as a kid I had high fever and I remember the feelings that I had then of nausea, weakness, and bewilderment. That's how I felt now—more bewildered and confused than anything.

I rode without speaking as a host of memories of Ben Jordan came back to me. I met the old lawman first some twelve years ago when, at the age of seventeen and new in town, I'd faced the muzzle of Jack Malone's double-barreled shotgun. The ancient single action .44 I wore that killed him on the spot had seemed to explode on its own. Blind luck saved me. There sure as hell had been no hint of skill involved, but the word spread like wildfire that I'd drawn in the face of a scattergun and brought down the fearsome Jack Malone. That is how my life as a gunfighter began.

I pushed my boots down in the stirrups and straightened my back, feeling the solid movement of my horse under me as I cleared my mind of the past. Then and there I made a resolution: *Never look back.* Even at the time I recognized that making these was considerably easier than living up to them.

Santiago Acosta, Benito's son, had Juan Suarez take our horses to the livery stable when we reached Concho Street in Santa Rita. The rest of us walked into the Lost Hope Saloon, where a sizable number of cowboys and townspeople had gathered. I've never seen it fail: a brutal killing excites folks; it draws a crowd.

The people became silent on our arrival, then parted into an aisle. We walked down it till we reached the bar. Then the hubbub began again, two dozen men all trying to talk at the same time. Mixed with the odor of stale beer and whiskey was the sharp smell of beef frying in a skillet, for John had an old mixed-breed cook, a woman named Jimmie. She had once been married to a buffalo soldier at Fort Concho, and now she prepared meals in a tiny kitchen which had been stuck on the side of the structure as an afterthought.

John Hope, the bartender and owner, dried off a thick glass and put it with a line of others like it on a shelf behind him. He had not named his place the Lost Hope Saloon for any philosophical reasons. He had wandered off the main trail two years before when he had been headed for San Antonio and had in truth been lost. On arriving at the raw settlement on the Concho River he had liked what he saw. There weren't too many people. John didn't mind being a bartender but it vexed him sorely when he had customers. Today, with the place jam-packed, he had a wild look in his eye, the way a raw bronc does when a cowboy steps down slow-like into the corral carrying a rope.

We exchanged howdies, and then John said tersely, "It has finally happened. Every damn man in West Texas has crowded into my place." On either side of him two helpers poured whiskey as fast as they could, and the sound of silver rang as dollars hit the oak bar. He added, "I don't know how much more of this I can stand." Then he added, "Max Hall and the rest are in the back room waiting for you." I thought then, as I have since I've known him, that this is a hard man to read. While I believe John Hope is a friend, I've never been sure of it. At least he's not an enemy, so I guess that puts me head and shoulders above most of mankind as far as he's concerned.

"My mouth's too dry to talk to anyone right now, John." While he reached for a bottle I looked at the mirror behind him, taking in the anxious faces of the people who stared at my back. Then I saw my own reflection: a sun-darkened face with very pale blue eyes.

John Hope slid a water glass half full of rye across the bar's rough-sawn oak surface without a word, and I paid him for it while I looked around for a place to sit down. I saw a table at the far end of the saloon where I could have my back in a corner, so I headed for it. Conscious of the weight of the matched .45s on my legs, I moved through the throng, which momentarily became quiet again. The rowels on my spurs made clinking noises as I walked, and out of habit I kept watching for quick movements, keeping my left hand ready just in case. I needn't have worried. Luis, Pepe, Santiago, and the rest were doing the same, but they had their rifles cradled in their arms, and it would have required a pure-bred lunatic to draw on me under the circumstances. They took up positions along the wall, standing in a menacing way, while I sat down. This seemed to dampen people's enthusiasm in the bar, and I decided to finish my drink and get out so they could relax.

Just then a deep voice boomed out, "I find it almighty difficult to enjoy my dinner when nervous-looking folks stand around me with their fingers on triggers."

Startled, I looked at the speaker, who rared back in his groaning chair at the next table. He was a hugely fat man, easily weighing three hundred pounds or more, and his normal-sized eyes looked small in his swollen face. His ears stuck out a little under his sweat-stained hat. It struck me that he'd probably been good looking as a youngster, for he had an aristocratic nose, straight and narrow, and regular features. But now, in his late forties, he carried at least a hundred pounds more than he should have. He straightened in his chair, and squared the biggest pair of shoulders I've ever seen as he roared, *"John."* Then he bellowed at the saloon's owner, "This steak's *raw."* Glancing over at me he complained, "If I ate it I'd feel like a damn cannibal." He glared down at the offending plate.

With a great sigh he shoved it toward the center of his table—away from him—with an expression of disgust. Looking up he saw me watching him, and he couldn't suppress a quick grin. He said, "When you go to town you have to raise all manner of hell or no one pays you any mind." He added, "I like my steak burned up so it don't seem like something a butcher hacked off the rear end of a poor, sufferin' live steer." Then he scowled again and looked dead serious, although I suspect he was playacting, that he liked having an audience. "If I stuck with bread and gave up meat altogether I suppose I'd survive. But when you think about it, bread's made of wheat, and wheat is nothing but seeds. And seeds are the stuff of life itself! What the hell am I to do?" he demanded in an aggrieved tone. "Eat rocks?" Then he shrugged and observed that most living things eat one another—or get eaten. "Since that's the case I reckon that it's best to be the one doing the eating," he remarked, "but I'm still going to be civilized enough to demand that my steaks are well done."

After that he said, "My name's Calvin Laudermilk, and I ranched near Fort McKavett until the bottom fell out of the cow business. Anybody who goes into ranching from here on out—after the black September of eighteen eighty-six—ought to have his fool head examined." He seemed pleased by this pronouncement and turned with care in order to face me more directly. "You don't have to tell me who you are. You'd be Tom English, the man who fenced his land and destroyed the open range in Texas." I must have looked surprised for he snorted out a laugh. "I got to blame somebody, damn it." He squinted his eyes at me and finally declared, "Well, you look harmless enough, though I understand you're known as the meanest man in West Texas." His belly shook with silent laughter after this, and then he protested, "Now calm down, *I* didn't accuse you of any meanness. I'm simply repeating what is commonly said, as you most surely have to be aware."

With that he rose to his feet and picked up his plate. Lumbering with it toward the bar, he said, "Now John, if you'd at least *warm* your steaks for me in the future I'd be much obliged."

The hot, raw whiskey warmed my stomach, and I waited for this first drink of the day to calm the wild, tumbled feelings I had. Many of the people in the crowd kept throwing quick glances my way from underneath their hat brims. I wondered if Ben Jordan's killer might be in that very room. Without thinking, my right hand slid from the glass and fastened on my six-gun, and for an instant a remembered sense of fierce elation spread through me—an unforgivable feeling that I've never mentioned to a soul, not even to Sally. It's the spasm of rage I've had just a few times: when I faced a man I truly hated—and knew I was going to kill him.

CHAPTER THREE

I sat with my back against the bar's wall looking out the open window as dusk fell gradually upon Santa Rita. A hint of fading sunlight streaked the roof of the Taylor Hotel, but the livery stable across from it and the other saloons and the ramshackle stores on Concho Street all lay in deepening shadows. Sounds drifted through the half-light: dogs barking back and forth at each other, windmills in the distance faintly creaking and chugging, and the constant gusting of the south wind.

A nod served as a signal to the Mexican men standing guard, and they moved with me as I rose and walked to the back room of the Lost Hope Saloon. John Hope had arrived with a bottle and some glasses just before I did, and as I went through the door I heard him say, "He's here." My cowboys, holding rifles carelessly, took up positions outside the room.

I took a chair and sat in the dimness beside the four men who waited for me around a scarred, octagonal poker table. I greeted them and they nodded in return and spoke to me in low voices. John Hope walked around the table, splashing bourbon in glasses, then he lit the coal oil lamp that hung suspended from the low ceiling over the table before returning to the bar. A warm, yellow glow fell like a fisher's net around us.

"What took you so long?" Max Hall asked.

"Max," Lewis Westbrook said to him when I didn't answer, "you know how cowboys are—when they get to town the only thing they can think about is getting hold of some whiskey so they can settle their nerves."

"It's been my experience that whiskey is a short-lived solution to nerve problems," Doc Starret remarked wryly.

Jedediah Jackson, the old lawyer, said nothing. I glanced across the table at him, and he looked sick at heart. With his head down, observing his task, he cleaned his fingernails carefully with a small pocketknife, then folded the knife and put it in his pocket.

For a little we simply sat there, not saying a lot, sipping on our whiskies while night crept up outside. I don't know why but a drink seems to hit me a little quicker than it used to. I welcomed the liquor's effect and I looked at one and then another of these four friends—the closest I've got left in the world. Gradually I stopped hearing the sounds of the dogs and the windmills and the wind, and I thought about these men in the strange silence that none of us wanted to break.

Doc Starret, in his sixties and never married, sat on my left. He always goes out of his way to stop at the Lazy E ranch to visit Sally and me whenever he can. Doc had made the difficult delivery of our daughter, Rebecca, ten years ago. I can't forget what he told us later: that Sally should never have another child for it would probably kill her. A new anxiety built up in me and I took a stiff drink to still it. I can't forget the grim way Doc had looked at me when Sally announced her pregnancy to him a few months back.

Jedediah Jackson sat on my right. A widower, seventy-three years of age and Tom Green County's only lawyer, he had come out to the desert dryness of West Texas, he invariably takes care to explain, for reasons of his health. Jedediah didn't want people to think he would live in such an uncivilized place by his own free choice. He had troubles with his lungs, he stresses.

Lewis Westbrook leaned back in his chair on the other side of the table. Lewis is four years older than I am, and at thirty-three he already has a few white hairs around his sideburns. Lewis has unusually large gray eyes with laugh wrinkles around them, and people feel comfortable in his presence. He owns the Westbrook Hardware Company, which serves settlers in the community and, in fact, for many miles around it. He sells hammers, nails, and building materials as well as skillets, chains, and dozens of unexpected products. In one section he stocks pistols, rifles, shotguns, and ammunition. In another he has windmill parts and supplies, and behind that a shed where he carries an inventory of leather goods such as bridles, halters, and saddles, not to mention a reasonable supply of barbed wire, salt cakes for cattle, and other miscellaneous supplies. The name of his firm no longer truly describes his store, for two years ago he moved to a larger building which he had built. He now devotes a substantial amount of his floor space to a stock of dry goods, including ready-made pants and shirts for men and bolts of cloth for women's dresses. His wife, Betsy, a happy, small woman with reddish hair and a sprinkling of freckles, recently started helping out at Westbrook Hardware. Lewis and Betsy have no children—a fact which saddens them—and on a few occasions they have talked to me about this. As the years pass they seem to grow fonder of one another. For some reason one particular memory of them stands out in my mind. I was on my way out of town and I rode by planning to tell them goodbye. When I reached the store, I saw Lewis and Betsy standing out front, looking seriously at each other, not realizing that anyone observed them. Then he held out a hand and she came up close, putting her head on his shoulder, her arms around his waist. An old woman with a sunbonnet on her head shading a sagging, wrinkled face paused in her passage down the street. She stood there very quietly for several minutes, gazing at them, and I saw a wistful expression in her eyes.

I looked at Max Hall, who sat to the left of Lewis Westbrook. Max had recently celebrated his thirty-ninth birthday. His round and happy face seemed to conceal an essentially cautious nature. He stands six-one and weighs around two hundred pounds. This makes him considerably larger than Lewis or me, for both of us are skinny, although we prefer the word *wiry,* and we have to stand tall to reach five-ten. Max owns and runs the First National Bank. He inherited, together with his money, an infectious grin and creative instincts. Most of all he enjoys applying his remarkable energies to business. He often states his belief that a banker can never have too much collateral, although as might be imagined, this puts him at odds with the West Texas ranchers who consider their word to be their bond. Max requires their word but he also generally takes in addition to that a mortgage, called a deed of trust in Texas. For some years he has given me more financial counseling than I'm able to understand; and the two of us own a fair amount of real estate in Santa Rita together. We're also partners in a good-sized wool warehouse on the south side of town. Max and Cele, his lively wife who is a good match for him, live with their three children in the only two-story house in Santa Rita.

For this brief period the five of us took what comfort we could from sitting together. Each of us avoided the pain that awaited facing the truth. Doc Starret, who sees suffering every day, took the first step. He raised his glass at last and said, "To Ben."

Solemnly we raised the hands that held our drinks in this last salute. Then the floodgates broke.

"We don't have any idea who did it," Max Hall said, turning to face me.

"Tom, it was so horrible," Lewis Westbrook blurted out, his voice strained. "Ben's sister Abigail sent for Doc—and I went with him. We got there just a short time after it happened." He shook his head as though to clear it of the memories that haunted him. "What kind of man would do something this awful?"

Jedediah Jackson said, "All of us were close to Ben Jordan. I've never known a finer man." He began to cough and leaned forward, shoulders heaving, until the paroxysm passed. "The question that plagues me is *why?* Why would anyone want to murder Ben?"

"And why kill him with acid?" Lewis added. The words of the question burned within our minds as we sat under a circle of light as though in the presence of death itself: confused and sick and angry.

I stood up abruptly, and the legs of my chair made a chattering, grating noise as they scraped back on the uneven boards of the floor. I paced over to a small window and looked through it at the darkness that seemed to isolate us in this small lighted enclosure. Then I turned and asked, "What's been done? Has anyone gone to visit with Ben's sister and his neighbors? Did you ask around to see if there have been any strangers in town?"

I met the haunted large gray eyes which dominated Lewis Westbrook's face. "Abigail is grief-stricken—she's hysterical. I tried to talk to her, but it was out of the question."

"Everyone has been milling around asking things like that, Tom," Jedediah said. "Several people claim they saw a Mexican cowboy, a stranger, ride through town. One youngster says he rode a rough-looking mare." The old lawyer sounded tired and defeated. "We've got a description of the mount, but no one paid any attention to the man. The kid described the mare as brown with a blaze face and white socks on all except the left hind foot. He didn't remember anything particular about the rider. Folks have been over Santa Rita with a fine-tooth comb and haven't found hide nor hair of the stranger or his horse."

Jedediah Jackson continued, "There is no evidence that this stranger committed murder. Other men could have passed through Santa Rita unnoticed. Or Ben may have had a bitter, life-long enemy living right here in town for all these years. You have to bear in mind that he has sent men to prison, has shot a few, and in the old days there was that man he hanged. We may never find the killer, that is what I'm trying to say, although God knows I hope we do—for we don't want suspicion and fear to tear this town apart."

We shared the tense stillness, gripped by a sense of denial, by a feeling that this couldn't have happened. Several spoke of when they had last seen Ben, and touched on the everyday comments that turned out to be the last things they would ever hear Ben say. This only made things worse.

At last Doc Starret said, "We're not lawmen, Tom. This whole thing flattened us, I suppose. We didn't know what to do." He stared across the table for a moment. Then he continued. "The men in town are drinking, talking about forming a posse—but no one's in charge, and not a soul has any idea where they'd ride if they could sober up and go out after the killer." He took a serious pull on his whiskey, and this made him narrow his eyes and twist his mouth. Then he said, "Old man Arch Hines was at Westbrook Hardware picking up supplies when he got wind of what happened. Two cowboys from his ranch were with him, and he sent them to Austin to ask for help from the Texas Rangers. He allowed that we needed some law here bad, and all of us agreed with that, although we can't expect help for five or six days at the earliest."

"Ben had two deputies, Tom, as you will recall," Max said. "One worked out of Sherwood and one lived in Villa Plata, but they didn't earn much and didn't have a hell of a lot to do. When they quit, Ben didn't hire anyone to take their places. With hindsight, I suppose we should have insisted on his getting new men, but Ben had always been able to take care of whatever problems that came along."

"He did until yesterday," I said.

Two days later, with Ben Jordan's funeral behind us, I walked into the First National Bank to see Max Hall. Luis and Pepe took up their stand outside the bank's doors, but the rest of our boys were busy saddling the horses over at the livery stable since this was my last stop before we headed for the ranch. I could see the frazzled expression on Max's face the minute I walked in. Harper Dent, all hunched forward in a chair, faced Max, who sat behind his littered desk. Harper seemed to be doing all the talking and he waved his arms around as he did so. Max glanced at me for half a second and then concentrated on the man before him. Well, I was in no particular rush. I leaned back against the wall and looked around. The First National Bank has a counter set up with four windows, but usually only one or two tellers stand behind it. Next to the counter, two benches and a scattering of chairs sit in front of a wooden divider with a little gate that fascinates me because it has a double set of hinges attached somehow so it can swing both ways. Max doesn't have a private office, and his desk sits behind the divider. This way he can see everything that goes on but still have a little protection so he can talk privately with his customers. His conversation right now, through no fault of Max's, sounded right public.

"What you're saying, you son of a bitch," Harper Dent pronounced loudly with a good bit of sincere feeling, "is that you'll loan money to people who don't need it but you won't spare a goddamn dime to folks who do." He jerked up to his feet, whirled around, and stomped out—going past me without a word although we've known each other for years. Harper ranches some thirty miles northeast of my homeplace, and a few months ago I sold him some Rambouillet rams and around four hundred ewes. At the time he told me he would never in this world have expected to put those greasy stupid animals on his range next to his nice clean cattle, but he'd do anything to save his ranch. I didn't place too much stock in what he said, for ranchers usually take the dark view when they are describing their prospects. But from what I'd just heard, it struck me that maybe Harper had dug himself a hole he couldn't climb out of.

Max swelled up like a bullfrog, mouth clinched and face red. "Well," I said, standing by the little gate, pushing it back and forth, "I can see why you need this thing to go both ways. Harper might have broken a leg getting out of there otherwise."

Max made a rumbling noise in his throat, and I said as I settled into the chair that Harper had vacated, "Before you get hostile, I want you to know that even if I came in here with the idea of borrowing money, I sure as hell wouldn't bring it up now."

"I'm sorry, Tom. Things like that upset me—I get so frustrated trying to talk sense to ranchers. None of you seem to pay any attention to reality."

"What in *hell* are you talking about?"

"I'm talking about trouble in cattle country, Tom. Real trouble, and it's as plain as the nose on your face."

Then he went into his sermon, and in half a minute I knew it was the same one he'd been preaching for the last few months. He went over the recent history of cattle prices and used that as the basis for his predictions about the future. I've noticed that most people accept the past, since they haven't much choice about it, and they have a fair idea about the future. The only thing that confuses the majority of us is what to do right now. But Max never appeared to be confused, and he often acted as if the Lord had anointed him as a prophet with clear information regarding how men who raised cows and sheep ought to behave if they wanted to get out of the wilderness and into the promised land.

"Tom," Max said in a tired tone of voice, as though he meant to try—one more time—to beat some sense into my head, "let's look at what has happened. A good many of you ranchers decided you were experts when you were doing business in a rising market some years back." He reared back in his chair and made a careful pause for emphasis. "An *idiot* can make money under those conditions. In eighteen eighty-one cattle were valued at around seven dollars a head, but in May of eighty-two the price for beef jumped to six dollars and eighty cents per hundred weight on the Chicago market. All of a sudden your seven-dollar-range steers were worth *thirty-five* dollars. Even when prices weakened, you did well. But then we had some drouths and stock died—and cattlemen began coming in here with excuses. But I'm used to that. You'd think that men who ranch in a place full of cactus and sand would wonder every now and then if a place that looked like a desert might not be one. But to put that aside, the market price for cattle went to hell in a hand basket in December of last year, and so far in eighty-six, beef prices have gone from bad to worse."

"Now hold on, Max," I said, feeling a little heat build up in my face. "We sure as hell are aware of these things, you haven't cornered the market on common sense. That's why most of us held our steers off the market this year—we'll wait 'til things get better."

"When is that going to be, Tom? And how do you plan to pay your expenses in the meantime?"

"We've always made it in the past," I said a little defensively.

"That has nothing to do with today," Max said, "and you know it."

He must have decided to give up trying to educate me for he leaned back in his chair and changed the subject. "I know how worried you are about Sally. Why don't you bring her and Rebecca into town until the baby comes. We've got plenty of room—we'd love to have them—and that way Sally would always be close to Doc Starret."

"Thank you, Max. When she gets nearer to her time we might do that. I'll talk to her about it."

"You do have a good many things to think about right now," Max said.

Later, riding with the boys back toward the Lazy E, I thought about them. Off to the west I could see what at first looked like a cloud, and for a minute my heart jumped. Then I realized that I saw a bad sandstorm headed our way. The rolling, boiling clouds filled the horizon and almost blotted out the sun, and the sky all of a sudden looked as though it had been stained by rust. All of us began to button our shirts up to the neck and we pulled bandannas over our faces as the first stinging whipped across us.

I kept my hat pulled down hard so I wouldn't lose it, and fixed my eyes through half-shut lids down on the trail. We rode this way for hours, with the wind getting worse as we went along.

All things considered, when an old friend is slaughtered, when all the other things you value hang in the balance, and then when nature swells up and acts as if it plans to sideswipe you, it makes the world seem a right precarious place to try to live.

CHAPTER FOUR

Old Mrs. Temple and her two married daughters, Felicity Halperson and Melanie Clement, finally concluded their shopping expedition and left the store, leaving Betsy Westbrook time to run down the street to her home. She had a wicker picnic hamper laid out in her kitchen, and she had thought about it with pleasure throughout the morning. On entering her yard she stopped at what she called the well house, a small stone shelter by the windmill which had a sunken floor. Betsy stepped down into the dank coolness of the well house, taking care on entering not to bump her head on the thick, rough timber that served as the short doorframe's lintel. Inside she moved past a shelf lined with jars of wild grape jelly she had put up during the summer, each sealed with a layer of waxy paraffin under its metal cap, and past the suspended coils of smoked deer sausage which Lewis bought each year when he went to see his sister in Fredericksburg. She stopped at the water-filled stone basin where the neighbor's boy brought that day's supply of fresh milk. He poured the foaming warm liquid through gauzy cotton cloth which strained it into a smoothly rounded tan crockery container that sat in the shallow, cool water. On a shelf beside the basin rested a large shapeless lump of whitish butter, wrapped carefully in a thin, moist cloth. Humming a melody to herself, she carried this to the house.

Betsy Westbrook enjoyed preparing small surprises for Lewis more than anything in the world. She had churned the night before, then made loaves of bread in preparation for the next day's baking. Earlier she had left her work at the hardware store during the morning so she could add logs to the fire in her iron kitchen stove and put the loaves in its oven. Bending forward, she opened the oven's door with a dishcloth in her hand so she wouldn't burn herself on the metal handle shaped like a shiny, twisted spring. With a happy sigh of contentment, she saw the steaming loaves within, their tops baked golden brown.

In a very short time she returned to the store, bubbling with enthusiasm. The sun made her red hair shine like burnished copper, and her exertions brought a glow to her lightly freckled cheeks as she burst through the familiar door of Westbrook Hardware. From the hamper on her arm came the compelling aroma of fresh bread, and her mouth watered at the thought of breaking a loaf and spreading butter into its hotness. In her mind's eye she could already see herself offering this gift together with a bright red apple and a slab of sharp, yellow cheese to her husband.

A slight frown touched her pretty face when she entered the store, for she saw that Lewis had a customer. Well, she decided, it makes no difference, thinking of the blue-and-white-checked gingham napkins wrapped around the bread, which would hold the heat for a time. A smile flickered across her lips as she saw Lewis looking at her and the wicker hamper curiously, then back at the heavyset man who stood across the counter from him examining a double-barreled shotgun.

The customer wore his dusty, wide-brimmed hat squarely on his head. It had an uneven oily-looking line around the crown where perspiration had soaked through the sweatband. The man's lank hair hung down over his collar and over the tops of his ears. He appeared to be in his middle forties, and lines creased his leathery face. He had a bushy, wheat-colored mustache which drooped past his fleshy mouth. Turning toward the door he raised the shotgun to his shoulder and turned with it as though leading a dove. Then he grunted, apparently with satisfaction, and put it down.

"Has a good heft to it," he said shortly, and then asked for some shells.

"You've made a good choice," Lewis Westbrook stated as he placed four boxes of cartridges on the counter. "The Greener ten-gauge is as dependable a scatter gun as you'll find." He looked at the weapon's twin hammers and twin triggers and at the elaborate engraving in the metalwork which held its sturdy wooden stock. Lewis said, "This is the time of year to sit down at a water hole at sundown and wait for the white-wings to come in." Laugh wrinkles formed around his expressive large gray eyes and he smiled broadly, obviously delighted to have made a major sale.

The heavyset man broke open the shotgun and shoved two cartridges into the chambers. Lewis paid little attention for he was writing up his customer's purchases on a small pad. However, when he heard the metallic clicks which the hammers made as they were pulled back, he lifted his head.

Disbelief etched Lewis Westbrook's face. He stood silently and slowly raised his hands above his head, eyes fixed upon the huge twin bores of the heavy shotgun.

"Is this a robbery?" he managed to ask.

The hamper fell from Betsy's hands and broke open on the floor, spilling its contents. Her startled scream resonated surprisingly in the shattered silence, rising very high then dwindling down. *"No!"* she cried, and began running toward her husband.

The ten-gauge shotgun exploded within the four walls with a deafening, echoing roar—ripping Lewis's chest, hurling him back as though he'd been struck by a cannonball.

The killer turned smoothly, as if making a second shot at ducks or doves or other game. The second barrel roared and a blast of birdshot at close range blew Betsy's face and part of her head completely away.

Reverberations from the violent detonations rang in the killer's ears as though multiple clappers were striking brass church bells. He stood for a moment, transfixed by the savaged corpses, eyes expressionless as marbles. Then he broke the shotgun open again, ejecting the spent cases, and walked quickly around the counter, taking care where he stepped, for the floorboards looked like those within a slaughterhouse. For his purposes he wanted cartridges with loads designed to fell deer and large game, not the fine lead pellets used for birds. Without a glance down at his butchery, he found some boxes of buckshot for the ten-gauge, reloaded, then snapped the twin barrels back in place. He stuffed the wide pockets of his denim coat with shotgun shells and clumped in the silence toward the door. As he did so he adjusted a Smith & Wesson .44 caliber six-gun in its worn, slick-leather holster at his right side. Though confident there would be no lawman waiting to confront him, he paused cautiously before leaving.

He cast one last look inside: Lewis had fallen behind the counter and could not be seen from the door, but Betsy's body lay twisted on its side, a large bright pool of blood growing about what remained of her head. An apple rested nearby, and beyond it lay a broken plate, soft butter, a thick wedge of cheese, and a blue-and-white-checked gingham bundle.

Junior Sims held the work-smoothed oak handle of his long-tined pitchfork in a frozen attitude as he stared through the open, barn-like door of the livery stable at the big man standing in front of Westbrook Hardware. What in the Sam Hill is going on? he wondered fearfully, suddenly very conscious that he stood alone beside the empty stalls.

The two explosions had attracted attention, and Junior saw three young boys run up. The big man swung a shotgun around, pointing it at them, and the children scattered like quail. Junior put his pitchfork down and advanced hesitantly to the front of the livery stable, standing on the trampled, crusted earth, not really conscious that his mouth hung open slackly.

"Come here, boy," the man with the shotgun said to him.

"Me?"

The man started toward Junior Sims and as he did he raised his shotgun until it pointed at Junior's belly.

Junior stood stock-still, his legs trembling, his features contorted by terror. His gaze went from the big shotgun to the dull eyes of the thick-bodied stranger.

"I've got a message here for Tom English," the man said, moving his left hand from the shotgun to his shirt pocket. He extracted a wrinkled envelope from it and pitched it toward the frightened youngster. He regripped the ten-gauge and cocked a hammer. "Pick it up."

Junior stumbled forward quickly and grasped the envelope to his chest. "Wha . . ." He gritted his teeth and fought against the stammer that had made him miserable throughout the seventeen years of his life. "What," he began again, speaking slowly and distinctly, "happened in there?" He looked beyond the threatening presence before him at Westbrook Hardware.

"I left something," the man said harshly, "in the only language that Tom English understands. He has to know I mean what I say."

Walden Doggett stepped down from his lathered dun horse and handed the reins to Sonny Cade—the nephew of J. K. Cade—who had ridden with him to Texas from Black Horse, Montana. They exchanged a few words, then the ordinary-looking young cowboy led the horse off toward the pens while Walden walked across the hard-packed, grassless earth toward the ranch house. Its owner, Jason Quest, waited for him at the door.

Jason wore his pant legs tucked inside high-topped boots and he held a brown bottle by its neck. He kept a plentiful supply of whiskey on hand for medicinal and social purposes. This eliminated the necessity of making the ride to the saloons of Santa Rita some twelve miles to the northeast when he felt the need for sustenance. He rarely went to Santa Rita, a place populated in the main by scoundrels in his opinion, although this was his view of most people who had no more sense than to live in towns or cities. He even avoided the nearby tiny community of Knickerbocker even though it had far too few people to be considered a town. It had no saloons, and even if it had, Jason would not have given them his business since he had yet to meet a man from there whom he did not despise.

Jason Quest handed the bottle of whiskey to Walden and watched him tilt it gratefully to his mouth before grimacing and wiping his drooping, wheat-colored mustache with his left hand. Then the broad-bodied man shouldered his way past Jason and entered the wide front hall of the house. Jason noticed that Walden carried a new double-barreled shotgun, and he looked at it curiously but said nothing, waiting silently for the other man to speak.

Walden put the shotgun in a corner and sat down in a rocking chair made of mesquite wood with the seat and back fashioned of spotted cowhide with the hair still on it. He took a long pull from the bottle and then began speaking dispassionately.

"Things worked out about the way we thought they would except for one thing," he said. "Santa Rita shuts down around noon on weekdays— just like Koestler had it figured—almost everyone goes home for something to eat. But Westbrook's wife came back to the store."

"You say his wife was there?"

"Jason, don't start looking pasty-faced at me. We figured that might happen, though we knew she normally spent the noon hour at home."

"God in heaven—"

"Shut your damn mouth, Jason," Walden interrupted him sharply. "You sat in this room and agreed along with everyone else that this was the one plan guaranteed to put Tom English in our hands. The first step was to get sheriff Jordan out of the way so he wouldn't interfere. When we found what good friends Ben Jordan and English were—that made it *perfect*. That's when Koestler came up with the way to kill Jordan that would jolt the hell out of Tom English."

Walden Doggett took off his grimy, wide-brimmed hat and slapped it down on the floor beside the rocking chair where he sat. He took another pull from the bottle, twisting his face as he gulped the fiery contents, then he continued speaking.

"Carl Koestler has the whole thing pretty well thought out, I've got to hand it to him. As you will recall, we had run out of ideas about how to get at that sunuvabitch English until Carl showed up."

"For Christ's sake, Walden," Jason Quest broke in. "What happened back there in Santa Rita?"

"It ain't Koestler's fault the woman surprised me. But gunning her down as well as the man ought to work out for us even better. I'd make a guess that this might be just what it takes to lure Tom English away from his guards."

"You killed the woman too?" Quest asked foolishly, his face oddly blank.

"Well of course I did, you idiot. What else could I do?"

Sonny Cade spent an hour alternating between a slow, rocking lope and a bone-jarring trot on the mean-spirited, sorrel mare which Jason Quest held in the corral as a night horse. As a rule Sonny only rode Sweetie, the illogical name borne by this contrary animal, to round up the remuda of riding horses kept in the horse trap, a small pasture near the house. In the two months since he and Walden Doggett had arrived from Montana he had worked as horse wrangler, fence mender, and general handyman on the ranch for their host Jason Quest in spite of his frequent complaints. "I didn't come all this way to work like a slave," he would say to Walden, "I came to help you put a bullet in Tom English."

Nervous excitement quivered in his stomach now as he rode over the final crest and headed down the low hill toward Tarpley's gulch. He saw smoke coming from a rusty stovepipe that issued at a slant from the shack by the dry draw. A sheet of ragged canvas hung between two liveoak trees off to one side and several men rose from its shelter as he approached. A rail corral held four horses, and a man who had been near it walked forward, his hands holding a rifle.

Sonny slowed his mare to a walk and waved, making sure the men recognized him before advancing too close. He knew Carl Koestler and Stoddard Landon fairly well since they had stayed at the main house of Jason Quest's ranch together with Walden Doggett and him for almost a month. During this period Sonny had observed big Walden assert himself. No doubt about it, Sonny thought at the time, Walden is the one who runs things. But in short order he had seen that Carl Koestler always came up with plans which the others followed. Walden accepted this without jealousy, and in fact on one occasion had stated, "Koestler here is our thinker."

When Bob Dawson had ridden in along with that hard-looking Mexican from Chihuahua, Koestler had said it might be noticed if too many people were seen to be staying at Jason Quest's ranch house. He decided that it would be best for some of the men to move to a remote section of the Quest spread where years before an old-timer named Tarpley had given up on trying to scratch out a living and had abandoned his dilapidated dwelling. Koestler picked the men who would go to that location with him.

None of this made any sense at all to Sonny, but the older men didn't listen to him. In spite of that he kept arguing with them. He said that the Quest ranch house lay a good two miles off the Knickerbocker Road, and with the hills and trees there was no way they would be observed. In addition, owing to Jason's well-known habit of firing rifle shots at strangers who approached his house, he had absolutely no visitors. Koestler had silenced Sonny with a single look. Then he said they mustn't give themselves away, so for the last three weeks Carl Koestler and Stoddard Landon along with Raul Ysleta and Bob Dawson had holed up out of sight of everything except an occasional range steer.

Sonny reined his mount to a stop when he reached the shack. Warily he eyed Raul Ysleta put down his rifle, propping it against the rails of the corral. The dark-faced Mexican wore a sheath knife and a six-gun, and the oversized rowels of his spurs clanked at every step as he walked nearer. He stopped about fifteen feet from the boy. Then Sonny saw Bob Dawson come from the shack's open door holding his arms out wide while he stretched. He yawned, scratched his stomach, and then sat down on one end of the thick, deeply scarred chopping log used for splitting kindling wood. An axe, its blade stuck in the other end of the log, raised its shaft at an angle toward the paleness of the late afternoon sky.

Sonny Cade dismounted and stood in the tattered shade provided by the skinny, slivered leaves of a gaunt mesquite tree. He tied his horse to a low-hanging limb, then turned to the waiting men.

Feeling nervous, Sonny saw the Mexican waiting not far from him. Raul Ysleta drew his knife and began to whittle on a stick which he held in his left hand, shaving dry curls off the stick's end which quickly developed a sharp point. Bob Dawson leaned forward from his seat on the chopping log. He spat between his boots, then propped his elbows on his knees and looked through half-shut but attentive eyes at the jittery-looking young cowboy standing hesitantly before the assembled group.

"Walden done it," Sonny Cade finally said.

Carl Koestler and Stoddard Landon stood beside him, waiting for him to continue. Raul Ysleta and Bob Dawson did too. These four men, like Walden Doggett and Jason Quest back at the main house of the ranch, and like the messenger they had sent, young Sonny Cade, all had one thing in common. They wanted to kill Tom English. They formed a strange alliance of outlaws, cowboys, and cattlemen, bonded together by their mutual hatred of the man who had gunned down their kinsmen or their friends.

"Walden killed Westbrook?" Koestler asked.

"Yep. Westbrook's wife was there—he had to kill her too."

Dawson winced, but the others waited impassively.

"The letter," Koestler asked, a trace of eagerness in his voice, "did he leave the letter?"

"Sure did," Sonny Cade replied.

"We have him now," Carl Koestler exclaimed in a low, exultant whisper. Then his voice rose. "We could never have got close enough to him, not with that pack of gunhands he keeps around him—but there's always a way. Always."

Koestler waited a moment and then continued, "Everyone has weaknesses. I've studied Tom English, I've talked to folks who know him. I've read all those newspaper and magazine stories about him and even the fool dime novels that make him out to be a kind of hero. I've learned a very simple truth from all of this: He's just like any other man, he has his faults. Tom English is overly proud, loyal to a fault, and he has a temper that gets out of hand." A thin smile, like a slit in rawhide, split his weathered face for an instant. Then he said, "A man's weaknesses can be the death of him."

In the distance a cow bawled, and Sonny Cade's mare nickered at the horses that looked over the top rail of the corral at her. However, the men staring at Carl Koestler only heard his words.

"I'd say that in two days, three at the most, Tom English will head alone for Mexico. And then we'll have our chance," Koestler said. He looked at the men about him one by one.

"There's no backing down now," Carl Koestler emphasized, biting down on the words. Then he added, "The fact that we have the blood of three people on our hands doesn't bother me a damn bit. We done what we had to do to cut that sonuvabitch out of the herd—to get him off where we can get ahold of him.

"We've all got good reasons to kill him," Koestler continued in an oddly matter-of-fact tone of voice. He fixed his eyes on Raul Ysleta and said to him, "English shot your oldest brother along with all those others around ten years ago in Mexico."

Koestler's windburned face darkened and he said, turning to the next man, "Stoddard, the best friends you and I ever had were Earl and Billy Dawson."

Glancing at Bob Dawson, he stated, "Tom English gunned your cousins down and two others that hellish afternoon in Santa Rita. I was there and I will never forget the sight."

Koestler paced toward the shack and then returned. "I don't guess that there has ever been anyone who has killed as many men in gunfights as Tom English, and how he's lived this long we'll never know. Up till now, regardless of the odds, he's slaughtered every man he's gone up against. But he's human—he can be killed—and he damn well knows it. That's why he has all those gunslingers around him day and night. What do you call a bodyguard in Spanish, Raul?" He kept speaking, not waiting for an answer. *"Guardaespalda,* right? The word makes more sense in Spanish— they call them 'back guards.' He wouldn't have all those men watching his back if he weren't *scared.* In my view his nerves are gone, so when the seven of us corner him alone he'll panic."

Again a smile without a trace of humor crossed his face. Koestler added, "That's the main thing, we had to come up with the one plan that would get him clear of all his men. And when he's on his own, we'll take him when he least expects it."

"We'll make the son of a bitch pay," Sonny Cade blurted out awkwardly, but nobody laughed.

Raul Ysleta didn't utter a word, although his eyes glittered. They looked very much as they had after he had poured acid down Ben Jordan's throat.

"It's hard to believe that one person could have killed thirty men," Sonny Cade said. "One of them was my uncle, J. K. Cade. Another was Bull Doggett, Walden's brother."

"We know that," Bob Dawson said.

Sonny Cade stood before the men feeling vaguely proud of himself. Suddenly the others weren't treating him like a kid. He reveled in this feeling of acceptance and only vaguely heard the voices of the others. Dawson was speaking, talking about the time English killed Ike Phillips, Jason's first cousin. And then Koestler told the story of the showdown that first made English truly famous—when he beat Joe Slade to the draw in Villa Plata—the fight when he also killed two more of Jason's cousins. Sonny tried not to listen to these scary tales. He concentrated on a mental picture of his dead uncle and tried to recapture the bittersweet, hot sense of rage that had fueled his energy in the long trip to Texas from Montana.

Carl Koestler broke in on Sonny's thoughts, saying harshly, "I'd like to see the look on the face of Tom English when he reads that letter I wrote him."

Sonny saw Stoddard Landon's bushy eyebrows knit as he scowled at Koestler. Then Landon moved forward, and Sonny paid close attention since this tight-lipped man rarely spoke.

"The thing I'd like to know," Stoddard said, "is how we're going to kill Tom English without his taking most of us with him?"

The five men waited in the awkward silence that followed this. The words of the question seemed to hang in the air. They had avoided it, but now that it had been expressed, it hovered about their heads and within their stomachs. All of them waited quietly, fearfully, as startled men do when a bolt of lightning has struck violently and unexpectedly nearby.

CHAPTER FIVE

I awakened early, and in that half world between sleep and wakefulness, I curled close to Sally, lying spoon fashion, my face cushioned in her long hair, and with one hand resting around her curved warmth upon the swollen tightness of her stomach. My eyes opened, and careful not to wake her, I sat up in the strange bed, staring without seeing. Then an acid bitterness clutched my stomach while dark images swept through my mind. An hour passed and very gradually the windows became dull gray rectangles against the blackness. Morning sounds began: a rooster urging the sun to rise, the quick chatter of sparrows, the sounds downstairs in Max Hall's house as someone stoked the kitchen fire. How is it possible, I was thinking, that everything goes on as though nothing had happened? As though Lewis and Betsy Westbrook had not had their lives ripped from them. Sick nausea gripped me as it had the day before, and in my mouth I tasted the sharpness of bile and the dryness of ashes.

In all the town only I knew why Ben and Lewis and Betsy were dead because I alone had read the letter. They had died for loving me. In a way of looking at it, that is what had happened. As I thought about it I found myself breathing shallowly, as though guilt were suffocating me.

I suppose I must have spoken to someone in the two days we had been in Santa Rita. I would have greeted friends and nodded at the curious who stood about staring at me. The life of the town flowed around me as if it were a stream and as if I were a stone sitting silently without feeling in its midst. Somehow everyone seemed to understand that I simply couldn't stand to talk to a soul about it, not even Sally. She held me for a very long time during the hollow, aching part of the night, those hours on both sides of midnight, and when at last I wept, she clutched me as tightly as she could.

I learned something about myself. For years I've played a part and have pretended to be as strong and hard as people say I am. But last night the gunfighter, the one called the meanest man in West Texas, broke down and cried with no more self control than a five-year-old. And now a sense of weakness has me by the throat, and I wonder if I'll ever be the same again. I doubt it.

During the funeral yesterday I stared at the patterns of the grain in the new-sawn pine boxes, seeing the people in my mind's eye who lay so still within them. The preacher droned on and on, and then he stopped, and I watched four men with ropes lower two nailed-together coffins into a single wide grave. A woman behind me began to sob at that moment, and I heard her say in a muffled, wet whisper, "It's good they're in the same grave—together—they'd like that." I concentrated then on holding on to my sanity. Crazed impulses whipsawed through me, just underneath the surface, and it was all I could do to remain still while all the others walked up and dropped a handful of dirt on the crude caskets lying deep in the wide hole. They had dug it by carving through thin soil and through a layer of caliche, the flaky, limestone-like rock that lies just out of sight in desert country. When shoveled back on top of the coffins, it would seal the tomb shared by two of the dearest friends I ever had.

That's when it happened. I walked as fast as I could away from the clump of people in dark clothing standing by the mound of fresh dirt and rocks piled next to the almost square hole in the ground. As I left the small cemetery I felt their eyes upon my back. I simply couldn't help it, and later no one asked me to explain or even mentioned anything about my behavior. I went to the room upstairs in Max's house where Sally and I were staying. Not long after that everyone came directly from the burial to the wake held in the large living room and adjoining parlor below, but I couldn't bring myself to join them.

The thing that none of them knew was that *it was all my fault.*

I sat in the guest bedroom with Sally and Max's wife, Cele, and silently I drank whiskey until the two women pulled off my boots and stretched me out on the bed. Then Cele left and Sally managed to undress me. After she had put on her nightgown she lay down beside me and pillowed my head upon her breast and spoke soft words to me as though I were a little child, stroking my head with one hand all the while. That must have been what finally broke through the armor I had tried to keep around me. That's when I felt a splitting hot anguish as my tears blotted into the soft cotton of her gown.

The night had somehow passed and soon the light would come. I rose and lit the lamp so I could find my things. Silently, then, I put on my clothes except for my boots. Sally stirred, something troubled her sleep, and a slight frown crossed her face. A wisp of fine hair trailed across her forehead, and taking great care not to wake her, I smoothed it back, then stood a moment looking down at her vulnerability. I couldn't stand it if anything happened to Sally. It came home to me just how much she meant to me when I realized that I could lose her.

My God, I loved her so!

Then I buckled on my gunbelt, tied down the right scabbard and then the left to each of my legs, and after blowing out the lamp, walked from the room in my sockfeet, carrying my boots.

Cele greeted me when I entered the kitchen. "I couldn't sleep," she said. She had me sit down at a round oak table with a lamp on it which burned with a dull glow. She bustled around, opening pantry doors and pulling provisions from shelves while humming softly to herself. During this time I pulled on my boots and then read the crumpled letter that the boy from the stables gave to me when I first rode into town.

The youngster had a funny look on his face at the time. He had said as he poked his hand up toward me with the note, "I seen the man who done the killing, Mr. English. He pointed his shotgun at me—like to of scared me to death—and he told me to give this to you."

I remember leaning forward from my saddle and taking the creased envelope with my name on it. It was sealed. I asked the boy what the man looked like, and he told me what he could. Then I asked if the killer had said anything else, but all the kid could remember was that the man told him that what had been done to Lewis and Betsy Westbrook was in some way "the only kind of language that Tom English understands."

I gazed for a few minutes out the window and saw a silver line at the horizon, that sliver of light which people call the "crack of dawn." In moments, I knew, pale colors would rise in the east. I glanced at Cele and our eyes met for an instant, and we shared the pain before each of us looked away. This morning she had her hair pulled into a bun at the nape of her neck and wore a soft slate-blue, corduroy robe with a dark sash. Cele is slight figured and has the fragile beauty of thin crystal. She turned and with ease picked up a great iron skillet and I had to smile, for with all her seeming delicacy, she was strong as a horse. While Cele addressed herself to stirring sizzling strips of bacon which sent their odor into the air about us, I spread the letter on the smooth golden oak surface of the table and examined it in the subtle light cast by the coal oil lamp. Though I knew its words by heart, I read it again.

To Tom English—

You can only stop the killing in one way. You are to meet me *alone* in Villa Acuña next Thursday afternoon. It's a long trip, but there is a reason for choosing that place. No lawmen will be in Mexico to stop the fight or to try to arrest me for what has happened in Santa Rita.

I'll be at Antojitos Cantina next Thursday waiting for you. If you don't come by yourself, you won't find me. But if you have the nerve to face me man to man, we'll settle this once and for all. You owe me your life for what you did.

If you don't show up, or if you try to trick me, every friend you've ever had will die. I'll kill your pregnant wife, and I'll either kill your daughter or take her with me.

Sooner or later you'll have to stand up to me, so it might as well be in Villa Acuña Thursday.

I read it slowly, carefully. "You owe me your life." These words stood out, and I knew that once again I found myself pursued by a man who could think of nothing but revenge. The letter, printed with a blunt, soft-lead pencil, looked crude. Even so, I sensed an intelligence behind it. As written, the note was designed to enrage me, and even on this, the sixth or seventh reading, it achieved its purpose. I felt the blood vessels at my temples pounding and made an effort to still the trembling around my mouth.

"Tom?" Cele paused in her cooking and looked at me. "What's in that letter?"

I didn't answer, and she brought me a cup of coffee quietly, then went back to the stove. She turned around and said, "You look so strange . . ." She broke off. "Your hand is *shaking*, Tom."

I looked down and saw, with some dismay, that she was right. Coffee spilled from my cup before I could put it down. Rising to my feet, I told her half the truth. I said I guessed I had a hangover—that, Lord knew, I deserved one.

"Sit down, you hear?" Cele said, in what seemed to me a bossy way, but I did what she told me. Then she smiled and brought me a plate of toast and fried eggs and thick-cut bacon with the rind on it, insisting over my protests that I'd feel better if I ate something. People don't die of hangovers, she said, but I would certainly not have made a bet of any size on that particular proposition.

I ate hurriedly and left the house, afraid that Sally might wake up before I could get away. I asked Cele to tell Sally I needed some time alone—that I was sorry—but that I'd be back by Sunday night.

Cele said, "You're going all the way to the ranch?" I didn't answer, but she went on, "I know you are—you always go out there when something's bothering you. Well, it's probably just as well. We'll enjoy having Sally with us in town."

None of the cowboys on the Lazy E can stand to ride Judge because he has a tendency to pace. This gait, which is when a horse lifts and puts down his feet on one side together, is probably the smoothest and most comfortable one possible. But a horse that paces can fall easily, so cowboys take their quirts and spurs to such a mount. If they can't break him of the habit, most will refuse to have him in their string. Judge is an example of the problem, but I like him. He has a dark, shiny chestnut coat, a jagged white star on his forehead, and he holds his head high, arching his muscular neck. It's still fun to ride a stylish horse, and Judge has his own brand of elegance. When he breaks into a run he has a tendency to raise his tail and let it flair out behind him like a battle flag. Riding him over rough ground might be a trifle chancy, but the trail from Santa Rita to the border town of Del Rio winds through fairly flat land with some low hills, and I anticipated no problems.

Another reason for appreciating Judge lies in the fact of his uncommon gentleness. It is a rare horse that won't go to jumping when you shoot from him, but I'd worked with this one for some time now, and he stood with very little flinching when I fired from his back.

Today I had my saddle gun in a different place. In the past I have tied the boot, which is to say the saddle scabbard, for my rifle on the left front side, slanted back under the stirrup leather but on top of the saddle skirt so it won't rub against the horse's side. Being right-handed, I've fretted about reaching over to the left side and hauling the rifle out butt forward toward the horse's head. That is plain awkward. Of course, some men put their rifle on the right, but I always keep my rope tied to the saddle strings there. Not long ago I hit on the idea of tying the rifle boot to the back of the saddle, with the barrel slanted down toward the front beneath the stirrup leather of my right leg. This permits me to lean back and get it free a little more smoothly and certainly much more quickly. There are situations where the time of a few eye blinks is all you've got between life and death. I think about things like this quite a bit.

Judge paced forward, swinging both right legs, then both left legs, rocking me along at a speed that on most horses would have been a fast, jolting trot. Sitting a trot the way we do makes it feel after a spell that your backbone is trying to jam up into your skull. So in spite of the slight risk of a fall, I looked kindly on Judge.

I glanced at the sun and figured it must be around seven or eight o'clock in the morning. It rankled that I'd fiddled around for so long, but it had seemed necessary to leave town heading north—toward the Lazy E—instead of southwest—toward Mexico. People get up early in our part of the world, and they damn sure notice things. The word would spread that I'd headed for home.

When I doubled back toward my true destination, it required me the better part of an hour to skirt the edges of Santa Rita on the west side. I rode through dry draws and ravines as much as I could, staying well out of sight until I got to the southwest of the town and the trail to Del Rio. Waiting for me at that border town lay a wooden bridge crossing the sluggish, muddy water of the Rio Grande, leading to Villa Acuña on the other side. There, in Mexico, I would face the one who had murdered Ben and Lewis and Betsy.

Once I walked through a slaughterhouse where a big-shouldered man with a sledgehammer crushed the heads of unsuspecting steers, one after another. The steers crowded forward, heads down in single file, forced up a narrow chute toward him by swearing workers with prod poles. Overpowered by the raw smell of so much blood, I had backed away. The clarity of that memory brought back the sounds, the heavy, crunching thuds, and most of all it brought back the smell of death, sharp and dark—which is like nothing else. In a strange way the road seemed like a chute, with hatred prodding me forward toward a waiting, faceless executioner. He had, in a way, sledged my unexpecting friends, and he lay in wait for me.

Once again a sense of weakness held me in its grasp as I thought of this, and I didn't notice a rider off to one side until he flapped his reins and moved out from the shadows of a brush thicket and pulled up his horse beside the ruts of the road.

Even from five hundred yards away he looked to be a giant of a man, sitting there in his long, dirty canvas duster. As the gap between us narrowed I noticed that his mount must have stood seventeen hands in height and looked to be as broad as a bale of cotton, though of course it wasn't.

Leaning back, I slowed Judge to a walk and made sure my saddle gun was loose in its scabbard. Then I did the same for my right Colt. The boy who gave me the letter after the bloodshed at Westbrook Hardware had described the killer as being "wide and square-built," but I hadn't figured on anything like this.

Judge whinnied out a greeting and the huge dappled gray the man rode snorted back at him. Then two things, relief and recognition, hit me at once for I saw Calvin Laudermilk, the oversized man I'd met a while back in the Lost Hope Saloon. Heaving a big sigh, blowing air the way a swimmer will when he hits the surface after being under water too long, I edged forward. I suppose I'd been holding my breath without realizing it.

"You took your own good time in getting here," Calvin Laudermilk roared at me. I was to learn that this was his normal manner of speaking.

I'm sure I looked thunderstruck, and this obviously tickled him pink.

"Surprised to see me?" He snorted in laughter, and his bulk quivered mightily. "I'll explain what I'm doing here. You see, from childhood I have been cursed with a curiosity that beggars description. The word had spread of a letter left for you, so I sought out the lad who works at the livery stable. Though he had orders to deliver the message only into your hands, I gave him four bits for the privilege of a peek at it."

Calvin Laudermilk sniggered at his own cleverness, or perhaps because all things human seemed lacking in reason and this amused him. He continued, "I told him he could reseal the envelope with some mucilage and no one would be the wiser. He did cotton to the notion of that half a dollar, so I read your private mail. That is not, let me say, the greatest sin I have ever committed. However, in order to pay for my transgressions, I decided I'd save your life."

I had no patience to waste on folks like this in the best of times, and now was decidedly not one of those. Once I heard old Arch Hines say, "A man can somehow get along with liars and cheats, but he must *never* try to reason with a fool."

I set my spurs to Judge and he jumped forward. In steely silence I rode west with my jaw set. But to my surprise Calvin's big-boned gray elephant of a horse lumbered alongside me.

"Yessir," my companion said, "I watched you standing first on one leg and then the other yesterday at the funeral, and I figured you'd be heading out early—though today is Sunday and Del Rio is not much over an easy three-day ride away. If you go through with this, you have until Thursday, so slow down some"—he paused to lean forward and clap his monster mount's thick neck—"or Sully here will be plumb worn to a frazzle by nightfall."

"Calvin, if you have read that letter then you know how important it is for me to ride alone into Villa Acuña."

"I know that." He cleared his throat with energy, sounding like a rusted-out tuba being blown by an asthmatic member of a marching band. That is to say, his wheeze had a strangely musical quality, running a ragged scale as he whooped. Calvin scowled at me. "Don't think for a minute that I intend to ride into Mexico where, more than likely, a dozen homicidal maniacs with rifles will be waiting to murder you and anyone fool enough to be at your side."

We rode in silence for a short way and then Calvin said seriously, "If you decide to go through with this, you'll ride alone." Then, in his joking tone again, he added, "But my idea is to trail along with you a spell and try to talk some sense into you."

His horse had hooves the size of pie plates, legs twice the size of Judge's, and a great barrel of a body. Yet he moved with surprising grace.

Calvin saw the direction of my gaze and he said, "This horse is a good and faithful friend." Addressing himself to the animal he added, "Ain't that right, Sully?" His mount made some low fluttery noises and Calvin seemed to be listening thoughtfully as he jounced along in the saddle. "We get along fine," he said, "even though we don't speak the same language. He pays heed with patience to what I say, and I extend the same courtesy to him. This may sound ridiculous to you, but sometimes I'll go months without seeing a human, and I would swear that by the end of that time Sully and I have a very fine understanding between us."

"What kind of horse is he?"

"Basically, he's a Percheron, a French horse originally, bred in the Perche region, I understand, although Sully has other blood as well which may account for his unusually easy gait. You can take a look at me and see why I have long had an interest in big horses. By the time I was sixteen—before I had begun to put on weight—I already carried two hundred and thirty pounds. I owned a little mare then who had her own manner of complaining if I got on her back: she simply laid down."

Calvin commenced at this point to giggle, an unseemly sound, I thought, coming from someone of his bulk. He sat his horse well, I noticed, and his tree-trunk thighs seemed to fit the broad arch of Sully's back.

Calvin continued. "Once I saw a contest in Fort Worth where they had Clydesdales, one Suffolk Punch, and a pair of the largest of the heavy horse breeds, the Shire. Yoked in tandem, two Shires have been known to move eighteen and a half *tons,* if you can imagine such a thing. A Shire stands over eighteen hands high and weighs more than two thousand pounds, but they have a stepping action that is shorter and higher than Sully's. They had some Percherons at the show, and I saw their movements were much smoother than those of the other heavy breeds. Anyway," Calvin concluded, "I bought Sully as a yearling at a good price since he was not a purebred, and brought him all the way to West Texas on a lead rope. That was eight years ago, and I don't plan to make a trip of that distance ever again."

We had stopped on a low rise and could see smoke behind us rising from cookstoves in Santa Rita, but the town itself was out of sight. Off to our right I looked down a shallow valley and could see the taller trees that bordered the South Concho, which wandered toward its junction with Spring Creek and then to the Main Concho.

With a great creaking of saddle leather, my companion dismounted and began to adjust the girth of his saddle. Sully turned, stretched his neck out, and began to nuzzle his pockets. Calvin said, "Dammit, leave me alone. You'll find no sugar there today, nor apples neither." With an embarrassed grin, he said, "I'm afraid this is one spoiled horse." He stroked the animal's head and commented, "Sully and I have a good bit in common that goes beyond our size."

He remounted and we rode without speaking for a few miles. A soft wind out of the south fanned across our faces, and some low-hanging dull clouds scudded across the sky giving a promise of moisture that would be denied. The gods of rain love to tantalize us, I suppose.

"You think I'm a fool, don't you?" Calvin Laudermilk said out of the blue. "You're thinking that you've run across a man with no more sense than to try to carry on a conversation with his horse."

I stammered a denial, but he cried out, "Aha! Caught you out. Well, when people say whatever that comes into their minds, others have every right to consider them foolish."

We rode without saying much for a spell, and I began to form a different opinion of Calvin Laudermilk. Then he spoke, not in his usual blustering way, but quietly—in dead earnest.

"This much I know: you're out after vengeance. But the peculiar thing is, whoever wants to kill you is also seeking revenge. It occurs to me that this is the type of situation that sets the stage for a feud, and those things last for generations. That ain't much of a legacy to leave for your children."

"Calvin," I said dryly, "I have lived with this problem for a good many years. You have thought about it, I suspect, for some hours. There is little you can say that sheds new light upon my situation. God knows I've tried to back away from this kind of life." I didn't want to take the time to tell him how often I'd put away my guns, rubbed neat's-foot oil on my gunbelts and scabbards, and folded them in an old shirt in a drawer. I didn't tell him about running from trouble twice, even changing my name when I went to Montana. But when folks start killing your friends, when they clearly plan to do the same to those nearest to you, the so-called "civilized" choices aren't available.

"There are times, Calvin, when it is not practical to be gentle."

He ruminated on that, and then he seemed to agree, for he said, "When you think about it, gentleness is not a design of nature. A kind black leopard would be savaged by ferocities that had not reached his level of civility."

"Talking like that," I said, "is what gives people the notion that you are, if not a fool, at least not sound in the head."

Calvin Laudermilk's wild laughter echoed in the morning air. Then he said, "We'll rest this afternoon by the river with my old friend, Tuck Bowlegs. He is the orneriest sonuvabitch in kingdom come, but my, he does know how to fry catfish."

CHAPTER SIX

Six men waited impatiently in the woods at the west bank of the river. Each had found cover for protection and they lay without moving, keeping their weapons trained on the ford. Sonny Cade propped the barrel of his rifle on the soft, yielding bark of a decaying log which lay at an angle before him and then, with great deliberation, aimed at an old willow on the other side of the South Concho, putting the copper front sight in the notch of the rear sight. He very slowly moved the barrel up and down, feeling the wooden stock at his cheek, eyeing the wavering bead with intense concentration. He picked a place in the tree trunk which had a branch sticking out about four feet off the ground, and as he moved the barrel past that point he would apply a very soft pressure to the trigger, being very careful not to pull too hard. Each time he did this he murmured "pow" to himself under his breath. Then, feeling foolish, he put the rifle butt on the ground and tried to relax.

He *couldn't* relax. Unable to bear inaction longer, he crawled through brush to the next tree where Bob Dawson sat calmly: chewing tobacco and rarely spitting.

"Where are the others?" Sonny asked nervously.

"Yonder," Dawson managed to say carefully, lips pursed, cheeks full, pointing out Walden Doggett and Jason Quest to his right. Then he spat a long brown jet of tobacco juice before saying moistly, but in a more normal tone, "Carl Koestler and Stoddard Landon are to our left, on the other side of the trail."

The two men gazed at the swiftly moving shallow water which rippled in its passage over the rocks and gravel beneath it. Sonny looked at this and remembered the time he had drunk his fill from just such a crossing and shortly after that discovered the rotting carcass of a dead cow not two hundred yards upstream. He had recoiled in revulsion, but an old cowboy with him had told him not to worry, saying that river water flowing over gravel purified itself every ten or twenty feet. He didn't know if this was true but at the time he had forced himself to accept it.

"As a kid," Dawson remarked, "we crossed some cattle here. We had tried upriver aways but kept bogging down. Then we came upon this natural ford. That must have been thirty years ago before this came to be part of the trail to Del Rio." He shook his head and commented, "I sure as hell would never have thought that I'd be layin' in wait to ambush an unsuspecting man at this spot." He looked sour and pulled his hat brim down a little in front.

Sonny Cade said, "Dammit, Mr. Dawson, if we don't take him off guard it could go bad for us. I know how you feel, of course, but just think of the kin of ours that English has killed in cold blood."

"Call me 'Bob.' That 'mister' business makes me feel old," Dawson said. He added a few minutes later, "Somehow I don't feel right about what we're fixin' to do."

They saw a horse about this time on the other side, and Dawson hissed at Sonny, "Get down!"

The younger man lay flat while the older one slowly craned his neck off to one side, edging around the tree for a better look.

"Son of a *bitch,*" Dawson exclaimed. "It ain't English, it's Raul Ysleta, who is supposed to be trailing him. Something has gone wrong."

Not five minutes later the six men holding rifles waited for the Mexican to dismount from his brown mare. Then they gathered around him, listening anxiously, wondering what had happened.

"I followed him," Raul said in his harsh accent, "when he rode out of Santa Rita early this morning the way Koestler said he would. He left by the far side and circled back. A few miles along the way a fat man, *un gordo inmenso,* riding a big horse joined him. Koestler told us English would be alone—I don't know who the fat man is."

"Where are they now?" Walden Doggett barked.

"Downstream about four or five miles. There wasn't much cover—I had to stay a long way behind so they wouldn't see me. I lost sight of them but picked up their tracks after a little. These led to a beat-up old house near the river which looks as if it might be some kind of hunter's camp. I got close enough to see their horses tied in front of it. No other horses were there, but two mules are staked out behind the place not far from a flatbed wagon."

Jason Quest spoke up. "Did the fat man ride a gray workhorse?"

The Mexican looked at him through his slightly slanted eyes. He nodded affirmatively.

"It has to be that damn Calvin Laudermilk," Quest exploded. "He has a way of poking into things that are none of his business."

"That's a good way for him to get his head blown off," Walden Doggett said tersely.

"What do we do now?" Bob Dawson asked.

Koestler ruminated a moment as the others automatically turned toward him. Then he said, "I would guess that they ran into each other by chance—and that English will ride on alone. However, a man on horseback can easily ford the river at a good many places, so it's not likely that he'll come all the way back here."

"Damn!" Walden Doggett roared, slapping his open hand sharply against his leg.

"I had figured that our best bet would be to cut him down when he tried to cross," Koestler said. "We're not going to take him unawares in the open country once he's on the other side." He began to pace back and forth, staring at the earth as though looking for a sign. Then he strode back to the waiting men. "I had a good idea where he'd ford the South Concho, but now we have to come up with a new slant. There's just one thing to do—gun him when he comes out of that house. I've got nothing against Laudermilk in spite of his being a troublemaker, nor do I know who might be the owner of that cabin where Raul saw the mules. But I value my hide and don't plan to get into a showdown with a man like Tom English. We don't have any choice—we have to take all of them by surprise."

"You mean kill two innocent men along with him?" Sonny Cade blurted out, his eyes wide.

"How do you know they're not friends of his who would put a bullet in your gut without thinking twice?" Quest snapped at him.

Several men started talking at once, but Walden Doggett silenced them. Then Koestler had Raul Ysleta scratch a rough map in the dirt with a stick so they could have an idea of just where "our game has gone to ground," as he put it.

Raul told them briefly how he had tethered his mount in a dry arroyo and then crept along it in order to approach the house. The gully, as it led down to the river, passed not far from the shelter. They decided that six men should go there: Walden Doggett with Bob Dawson, Jason Quest, Stoddard Landon, Carl Koestler, and Sonny Cade. They could tie their horses at the head of the ravine in a stand of scrub cedar which Raul described, saying that it lay out of sight of the old house. Then they would enter the draw and follow its sunken, rocky path as it meandered toward the Concho. This would bring them within fifty yards of the house where Tom English and the fat man and some stranger stayed. When their prey came outside, they'd cut them down.

As a precaution, Raul Ysleta would stay on horseback on the low hill behind the place. If by any chance English got away, Raul would trail him.

The horses surged into the water as their riders spurred them, and in moments they lunged forward, throwing spray, until they reached the other side. Sonny Cade brought up the rear, and he leaned forward as his mount climbed the bank as they backtracked. Then they circled, with Raul leading the way.

Sonny closed the gap and pulled even with Bob Dawson. Swift currents of excitement ran within him, blending with rushes of sharp fear. He rode with his rifle clutched in both hands, the reins snarled around it.

"Put that thing in its scabbard, you idiot," Dawson said in a muted yell. "You want it to go off and give us away?"

Sonny pulled to a halt while he fumbled with his rifle until he slid it down securely in its leather boot. Feeling that a thousand butterflies fought within him for release, he urged his horse into a lope so he could catch up. He wanted to stop so he could relieve himself behind a tree, but he didn't want to fall behind the others. A hunting fever gripped him, and he said to himself, feeling awed by the thought, I'm going to kill a man today, but he began stammering and couldn't get the words out.

"It must be getting on toward noon," said Calvin Laudermilk, "and I can't for the life of me figure out where Tuck might be."

He and Tom English left the crudely built board shanty and headed for the river. "Let's see if he's not down here catching some fish." Calvin huffed out the words as he labored over the broken ground.

They walked almost a mile along the tree-lined South Concho in their search, with Calvin speaking ceaselessly. "Tuck Bowlegs is a descendent of a Seminole Indian scout who fought with the U.S. Dragoons and later the Cavalry against the Comanches. His father ended up with a Comanche squaw, strange to say, and the two of them pulled up stakes and went to New Mexico, where they found the remnants of her tribe. That's where Tuck was born—after his father died—and his mother's people raised him. He lived as any other Indian boy would until he was around twenty years of age. Throughout that time they moved every few months, dragging their lodges from one place to another. What they did, as I guess you know, is follow the game that they hunted. When it played out they had no choice but to move on. While they were over by the Canadian River in the Texas Panhandle, the army rounded them up and put what was left of their tribe on a reservation in the Oklahoma Territory. He got good treatment there from an Indian agent who found out that his dad had worked with the cavalry, and Tuck learned how to speak our language fairly well."

"How is it that he ended up on his own down here?"

"Well, Tom, at the reservation an outfit showed up with a contract to supply beef for the Indians, and they needed a cook. The agent recommended Tuck and he rode with them for some years. They went on cattle drives that would start in South Texas and wind past Fort Concho on the way to Indian Territory. Maybe seven years ago Tuck was passing through and he took up with a widow woman who is black African and red Indian and Lord knows what else, name of Jimmie, who had once been married to a Buffalo soldier at the fort."

"Is that the cook John Hope has at his saloon?"

"The very one. Well, they make quite a pair. Tuck doesn't say a hell of a lot and Jimmie hardly speaks at all, so I don't know how they communicated the fact to one another that they wanted to live together, but nature has a way of lending a hand to the most helpless of us. When I see that the hippopotamus and the rhinocerous and the pachyderm are able to find mates in spite of their apparent hindrances, it makes me believe that all creatures are so constituted that they find ways to overcome the greatest obstacles in order to fulfill the biblical injunction that they should be fruitful and multiply."

"There are times when I find it a trifle hard to follow you," Tom English said with a slight smile. He sat down upon a limestone ledge that lay below an old salt cedar tree.

Calvin Laudermilk looked at him and then, raising his eyes, he peered through the fragile branches with their fringed, light green leaves at the blue clarity of the noonday sky. Lowering his gaze, he replied, "Don't worry about understanding me, son. It's enough for me if you just listen."

Calvin sat ponderously on the cool ledge beside Tom with a gusting sigh of relief. The great folds of his belly lapped forward and rested on his thighs, and he took a red bandanna from his rear pocket in order to mop the small rivers of sweat which rolled down his face and neck. Then he whispered, "Be quiet—I hear something."

They saw movement in the brush, coming around a bend in the river. A man with a quiver on his back appeared. He raised a steel-tipped dogwood shaft, his arm straining as the short, thick cedar bow bent, and then an arrow hissed through the silence, spurting as it penetrated the shallows beneath him. The man plunged into knee-deep water where white splashes broke the surface, and grasped a sun perch from it, holding the fish and the arrow which pierced it in his hand as he turned to face the men behind him.

A hooked, aquiline nose dominated his creased, walnut-colored face. A small leather strap secured his long black hair with gray strands in it behind his neck. He did not change expressions as he spoke. "I been watching you, Laudermilk." The fish in his hand twisted in an arc, gills straining open and shut. Tuck Bowlegs held it firmly to avoid being finned, and addressing himself again to Calvin, he said, "You only come to see me when you're hungry." He withdrew his arrow, rubbed its point with his fingers to clean it, and slid it into his quiver. Then he climbed to the shore and picked up a length of rawhide cord. He pushed the end of it into his catch's mouth and out a gill, then slid the shimmering, flat sunperch down his stringer where it dangled like an added, heavy scalp along with eight other small fish. "I got enough here to feed you and your friend," said Tuck Bowlegs.

Sonny Cade lay at the edge of the draw, his head under a gray cenisa bush. Through its branches he could clearly see the cabin, which had smoke coming from its stone chimney. The six men had waited in frozen positions, clutching their weapons for over half an hour, and the tension had become more than Sonny could bear. In an effort to break it he asked, "Who lives there?" in a loud whisper to Jason Quest, who crouched beside him.

"A crazy Indian called Bowlegs," Quest replied in a low but matter-of-fact tone, apparently relieved to have something which might occupy his mind.

"Crazy?"

"I recall a time," Quest recounted, "when he had not been around here for many years, it must have been about eighteen eighty. It was in the spring, I'm sure of that for we'd just had the first real rain of the year. Anyway, he got drunk and rode a paint horse full tilt up and down Concho Street right in front of everyone till they caught him and put him in jail."

"For riding a horse?"

"He was buck nekkid, squawlin' like a panther, and hanging down off the horse's neck, first on one side, then the other, like a Comanche."

"Oh, my Lord," Sonny murmured.

"Colonel Grierson came over from the fort and got him freed. Said his daddy had served with him as a cavalry scout. Santa Rita didn't have a jail cell until they built the sheriff's office a few years back, so they had this nekkid Indian chained to a mesquite tree. His woman brought him a pair of pants for the sake of decency. The men in town were fit to be tied, but the colonel got things settled down."

"Does he work for someone?"

"Hell, boy, who'd have him? No, he hunts and fishes mostly, and lives off the earnings of Jimmie, that's his woman, who is a cook in town. He does sell venison and various fish now and then for pocket money, but Jimmie makes him come out here when he plans to get drunk. At least, that's the word in town," Quest concluded.

"Hold it down," Walden Doggett growled. Then he hissed, "Look out! Somebody's coming through the door." Cold-steel, clicking noises sounded as he cocked both hammers of his heavy ten-gauge shotgun and held it in readiness.

An Indian with tied-back long hair emerged and went to the back toward the two mules. He wore faded brown canvas work pants with a beaded belt. He had on moccasins but no shirt, and his hairless upper body, even at this distance, could be seen to be compact and smoothly muscled in spite of his years. He harnessed his team, then backed the two mules skillfully to the wagon and hitched them to it.

"What's he going to do?" Jason Quest asked in a querulous way, not really expecting an answer. He glared in perplexity at the Indian.

They watched him roll two wood-staved empty barrels up to the side of the wagon and hoist them into it.

Carl Koestler stepped on a small branch, which made a dry cracking sound as he moved between Sonny and Doggett. Koestler put his hand on Doggett's arm and said, "Don't shoot yet. Wait for all three of them to come outside."

The Indian drove the wagon around the house, its steel-rimmed wooden wheels clacking over stones. It creaked and groaned and tilted on its way down to the river's edge. On reaching water, the flop-eared mules came to a stop and dropped their heads to drink. Each swallowed with jolting, uphill ripples showing in their necks. Then the driver slapped his long reins and they leaned into the traces, pulling the wagon without difficulty down into the shallow water of the South Concho.

The men in the arroyo watched the Indian pull his team to a halt. The river's mirror-like surface wrinkled as it swept about the wagon and the mules.

Sonny tensed, his fingers whitening with pressure on his rifle, for two more men came out of the shack.

"Hold your fire," Walden Doggett husked. A long, drawn-out sigh came from his mouth. His dull, leaden-looking eyes half closed, and he said exultantly, "They took off their weapons—God almighty *damn.*" Then, breathing heavily, he added, "Looks like they plan to go fishing—they're carrying a seine."

Two figures, one huge—his shirt seemingly swollen beyond all reason—the other slender, came from the shack and walked in single file. The fat man carried a four-foot-long, rolled-up net—a seine—upon one shoulder.

The six hunters holding rifles and handguns in the dry gully listened to the sound of voices from the men they planned to kill.

"Wait till they get in the water, then we'll have that bastard where we want him. Jesus Christ!" Walden Doggett snarled, "I've finally *caught* the sonuvabitch in a trap. Don't none of you shoot English—I plan to use my knife on him!"

Calvin Laudermilk labored down the steeply inclined path which twisted from the cabin to the water's edge. Tall trees, primarily pecans and oaks, towered above him. He let the heavy seine tumble to the ground. "Let's get out of these clothes and into the water," he hollered.

"Hush up," Tom English warned him, "you'll scare the fish."

"I've heard that all my life," Calvin grumbled as he sat down to pull off his boots, grunting with the effort this cost. "It's my opinion that fish can't hear us any more than we can hear them."

Tuck Bowlegs drove the wagon into deeper water and then tipped over both barrels. He righted them when each had half filled, and then he drove the wagon up to a slightly higher level, allowing the current to flow just under the wagonbed. He called out, "You two can have the fun of seining, and we'll put your catch in the barrels. My plan is to sell fish in Santa Rita for enough money to buy their weight in tequila and mescal."

The two men on the bank stripped rapidly and then walked into the river in the shaded, waving light that streamed through the canopy of leaves arching above them. Dappled shadows fell across their contrasting bodies: one with herd-bull shoulders above a voluminous belly which draped in massive folds down toward tree-trunk legs; the other, with less than half his breadth, had well-defined muscles in his back and arms and legs.

The two men stepped gingerly into the slowly moving water. They each held one end of the long seine, which had twisted again even though they had unraveled it on the bank before entering the water. With a deft movement, Tom straightened out the snarled netting then stretched it tight, backing away from Calvin Laudermilk.

Soft mud pressed between Calvin's toes, and unbidden childhood memories passed vaguely through his mind. He dismissed them and moved forward, conscious of a host of sensations: the pressure of small waves circling each leg, his feet slipping on moss-slick rocks, then pressing upon rough gravel. The river, warm on top, became much cooler as he descended. It slid between his legs and sent shivers from his thighs up to his waist. The seine bellied out into a wide curve as they slowly moved upstream against the tugging current.

"We got something!" Calvin yelled, and both men felt the weight. They moved faster, closing the opening between them, letting the mesh pull into an ever-narrowing, long semicircle until they closed it and lunged toward the slick bank, stumbling and splashing—calling to each other in excitement as if they had known each other all their lives and not simply for a few days.

Calvin sank to one knee as he reached into the net. Fumbling with both hands, he succeeded at last in hooking his fingers in the gills of a twisting yellow catfish—a monstrous freshwater creature fully four feet in length. "Lookee here," Calvin howled, lifting his slippery, slick-skinned catch high. He caroled out, "he must weigh nigh onto forty pounds!"

He struggled to the wagon and plopped the whiskered, flopping fish into one of the barrels. Returning to the net, he plucked perch and crappie from its folds, throwing some back into the river but keeping the large ones. He seized an alligator gar that had severed several of the net's tough strands with its wicked teeth. "Even Indians won't eat these," Calvin declared, laughing maliciously at Tuck Bowlegs. He added, "I seen some starvin' Tawakonis once, and this is what they done to keep these here gars from getting other fish." He stumbled to the bank and thrust the gar's long, bony beak into wet sand and snapped it off; then threw the remains into the river.

Back in the stream, they moved deliberately forward under the overarching shelter of wind-ruffled leaves. A turtle slid sideways from a log, plopped into the water, and sank out of sight; and off to their left a large water moccasin wriggled its fat, sinuous length through the shadows, only its head showing ahead of a trail of quickly disappearing V-shaped ripples. The hot wind felt cool upon Calvin's wet skin as he and Tom swept the seine time and again through pools and shallows. They caught a big buffalo fish, perhaps a twenty-five pounder, and half a dozen black bass, each one measuring more than a foot in length. On their last try they brought to the bank two more long-whiskered, heavy catfish, one of them a flatheaded Appaloosa cat. "Lord have mercy upon us poor sinners," Calvin sang out gleefully. "After working this hard, we're going to have to force old Tuck to skin one of these catfish and fry him up for us."

Tom stood in the wagon with Tuck, peering down into the two barrels, watching the fish thresh about in frothing confusion. Calvin drug the last seine-full of fish toward them, preparing to hand them the slippery haul one by one. The team of mules stood patiently in water which almost reached their bellies. One of them raised his head, perking his long, shaggy ears forward, and looked sideways at the shore. The other snorted and did the same.

Calvin stopped talking and looked up the steep bank. "My God," he gasped, "what in the name of all that's holy have we got here?"

Six armed men stood above them, their dark silhouettes looming against the clear-blue sky. One of them raised a rifle and barked out, "Don't move a muscle—just raise your hands up over your heads real slow."

The six men scrambled closer, sliding down the bank until they reached the water's edge. All held weapons. One of them, a thick-bodied man with a bushy, wheat-colored mustache, carefully propped a double-barreled shotgun against the exposed, curving roots of a cottonwood tree, and drew from a sheath at his belt a curved, wide-bladed bowie knife.

"Keep your rifle on 'em, Stoddard," the one holding the knife commanded. A strange expression played over his face as he walked to the side of the man who had his rifle up against his shoulder, swinging its muzzle slowly back and forth, covering the three astounded fishermen. The other four hurriedly placed their rifles on the bank and drew their six-guns.

CHAPTER SEVEN

I bent my knees, holding to the top of a barrel, and felt the rough wood beneath my bare feet. Black snakes of fear twisted up my legs and sank their fangs in my belly. In front of me Tuck crouched, reaching down on the floorboards for something.

My eyes met those of the rifleman on shore. He raised his head, then deliberately put his cheek to the stock and leveled his sights on my chest. Off to one side of him I saw Calvin—pulling the seine behind him—sidle toward the men with pistols. He and Tuck must have been aware that the gunmen all had their attention fixed on me.

"Tom English!" the thick-bodied man holding the big knife yelled. "My name is Walden Doggett. That name mean anything to you?"

At that instant Tuck Bowlegs dove from the wagon—making a big splash as he hit the river. Gunfire exploded, slapping bullets into the ruffled surface where Tuck had disappeared. I grabbed the long reins and used them as a whip, lashing and yelling at the mules. They lunged forward, heaving against the traces while I sank as low as I could behind the barrels. But the wagon's wheels had sunk in the mud and we hardly moved at all.

"Don't shoot him if you don't have to," the leader with the knife bellowed. "Take him alive if you can."

Two men came into the river, high-legging it at first, then wading out, leaning forward waist-deep, leaving a rippled wake behind them in the water. One caught the headstalls and bits of the two mules and held them fast, and the other, a very nervous-looking kid with his face turned red from fear, circled to the side and came at me, holding his handgun forward in a very unfriendly way.

The men on shore watched all this going on, not noticing Calvin Laudermilk edging toward them, mother-naked just like me, leaning down and sticking his right arm in the seine. He pulled out a three-foot-long catfish from the net and fastened his hamlike hand just above the tail. Then he twirled it around his head like a slippery, limber shillelagh and, with an enormous heave of his huge shoulders, smashed the long-whisk-ered head of the big catfish into the face of the nearest man to him. It sounded like the flat side of an ax hitting a ripe watermelon. I have heard of someone being knocked for a loop, but until that instant I had never fully appreciated it. His feet flew out before him and he flipped over back-ward, landing on the back of his neck, going tail over teakettle as they say.

Calvin swung the bloody catfish in a wide arc and caught the man next in line—who was raising his Colt—right in the gut, knocking the wind from him and doubling him completely over. He splayed his arms out as he fell backward, open mouth working like a fish out of water as he tried to breathe. Calvin went to the attack in earnest then, spinning about and allowing his full weight to fall on the helpless man. Calvin's formidable, unclad rump landed squarely on his victim's chest, driving him deep into the moist sand.

A pistol shot whined past Calvin's head and he lurched to one side, rolling and staggering off-balance, and then he launched himself out into a prodigious belly flop that threw a startling wave, a far-flung sheet of silver spray, as he sank from sight in the murky olive-green waters of the South Concho.

The scared-looking kid by now was crawling up the side of the wagon toward me, waving his big .45 in my direction. Toward the front of the wagon I saw the other man climbing in, an older man, dripping wet and glaring, and he too pointed a pistol at me with a shaking hand. I started forward but then stopped as a wave of gooseflesh washed across me from head to toe. There is something about being barefoot all over that limits your aggressiveness.

Then the damndest thing happened: It seemed to me that the world had jerked off its axis, for the wagon tilted abruptly off to one side. I saw my two assailants whipping out their arms automatically, trying to keep their balance. The kid next to me dropped his gun and a yell started from him. Then we were hurled head over heels as the wagon spun over, and I found myself flung with fish barrels as well as the two men into the abrupt coldness of the river.

I fought my way to the surface, gulping for air, and saw a strange vision: Out of the river bottom came Calvin Laudermilk like some monster from the deep—dark moss caught in his hair and a crazed gleam in his eyes. He immediately upended his broad, pale beam as he dove once again, like the great white whale of the story I'd struggled so to read as a youngster.

I ducked and swam under water frantically, all of my senses screaming out, as bullets splashed the stream inches above my head as well as all around me.

A hand had me by the hair! I grasped a wrist, came up, and then a wet pistol barrel pressed deep into the side of my neck. Blinking the water away so I could see—I looked into the cruel eyes of the older man who had been in the wagon with me.

"Hold it right there," he snarled.

"You got him, Jason! Bring him out of that river to me," the man on shore with the bowie knife cried out exultantly. He waited without moving, his eyes like dark, dull stones. His thick, wet lips beneath his drooping mustache hung open slackly.

The man called Jason let go of my hair and shifted behind me with the intention, I suppose, of herding me ashore. That move proved to be a mistake for him. Calvin Laudermilk came up for air with Jason folded in his brawny arms. I saw Jason's eyes bug out, his face turn purple, and I heard a terrible cracking noise as if dry sticks were breaking. Then Calvin pulled him down into the foaming stream and they disappeared from sight. The rifleman and the leader with the knife stared at the troubled water a moment, thunderstruck, and then switched their attention to me. The rifle swung my way, but I plunged under water again, starting downstream toward a willow tree which drooped toward its mirrored image.

Groping at the slickness of the bottom leading out, I cautiously slipped my head above the surface, hugging the slight protection of the bank. I reached above my head, clutched a willow's limp branch, and pulled it between me and my enemies. Looking through a screen of leaves, I saw Tuck Bowlegs standing high on the bank behind the thick-bodied leader and the rifleman. I saw him notch an arrow, and in his hands a short, thick cedar bow bent almost double.

A shaft of sunlight reflected off the water and I had to squint my eyes to see in the glare. Things happened so rapidly I couldn't understand them: a rifle spinning in the air, hitting in a clatter on the ground. What the hell is going on? The man who had seemingly thrown the weapon took three steps toward my hiding place. He stopped and slowly faced away. I watched in bewilderment. Then I heard his awful screams, and when he turned I saw him reaching desperately for his back. An arrow's feathered shaft protruded from between his shoulder blades. He kept turning—he faced me now again. Frozen by the sight, mindless of the danger, I stood in the river as the man crumpled facedown in the wet sand. He kept scrabbling with both hands at a point in his back he couldn't reach, and his hoarse screams went on and on.

Only seconds had passed although they seemed much longer. The leader dropped the bowie knife and clawed at his pistol, but an arrow tore away a section of his ear. He had his six-gun coming out when a second arrow chunked into the fleshy part of his thigh. He went down hard, squealing like a stuck pig.

Clamping his mouth shut he grabbed the arrow and jerked at it. The point pulled free but the barbs tore out a small chunk of bright, red muscle. Blood pumped from the wound, and the leader's face changed into a mask of corded agony. A fine red mist sprayed his neck and shoulder from the tattered slot where his earlobe had been before.

I had not been conscious of the mules, but now I saw them struggling to their feet in the twisted traces, making an infernal racket. Their braying sounded like bagpipes played with discordant abandon by drunken pipers. I'm sure they were just as upset with their conundrum as I was with mine.

I saw the man named Jason struggling from the water. He crawled out and pitched forward on his face. Down the bank to my right, maybe seventy yards away, I saw the kid who'd dropped his six-gun when the wagon turned over. He grabbed up a rifle as he sprinted past the two men Calvin had felled with the catfish when the scrap started. One of them was on all fours retching, and the others sat with his legs apart, looking dumbly about. In all likelihood he was wondering what the hell had hit him.

Calvin lumbered up behind me and we struggled up the bank toward the shelter of the trees.

"Quick," Tuck called out to us, "head for the cabin. There's a rider behind me in those trees." He stretched his arm out, pointing. "Another man is off to the right with a rifle, and in a minute or two the big one back there will get his hands on that shotgun."

As if to confirm his words, I heard whistling sounds and air shrieks as hot lead spat by us. Then there came a booming like a blunderbuss as the shotgun came into action, and buckshot splattered through the branches right over our heads. Like most cowboys I had never before laid claim to being fleet of foot, but at that instant I do believe I came very close to flying. Tearing through the trees with not a stitch to slow me down, I spun from tree to tree, sliding down and rolling once when I lost my footing.

A man on horseback rode hard at us, firing as he came. While reason told me that he had no chance of hitting anything from the back of a running horse, I didn't pay a speck of attention. Reason had no part in the drama in which I was an unwilling player; and at the time it seemed he couldn't miss. Head back, arms pumping, I increased my speed until I reached safety and hurled myself into the cabin a split second before Tuck did. Behind us the shooting continued, and I pulled my Colts free while I craned my neck around the door in time to see Calvin Laudermilk blundering up the trail with all the grace of a juggernaut. When he stumbled inside with us he bent over till his head hung clear down to his knees as he fought to catch his breath. The sounds of his torn wheezing sounded like a rusted sawblade screeching through wet wood.

Tuck pulled out a deer rifle and began to shoot through the door. Calvin grabbed his hog leg of a handgun preparing to go to the attack when the shotgun roared again, and at the same time the only windowpane in the cabin blew into a million pieces, stinging my bare back as if I were standing in a glass hailstorm.

While the others fired blindly into the out-of-doors I scrambled into my clothes, hardly aware of the slits and glass-sliver punctures along my spine and shoulders. Though not of any real protection, the difference having a layer of cloth on was as if I had donned a suit of armor. I pulled on my boots, strapped my gunbelt to my waist, and quickly fastened the tie-down strings of the two scabbards to my legs. Throughout this time Tuck and Calvin kept up their cannonade. I picked up the balanced Colts, checked their cylinders, then holstered them.

Calvin donned his pants and shirt and—after some heartfelt swearing— managed to get into his boots. Outside we heard men yelling. It dawned on me that our horses were gone. Looking through the door, I saw the tree where we had tethered them, and I saw the ends of Calvin's and my reins hanging down. They'd been cut.

The firing slowed, then stopped. Holding my Winchester in my left hand and a Colt in my right, I made a run at the door and dove through it. I hit rolling and came up behind a big, half-dead mesquite with a large black seeping stain on its side. I slipped around it and dashed for a liveoak, pressing my back so close to it that it must have appeared that I wanted to squeeze between the bark and the sap. Forcing myself to slow down—to concentrate—I holstered the .45 and levered a cartridge into the rifle's firing chamber. The combination lever and trigger guard of the rifle made a cold-steel sliding noise in the silent air, sounding a little like heavy scissor blades clashing. Quivering with pent-up rage and fear, I threw myself around the tree, holding the weapon chest high. Eyes flicking through the trees and shadows, I found no targets. Behind me I heard movement, then saw Tuck zigzagging off to my right and Calvin on my left. Calvin advanced straight ahead, looking like a herd bull heading toward a rival.

We had scarcely reached the river when we heard the drumbeat of a bunch of horses running in the distance. Tuck's eyes met mine. I said to him, "You take the lead." He knew the lay of the land better than we did, and he had Indian eyes. He'd be able to read signs and tracks as clearly as a city-bred man would a newspaper.

We went in single file down the path to the river. Below us lay the still figure of a man facedown near the waterline, no longer moving at all. A dogwood shaft stuck up at an angle from his back. The bright feathers of the arrow stood stiffly out above the scarlet wetness which glistened on the man's faded blue shirt. I knelt beside him and touched the gray skin of his neck. There was no pulse and his flesh was cold. He was stone-cold dead.

Not far away two furious, wet mules snorted helplessly, hitched as captives to a twisted, upside-down wagon. We saw no sign of any of the other men who had attacked us.

We went upriver after this and followed tracks that led to a deep draw which runoff water had dug over the past century or so. The draw, a jagged, steep-sided gully, led from the river in an ascending, winding path off to the east of Tuck's house. Every few minutes he hesitated while he pointed out to us pressed-down grass, a broken stick, and scuff marks in the stones.

Tuck said, "They laid in wait here, watching the cabin." He pointed to faint indications near the edge of the ravine that told him this story.

"Why didn't they just shoot us from ambush?" Calvin asked.

"They would have seen us leave the cabin unarmed on our way to the river," I said.

"They were after you," Calvin remarked. It was a statement, not a question.

"Yes," I answered, "they were. Looks like the man who wrote that letter had no intention of facing me in Mexico. What he had in mind was to waylay me while I was on the trail."

Tuck had left us behind and we hurried to catch up. He bent forward, running his fingers lightly over rocks and dust and random weeds. "Two men walking together, one dragging his feet," he said, letting us interpret that any way we wanted. He kept speaking, pointing here and there. "Blood on the grass again. Must be from the big man who had the knife."

Tuck sat down on his haunches examining his find, a scowl darkening his face. "I wish I'd had my deer-hunting arrows—they're heavier, have bigger heads and wide barbs. The only ones in the wagon were the arrows I use to hunt squirrel and fish. They have little heads . . . small barbs. The kind of arrowheads that children use." He twisted his mouth, disgusted, before he said, "Too bad I didn't kill the big man too. Well, he's like a wounded deer. I'll have to track him down and finish the job."

Tuck said, "You know, I was lucky that I hit the one with the rifle in a vital spot. Then I aimed at the big man's ear—had in mind driving the arrow right into his brain, but he ducked and I only nicked him. Then he went to floundering around and my next arrow—which I aimed for a gut shot—caught his upper leg."

The three of us fanned out as the draw widened, and then we came out its shallow end at a thicket. Tuck inspected the trampled earth and said, "Five men on foot came here where they had their horses tied." He walked away, leaving Calvin and me in the shade of the small stand of trees.

This time I didn't follow him as he walked in widening circles around us. I felt completely drained—as if I'd run a ten-mile race. There is nothing on God's green earth, I realized, that can tire a man the way fear does. "It appears to me that they've run for it," Calvin said. "Gone off to lick their wounds."

"Or get reinforcements," I remarked.

Calvin said in a low, threatening manner, "Well, by God, I hope they *do* come back. I'll declare, it would be nice to face those sons of bucks when I had a gun in my hand and not a blamed fish."

I had to laugh at the pictures his comments brought to mind. I said, "Calvin, that reminds me that I forgot to thank you for saving my life back yonder. It has just occurred to me that I didn't let loose an arrow or swing a fish during the fight—and I'm beholden to you and Tuck for defending me."

Calvin Laudermilk chortled, "Men will remember this as 'The Great South Concho Fish Fight.' "

Tuck returned and told us that a seventh enemy had been on horseback. He had joined the other five men when they mounted their horses at the head of the draw. We decided that he must have been the one shooting at us with a pistol when we made our run for the cabin. Tuck went on to say that six horses left together—moving fast—and a seventh trailed behind at a walk. He figured that would be the dead man's horse. They were in too much of a hurry, he decided, to worry about leading it.

Tuck left to track down our horses, and Calvin and I made our way back to the shack, where we kicked through a junk pile out back until we came up with some tools that would have to do: a rusted post-hole digger and a garden spade with a cracked handle. With these we returned to the river, dug a shallow grave high enough to be above the water level even in case of a big rise, and hurriedly buried the man Tuck had killed. He carried no identification, and I said, "We don't even know his name," but Calvin replied, "When they first surprised us someone called him Stoddard." The name rang a bell, but for the life of me, I couldn't place him.

After this we stripped again, although damn nervously I'll have to admit, and went back in the river to rescue the mules and the wagon. This was not a simple matter, for the mules had developed a terrible temper and kept trying to bite us as we struggled to unhitch them. However, we finally succeeded, led them to shore, and tied them to a tree. Then I splashed back to the upside-down wagon and grabbed hold of it. I might as well have tried to pick up a horse. It didn't budge. But then Calvin joined me, squatting down till only his head showed, then heaving with his legs and arms—while I tried to do the same—and the dripping wagon heaved up on one side, balanced an instant there, then flopped over. Breathing hard, I looked at Calvin, awed, and realized the muscles in his arms were probably bigger than those in my legs. Without a doubt, this was the strongest man I'd ever seen in all my life.

"Calvin," I said while we pulled our clothes on once again, "I didn't think we'd get Tuck's wagon out, and had decided we'd have to get a rope and pull it with the mules. However, I don't know if they have your power. What have you done to build up your strength?"

"Nothing," he replied. "I have all my life been firmly opposed to physical effort. It may be," he added, "that by saving myself for all these years I have a little extra available for the times when I need it." He made his throaty chuckle then as we hitched up the mules before driving them back to Tuck's place.

By the time we got there we saw Tuck returning on foot leading my chestnut, Judge, and Calvin's monumental gray plowhorse, Sully.

"Found 'em grazing not half a mile to the north," Tuck said.

In a short time I had spliced the cut rein ends off the tree back on the bridles, repairing them almost as good as new. Cowboys learn things like this from necessity, since leather tends to dry and can then break easily.

I pulled a brown quart bottle from one of my saddlebags as we started inside, saying, "I for one am ready for a drink—and being of a generous nature, I'm prepared to share this with you."

Tuck and Calvin took me up on my offer without an instant's hesitation. However, Tuck didn't like the taste of bourbon so he went out to his woodpile, moved a few logs, and came back with a bottle full of cloudy liquid with what appeared to be a dead grubworm or caterpillar—fat, white, and curled—at the bottom of it.

"That's disgusting," I said.

"Not to Tuck it ain't," said Calvin. "It's mother's milk to him."

"The Mexicans make this," Tuck said, "from the agave or maguey cactus. They call it mescal—or maybe it's pulque. I get 'em mixed up. Now tequila, on the other hand, is an entirely different matter."

I had not heard such a lengthy statement from Tuck before. He had, it seemed, finally come upon a subject of conversation that merited his full attention.

"There's all the difference between daylight and dark between mescal and pulque," Calvin protested, adding, "What on earth does a damn Indian know about taste anyway?"

Tuck ignored Calvin for his concentration centered solely upon the bottle which he clasped protectively as he sank down on a pile of moldy Navaho blankets in a corner by the smoke-blackened fireplace where he cooked his solitary meals. He twisted the cork from the bottle's mouth, took a big gulp from it, then—after shuddering with either pain or pleasure for a minute or so—he said, "That's better."

He sat cross-legged with the bottle propped between his legs and said, "I been saving this mescal." He lifted it to his mouth, giving a clear sign that his days of thrift had passed by.

I noticed the slivers and shards of glass all over the dirt floor, and all of sudden felt the stinging on my back from the cuts I'd received when the shotgun blew out the windowpane. Pressing Calvin into service to doctor the places I couldn't reach, I pulled off my blood-spotted shirt. Without hesitating he applied his blunt and calloused fingers to the task of plucking all the small fractured spines of glass he could extract, then he roughly rubbed and brushed at the others, complaining as I winced that he wanted me to be still so he might attend my injuries. Then he judiciously patted touches of whiskey on most of the little wounds. He and Tuck had only suffered pinpricks from smaller bits of glass, but I'd been closer, though fortunately facing away from the window when it exploded, and had been the worst hit.

"That's it, thank God," Calvin murmured. "I feared you might be more badly hurt, which would have required an even greater waste of this scarce whiskey."

I forced a laugh, put on my shirt, and accepted from him a coffee cup full to the brim with bourbon. It took several drinks to scald out the nerves in my mouth and throat so the sipping could take on the nature of a pleasurable pursuit instead of a grim choking down of the stuff in the hopes it might bring a drugged relief. After two or three more cups I felt the teasing approach of the ease that I sought—and waves of sudden tranquility at last washed over me, leaving a dull buzzing in my ears that I took as the sign that absolute comfort must be approaching. In all my years of drinking I'd never quite got my arms around that elusive promise of tranquility, but there was an early age where I sensed that it was near, and at such times I had the compulsive feeling that if I kept on drinking I would get the ghost of comfort close enough to grab hold of it with both hands and clutch it to me.

Then worry, which is comfort's enemy, crawled out from its hiding place and scratched its way into my thoughts. I wondered if I might no longer have the *edge* that keeps a gunfighter alive. There is, I knew, no such thing as a fair fight. The few top guns I've known had a coldness, a quickness, an absolute concentration, and a willingness to pull the trigger without a hint of hesitation—all these things that I wrapped up in the word *edge;* and this, I was deeply convinced, gave them that slight advantage which spelled the difference between life and death. Could grief and fear have so weakened me that I'd lost it? I sat on a rickety chair, the only one in the place, elbows on the pine box that served as a table, and brooded about this.

Calvin reached out beside him and dragged to him Tuck's ancient saddle as a prop for his back. Thin, dry leather had peeled away from the saddletree in places, leaving bare wood in sight. He sat on a saddleblanket and settled himself like a giant bird wallowing into its nest before directing himself to me.

"Your body has no padding to it. It must be uncommonly painful to ride horseback all day when, instead of a sensibly sized butt, you've got such a pitifully small one." He leaned over on one hip and slapped his ample, well-cushioned rump, saying, "Now, *here's* a rear end as God designed it, one that can withstand the shocks and discomforts of a cold, hard saddle and of a slapping cantle." He shook his head in pity for one born with such a malformation as mine. He squinted his eyes at me. "Another thing I noted when we shucked our clothes at the river is that you've got almost as many scars as I've got freckles. I know the sign of a bullet wound, and I would not have thought a man could live who's been hit as often as you."

He had seen the humped bluish-red scar on my back, the small purple one almost in the center of my chest, the discolored, hairless round dents on my leg and left arm—and the terrible jagged white patch of skin which marked the place where a bullet had once shattered my right forearm. Remembered pain augured into the center of my brain, and the terrible reality of certain bone-deep memories ached within me.

"In addition to all those gunshot wounds I couldn't help but see the long white and red scars that snake all over your back and neck, and particularly on your arms and hands. I suppose it's not polite for me to comment, but they are enough to make my gorge rise. Looks like you got rolled up in bob wire and dragged for twenty miles. You know how curious I am—I had to ask you about them."

"They came from a bullwhip," I said shortly.

"A whip?"

"Yes." I shouldn't have said a thing for now I would have to explain. The conversation even had Tuck Bowlegs' attention, and it took a good bit to get his mind off his liquor.

"I was with Hap Cunningham in Montana when he got killed. I trailed the men who did it, the Bull Doggett gang. They wired me up on a tree where they skinned deer—planning to do the same to me—but the one called Bull used his whip on me first."

"Jesus," Calvin said, making a face and wincing, "I'm sorry I brought the subject up. Come to think of it, I read something about that in a newspaper. As I recall, you got loose somehow and killed the three men who had you."

Tuck grunted in approval and directed his attention back to his bottle.

Calvin said, "The leader of the bunch that tried to bushwhack us at the river called out your name—then said he was Walden Doggett—and asked if you knew the name."

I nodded as I replied softly, "I heard him."

Methodically I took the rumpled, creased envelope from my shirt pocket, then dug out the stub of a pencil. I withdrew the letter which had drawn me toward Mexico and turned it over. I had no other paper—I'd use this. Lost in thought, I held the short pencil. Then I began to write. When I'd finished I put it back in the envelope. Then I drew a line through my name and wrote on it, "Walden Doggett."

Calvin and Tuck both were watching me as I looked up, probably wondering why on earth I'd select such a time to write a letter.

"Tuck," I said, "can you track down those men?"

He made a grunting noise which I took to mean that he thought he could.

"Take this," I said, handing the envelope to him. "I want you to be careful—there are six of them; they're armed and looking for trouble. You'll have to sneak up, taking care not to be seen."

I looked into the blackness of his eyes and saw a light come into them. I have sat late at night by a campfire that has burned out, when the logs that flamed have turned to black stubs. Then a wind strikes up and one of them begins to glow, it turns white around the edge, and little sparks drift off, carried by the breeze. Tuck's eyes were like that; they had the same dark heat in them. He was obviously mad as hell, and I hesitated about using him for he might do something foolish. But I had no choice—I needed his help.

"This is my fight, Tuck. I don't want you getting mixed up in it. These men have killed the best friends I ever had." I had to stop talking for a minute for a haze of rage burned reason from my mind and I found it difficult to speak. "All I want you to do is wait for them to sleep—then leave this message where they'll be certain to find it. They'll have someone on guard, so you'll have to watch yourself."

Tuck rose and went to the opposite corner. He pulled the arrows from his quiver and put in six larger ones. Then he put his unstrung bow in with the wide-barbed deer arrows and slung the quiver around his back. "Hand it to me," he said.

CHAPTER EIGHT

Sonny Cade sat dumbly in a ladderback chair in the wide front hall of Jason Quest's house at the Quest Ranch, tasting the acid bitterness of bile which rose in the back of his throat. He wondered if he had ever been this tired or this confused.

Looking about him he saw big Walden Doggett slumped down in his accustomed mesquite rocking chair, the one covered in spotted cowhide. Doggett's eyes were squinched up in pain. He held a bottle and treated his case of the misery as best he could. Carl Koestler had attended to him earlier, putting sticking plaster on his ear to try to stop the bleeding, and then wrapping strips from a torn set of old long-handled underwear tightly around Walden's upper leg.

Koestler, who had earlier assumed with quiet authority the role of the group's thinker, now turned out to be a pretty fair doctor as well. For one thing, the others had confidence in him since he acted as if he knew what he was doing, so this helped. At the moment he knelt on the dusty boards of the floor beside the stretched-out form of poor Jason Quest, unbuttoning his shirt, then probing carefully with his fingers about his patient's ribs. Each time he pressed down, Jason grimaced and made a sputtery sound through lips he'd pressed tightly together to try to keep from groaning.

Sonny and Jason Quest had gone into the river after Tom English. They had climbed from the water and had been standing in the floorboards of the wagon, holding their six-guns on him, when all of a sudden their footing went out from under them. The next thing Sonny knew he had been swimming for his life. He had escaped, he figured, by the grace of God, but the hulking brute with the big gut that hung almost to his crotch had caught Jason from behind and damn near crushed him. Sonny shook his head to rid it of the awful memory and then observed the sight before him.

"I've worked on many a broke-up cowboy who's been throwed from his horse," Koestler said, perhaps thinking that this revelation of his past medical background might serve to make Jason feel he was in good hands.

"Come to think of it," he proceeded to observe, "don't know that I ever had one with this many ribs busted. Not one hell of a lot I can do except wrap you up. You'll just have to grin and bear it after I'm done. If a splintered rib don't puncture your lung, you have a fair-to-middlin' chance of surviving."

Sonny decided that their self-appointed doctor needed to work on his bedside manners. In Koestler's defense it could be explained that he probably had some fractured ribs of his own. He had been the one whopped in the stomach by that maniac swinging the catfish, who had then whirled around and sat upon him. "Thank God I was on wet sand and sank in," Koestler had said later when talking about it. "If I'd a'been on hard ground he would most certainly have crushed the life out of me." He had used up most of the sticking plaster that Jason Quest had in his medicine cabinet on his own ribcage before directing his attention to the injuries suffered by his associates.

Bob Dawson, who had been knocked head over heels by the fish-wielding giant, a memory that still astounded Sonny Cade, sat on a butt-sprung old couch by the wall, the left side of his face swollen beyond recognition. Angry red and blue contusions had closed one eye and the other stared dazedly at the floor.

Only Raul Ysleta looked as he had earlier in the day, lean and stringy as whitleather, frustrated and angry. In his broken English he blurted out, "What happened? Can anybody here tell me that? I heard gunshots and stayed on the hill for a little—that's what you told me to do. Then when I heard more shots, I rode down to help. Now you're telling me that six of you with guns had the three we were after trapped in the river, without guns or clothes, *completamente desnudos, desarmados—Dios mio,* and you let them get away! How can that be?" He stalked back and forth, the silver-dollar-sized rowels on his big spurs clinking with every step.

Walden Doggett heaved himself out of his chair and fixed Raul with his dead-looking eyes. Raul stopped in his tracks, looking for the first time a little unsure of himself. "There's to be no more talk from you, Meskin," Walden snarled. "I wanted to carve up English—make him really suffer—before we killed him. I won't make that mistake again." In a low growl, coming as close as he ever did to an apology, he said, "The son of a bitch butchered my brother was why I wanted to pay him back in kind."

The tension in the room grew until Sonny Cade felt he could almost reach out and touch it. Jason Quest forced himself out of his chair, gasping from pain at the effort, then went to the kitchen and limped back with another bottle and some glasses. When he had put these on a table, he poured a drink for himself and asked, "What happens now?"

Bob Dawson said, "I didn't come all the way back to my senses till we had almost got back here to the ranch. It was then I realized that we'd left Stoddard behind. We have to go back tonight for him—he might still be alive."

Koestler shook his head. "Stoddard Landon is dead as a doornail. I checked him just before we grabbed our rifles and went for the horses." He shook his head in bewilderment, "The thing that floors me is the way he died—being shot with an arrow by an Indian." In a baffled voice he added, "Who could imagine such a thing as that in this day and age?"

Dawson's good eye closed tightly, and he settled deep in his seat. Finally he said in a choked voice, "I grew up with Stoddard. He and I, along with Earl and Billy Dawson, were like brothers." He opened the eye and said, "The only reason we joined up with you fellers was to get Tom English for gunning down the Dawsons." Several minutes passed before he said, "I can't believe that I'm the only one of our old bunch that's left."

Jason Quest said, "If it wasn't for Tom English, they'd all still be alive."

Bob Dawson said, "You're right about that."

Night had fallen and an unseasonably warm breeze came up from Mexico, making unseen branches outside the house rattle against each other. A sheet of heat lightning flared across the western sky and then, as swiftly as it had come, it passed back into the darkness of the moonless night.

"What do you know about that Indian who stayed in the camp by the river?" Carl Koestler asked Jason Quest. They sat in the caverned rectangle of the big room where pools of amber light fell about the two coal oil lamps, leaving the corners in deep shadows. A sudden gust made tree limbs outside thresh violently, and the two looked at each other uneasily.

"I've told you all I know of him. He and Calvin Laudermilk are known to hunt together now and then. Folks have laughed about it—they seem an unlikely pair. The Indian has an odd name, Bowlegs I believe it is, and his mother was a Comanche."

"He could track us," Koestler said quietly.

"Hell, how could he?" stormed Walden Doggett. "It was dark before we got here."

"Injuns got their own ways of doing things," Bob Dawson said. He took a cloth sack of tobacco from his pocket and a little sheaf of papers. Wetting a fingertip deliberately with his tongue, he carefully sorted out one of these. Then, curling it with yellowed, nicotine-stained fingers, he held the paper with great care as he filled it with tobacco, ignoring the granulated brown shower that fell in his lap and on the floor. With a flourish he licked the paper, rolled the limp effort into a lumpy cylinder, then scraped a match on the sole of his boot and lit the cigarette. Squinting his one good eye against the blue-gray smoke which wafted into it, he rose with difficulty from the deep depression in the horsehair couch. He put a hand up to test his battered face with careful fingertips before muttering, "I got to go outside to take a leak." Then he stepped out the door to the porch and clumped down the steps.

Dawson walked to a tree not far away, unbuttoned his fly, then leaned with his left hand on the rough bark, conscious of the pain around his right eye that seemed to surge with each pulse of his heart. He inhaled deeply and his cigarette glowed like the eye of a bobcat reflecting the flare of a torch.

Bob Dawson never heard the sharp twang of the bowstring or the shrill whiffling sound of the heavy deer arrow that whacked squarely into his breastbone, splitting it as it plowed on, ripping through his heart and then out beside his spine. Dawson's body spun down like a shot, the cigarette smoldering as it left his nerveless lips to land a foot away from his head.

A shadow moved from one tree to the next, then bent down and placed a wrinkled envelope next to the dead man's limp left hand.

Almost fifteen minutes passed. The cigarette had burned out. The wind made moaning noises overhead, and silent sheets of lighting flashed off toward the west, making lying promises of rainfall.

"Bob?" a man called out from the house. More voices sounded at the front porch as men gathered there. Then, from inside, someone picked up a lantern. It bobbed forward, held out at arm's length.

"Where in hell do you reckon he went?" Carl Koestler's voice could be heard complaining. "Do you suppose the silly sonofabitch actually went back to see about Stoddard? God *damn*," Koestler snapped, "if that don't beat the Dutch."

"Whoa . . . look here," Sonny Cade burst out, stunned by the sight. He held the lamp down so that light fell upon Bob Dawson's body.

"Madre de Cristo," Raul Ysleta whispered, and the others heard the sliding sound of steel on leather as he drew his Colt.

"Get rid of that light!" Walden hissed. "Fan out—and watch yourselves —they're more than likely lying in wait for us."

After a half-sobbed intake of wind Sonny said, "I don't have my gun."

"Then *get* it. And warn Jason—he's still inside."

The frightened men, all of them injured except for Sonny and Raul, crept about the main house and down to the pens. They startled each other repeatedly, and several broke out cursing—more in relief than anger—when they saw that a companion rather than some savage had been the form which had terrified them. Then they retreated in a group, backing from the barn until they reached Bob Dawson's body. When they picked him up, they noticed the envelope, and they brought it with the corpse into the house.

Cursing monotonously, Walden Doggett pushed the arrow until he could cut off the head. After that he jerked and pulled until he got the arrow's shiny, blood-reddened shaft drawn out from between the shattered bones which held it. With the help of Sonny Cade he rolled Dawson's stiffening body in a blanket, and they put it on an old Navaho rug in a tiny parlor off the hall. The rug had a black border with an interior of gray and faded natural wool inside black sawtoothed designs which made jagged triangles. Two geometric splotches of grainy, watermelon red appeared at either end of the threadbare rug. Walden straightened with difficulty, favoring his injured leg, and they left the darkened parlor. "We'll tend to the buryin' tomorrow," he said. The others didn't answer.

The five men huddled in the main hall, a place without windows, as though it were a sanctuary. In the lighted room, in the company of others, they felt safer.

Walden Doggett sat at a table and read the letter. "I'll be damned!" he exclaimed. "English is going on to Villa Acuña anyway."

"What?" Koestler burst out, perplexed. "I don't understand."

"Read it for yourself," Walden said, flipping the letter across to him.

While the others waited, Koestler smoothed the sheet of paper carefully, for it had torn in two places at its folds. Holding it under the lamplight, he examined the message. He read it twice: first to himself and then out loud so the others would know what it said.

> To Walden Doggett:
>   You and I are going to face each other.
>   I will ride to Villa Acuña and be there Thursday at Antojitos Cantina—the place you chose. I know you never really planned to go to Mexico, but now you don't have a choice. I can find you anywhere you try to run—and you're bound to realize you have a better chance in Villa Acuña than if I have to slip up on your blind side later. At least

you'll know where I am and can make your plans. That might sound better to you than finding me at the foot of your bed some night.

I don't believe you'll come unless you think you have an advantage, so I'm going to offer it to you. If you want a stand-up fight between the two of us, ride at the head of your men. Have them stop at least three hundred yards from me. Then walk forward by yourself. If your idea is to have them join in, we won't set any rules.

Here is your advantage: You are free to draw your weapon well before you get in range. Mine will be holstered. The closer you get, the bigger advantage you'll have.

Tom English

"What do you think?" Doggett asked.

"You wouldn't have a chance," Koestler replied dryly.

Sonny Cade broke in, saying, "My uncle and two of his men had their guns out when Tom English faced them in Black Horse. He killed all three of them before—"

Doggett jerked up his hand to silence the boy. "I'm not fool enough to go up against him alone, you half-assed idiot." He made a quick gesture, demanding silence, and turned to Koestler. Addressing him he asked, "What'll we do now?"

Carl Koestler didn't speak at first. He stared meditatively at the floor before replying, "English knows what all of us look like—except for Raul. I expect that Raul can get there easy by Wednesday night if he leaves early. He should take the kid here," he said, nodding at Sonny Cade, "who, other than him, is the only one of us who isn't bunged up. Put the kid in a hotel or upstairs room or someplace where he can get a rifle on our man. Then Raul can come up behind him and make sure English is alone before he makes his move."

"It sounds good to me," Raul Ysleta said. "Are the rest of you going to Mexico, or am I to do it by myself?"

"Let's talk about that," Koestler hedged. He said, "Now, here is what I suggest."

The men in the protective main hall of Jason Quest's ranch house listened carefully as Carl Koestler began speaking rapidly.

· · ·

The cavalrymen sat or stood in patient clusters in the grayness of dawn around four small fires, waiting for water in thin metal pots to bubble. When it did they would boil coffee and make do with hard tack and beef jerky on this last trail breakfast before reaching the relative comfort of Fort Concho. The soldiers, all negroes except the lieutenant, were bone tired and anxious to get out of the field. The Indians called the black men "buffalo soldiers" because their hair turned bushy when uncut, giving them the fierce appearance of buffalo bulls.

They had been on patrol for three weeks. Their presence discouraged the thieving Mescaleros of New Mexico from raiding in Texas, and helped control the few roaming, ragged packs of renegade Comanches who had fled the distant reservations.

A sergeant with long yellow chevrons forming three broad, shallow vees on each arm sat on an outcropping of limestone. His pipe jutted from a mouth framed by a bristling, wiry jet-black mustache. The front of his hat brim turned up in a permanent, defiant flap as did the back. Each soldier's individuality found expression in the way he creased his hat, or how his brim curled.

The horses had been picketed nearby the night before. A few now bore cavalry saddles on their backs with tightly wrapped bedrolls behind them, and these had their reins tied to trees. The majority of the horses had not been saddled, and they waited patiently with leather halters on their heads, a long picket line passing through an iron ring below their jaws.

Lon Watt, hat turned up in front like many of the cavalrymen, and with two cartridge belts crisscrossed at his waist—one supporting a knife, the other a fringed leather holster with his six-gun—leaned back on his heels while his hands waved before him. Lon's black eyes snapped as he talked, his expressive dark brown face shone. Lieutenant Crocker had finished trimming his blond beard and now adjusted his suspenders as the trooper talked excitedly.

"I'm tellin' you, sir, I thought we had come up on a massacre. Sounded like five guns all firing at once. Me and Billy had been out on patrol for four hours when we heard it. We jumped off our horses, tied 'em, and went ahead on foot. We were maybe two days' ride from the Rio Grande, I'd say, and had talked to some of the cowboys who work for Minor Cain. He's the one who's been complainin' about rustlers coming up from Mexico and stealin' his cattle. Anyway, we climbed through some rocks and peered down in a canyon, and that is when we seen what was going on."

The lieutenant had already heard the story the night before when the two-man patrol returned to camp. He only half listened as he finished dressing in preparation for the entry into Fort Concho late that day. He put on his dress cape—blue on the outside with a golden yellow lining. He had a flat-topped cap on his head, a squashed, kepi-type hat with a leather visor.

"You already told me this, Lon," Lieutenant Crocker complained.

"Not all of it, I ain't," the soldier said in an aggrieved tone. Then he brightened as the officer hunkered down, prepared to listen.

"Me and Billy saw this man on foot. He wore two guns and had set himself in front of a cholla, the one some call a 'walking stick' cactus. You know what I'm talking about, the kind that has a stalk with short branches covered with spines that stick out from it. Well, the man whipped out both guns at once, cut down on that cactus, and proceeded to blow it apart. He let loose all twelve shots before you could say jiminy Christmas. Billy looked at me and kind of rolled his eyes the way he does, and I said, 'My oh my.' We could not for the life of us understand why anyone would be out here in the middle of the desert attackin' a cactus."

Lon raised his eyebrows and his story took on a singsong quality. "Well, old Billy he nodded at me and said, 'We done found ourselves a crazy man.' And I said, 'I 'spect you're right.' And Billy said, 'What we gone do now?' And I said, 'We got to talk to him.' Then Billy asked me why was that and I said I thought we just ought to, so we did. We stood up and called out first and waved, you know, to let him see we was friendly—and to see if he would start shootin' at us."

"What happened?"

"Not much. He stood there, loadin' his guns while we walked down a cowpath and came up to him. When we got close we saw a cowboy-lookin' type of man, maybe thirty years old or thereabouts. Hard to say. Had a harsh face, dark as a Meskin's from the sun. He stared at us with eyes that looked like a hawk's: real pale, steely-looking eyes. I want to tell you, that was one mean-looking *hombre,* as my Meskin friends might say."

Lon Watt smiled. He prided himself on his ability with Spanish, and when on a pass he sought out Mexican girls at the saloons who shrieked with laughter as he spoke to them. "I got a way with them Meskin gals," he often confided to his good friend, Billy. He put the thoughts to one side and proceeded with his narration.

"Anyway, he watched us walk up to him, and then he said, 'Boys, I didn't figure anyone would hear me practicin' way out here.' And I said,

'Why you doin' that?' And he said, 'Well, if I don't practice I get bad dreams.' Then he smiled at us—and all of a sudden the meanness went clean out of his face." Lon's brow wrinkled. "The man turned and walked back to where he'd tied his horse, got on it, and rode off. I called after him, 'What's your name, mister?' and he pulled up his horse and said, 'Tom English.' "

Lieutenant Crocker's head came up. "Well, I'll be damned," he said. Then he added, "You left out that part when you told me about him last night. It sounds as if you and Billy ran across the best-known gunfighter in Texas." Then, almost to himself he said, "Now why would he be riding off alone toward Mexico?"

"Do you think they saw us?" Sonny Cade asked Raul Ysleta.

"No, those soldiers aren't thinking about anything except getting back to the fort."

The two men led their horses from concealment, scratching past clinging cedar branches, remounted, and rode on in silence. Before them, stretching to the horizon, lay brown land broken by an occasional yucca and at times a tall century cactus, its stalk crowned by a large yellow flower. A hawk rode wind currents above the riders when they came up a swell, and then they saw below them three blacktailed deer, bounding as if on springs, leaping gracefully up the rocky slopes toward escape.

"We'll be there before dark," Raul commented. "If we're lucky we'll kill him tonight."

Sonny gulped nervously. "Don't you think we ought to wait till tomorrow?"

"Why should we? He won't be expecting anything this quick. It might be our best chance."

CHAPTER NINE

I sat at a table near the back of a narrow saloon in Villa Acuña. The room measured no more than fourteen feet from one side to the other, and it stretched some forty feet in length. A wide pine bar without stools ran from near the open front doors about thirty feet into the room. Three rough tables with chairs around them ranged from the end of it to the far wall of the cantina. Seven or eight Mexican cowboys drank beer or tequila at the bar, standing back from it or leaning their arms and elbows upon its stained surface. This left only a narrow aisle between them and the wall as a way out of the place.

I examined the short bartender who couldn't have stood more than five feet tall. The man's head looked out of proportion to his body as it was quite large, and it sat directly on his thin, pinched shoulders since he hardly had a neck at all. He compensated for his wretched physique with a scraggly mustache and maybe a twelve-hair beard, and he worked without speaking as he measured out drinks and collected money. As in most border towns, he didn't care if he got paid in pesos or dollars, although it has been my experience that the cost of a drink can vary a good bit from one place to the other regardless of the currency used. A guitarist near me plucked the strings of his instrument and occasionally sang softly, as though to himself; and a few lanterns suspended from holders on the walls flickered enough to shed a wavering light upon the solemn assembly. If the people in the bar were celebrating, it struck me that they were doing so in a particularly joyless way. Since I'd sat there, trying to choke down their terrible-tasting whiskey, I had not seen a smile nor heard a laugh.

I had found a place to stay at a one-story hotel about half a mile away. There wasn't much to the town, but what they had was well spread out. The hotel sat on a corner and folded around an enclosed stable yard, so I'd been able to put my horse, Judge, there. Then I wandered around the dirt streets for an hour or so, trying to get the lay of the land. It felt good to walk after spending the better part of the last three days on horseback, and

I enjoyed stretching my legs. Then, as twilight approached, I asked a few questions, and a boy directed me to Antojitos Cantina.

The guitarist stopped playing, tilting his instrument and fiddling with its knobs, tuning it. Of the people in the place, only he and I were seated. The presence of a lone gringo in their midst must have been a rarity, and this fact caused some of the Mexicans to level hostile stares at me which I ignored. They all had hats squared on their heads and straight black hair hanging down their necks. Most of them did not wear six-guns, I was relieved to see.

Looking up, I saw a thin young girl with dirty, bare feet walk past me and open the back door. Through it I saw a small, enclosed patio and a ten-foot-high adobe wall topped with shards of sharp glass which surrounded the small courtyard. In case they ever had anything inside the cantina worth stealing, they would be well protected. The girl had built a fire in a blackened circle full of charred logs and ashes in the center of the patio, and now pushed the glistening carcass of a skinned kid goat on a sharpened wooden stake which had been stuck in the ground. She angled this so that the flames would almost reach it. After that she rigged two smoke-darkened poles with rings on top of them on each side of the fire, stuck an iron bar through the rings, and suspended from this arm a heavy kettle half-full of frijoles so that it would hang over the growing, reaching flames. As hungry as I felt, a meal of cabrito and frijoles would be more than welcome.

Giving up on the rot-gut whiskey, I bought a bottle of tequila, and the bartender gave me a saucer of salt, two quartered limes, and a glass. I know the foolishness of too much liquor the night before a fight, and I have been told all too often by Sally that my drinking is getting out of hand. Talk like that makes two things happen: I get mad because I sense she may be right, and I get thirsty. I told myself that I possessed much more self-control than Sally gave me credit for having; that I would allow myself only two more drinks—maybe three—so I could relax, then I'd quit. Besides, I found myself arguing, although no one sat in opposition to take the other side, when a man is tired he *owes* himself a drink. With all those excuses at hand I had no difficulty in convincing myself of the justice of my cause.

I put some salt in the hollow between my left thumb and forefinger, then picked up a wedge of lime carefully with that same hand. The object is to lick the salt, throw down the two fingers of tequila with your right hand, then instantly bite hard on the lime. This isn't as easy to do as it sounds, and to master it you have to concentrate. The salt before and the acid of the lime juice afterward somehow take the kick out of the tequila, which means that your throat still feels like someone branded it, but you have so confused your tastebuds that they don't know what's going on. Caught up in the spirit of the game, I had done away with almost a third of the bottle before I got the hang of it again, for it had been some years since I had worked on this particular skill.

Feeling pleased with myself, I walked out to the patio to watch the girl who crouched, her colorful skirt almost touching the ground as she wrapped a piece of cotton cloth around the end of a stick. She stuck this in a dented, shallow pan full of a sauce made of melted butter and lime juice and peppers and, I suspect, other things, and with the dripping swab she basted the crackling, fire-browned, smoking flesh of the kid goat. I had the bottle and glass with me so, without benefit of all the falderal of the salt and the lime, I poured some tequila, neat, as a man might do with whiskey, and took a big drink. I remarked, blinking the tears from my eyes, "They say that a man can get used to anything, but I don't hold with that. What do you think?"

The girl looked up, brushing the hair back from her eyes with the back of one hand, then busied herself once again with the cabrito. She obviously didn't speak a word of English. I knew enough ranch Spanish to get along with our cowboys, but my vocabulary was limited, and it didn't fit this occasion. I drank some more, refilled my glass, and tried again to communicate, using great patience, speaking slowly in English—which is surely the language that all men ought to understand since it is more sensible than others. I pronounced every syllable of each word. That, I reasoned hazily, ought to do the trick. The girl smiled and shook her head. She shrugged her shoulders, and went back to work. She had not, I decided, been able to concentrate; otherwise we could have had a nice conversation.

Leaning against the adobe wall of the patio, smelling the wood smoke and cooking meat and frijoles, and looking up at the endless sweep of night, I felt a sense of peace climbing within me. The fear, a feeling I refused to recognize by thinking about it, pulled in its horns a little bit. At least it stopped poking me in the pit of the stomach the way it had all day. Beyond the inner walls came sounds of confusion from the bar, and within my head I heard a ringing in my ears.

A giant form filled the back door of Antojitos Cantina; I stared at it for several minutes, trying to focus.

"Calvin Laudermilk," I managed to say, my mouth feeling dry, "what in the *hell* are you doing here?"

He did not say anything at first. He stood there at the door, raring back a little, and put his hands on the bulge that fell over his belt. "What have we got for supper?" Calvin finally asked. He said, "I feel like I've been rode hard and put up wet, and I'm *hungry.*"

We made our way back to my table inside the cantina, ignoring the Mexican cowboys who backed away from the bar, glaring at us. I suppose they figured we had invaded their territory, but all we really had in mind was to share it for a spell.

Calvin refused my advice about the salt and the lime juice and drank his tequila straight. "I have to think about my health," he said, throwing down a stiff jolt of the clear, white lightning. "I have heard that salt is bad on a man's constitution. I don't allow it in my body. Neither in food nor in drink."

I had earnestly wanted to have a conversation with someone only a short time before, but now Calvin began talking and I couldn't get in a word edgewise. It occurred to me that it had been more fun talking to the Mexican girl, who would do no more than nod and smile every now and then.

"When you gave that letter to Tuck and asked him to deliver it," Calvin said, "I walked outside with him. He was putting on what he calls his running moccasins when I came up and told him I wanted to read what you wrote. Naturally, he let me."

Calvin went to the bar, bought another bottle, and returned. He continued, "I departed a few hours after you did, after leaving a note for Tuck. By the time I got halfway here, he had caught up with me." He added by way of explanation, "When Tuck's in a hurry he doesn't use his team. That's why he keeps a saddle. He usually rides Cautious, that's the off mule that's a little taller. The other one is called Jug. As a matter of fact, I gave those mules their names; Tuck doesn't bother with things like that."

"Cautious?"

"That's correct," Calvin said. "I saw how carefully that mule could walk when we went hunting, stepping over sticks when we tried to sneak up close to a deer. And when he isn't hitched up with Jug, he doesn't make such an infernal racket either."

"Lord, Calvin," I said to him, for I'd only been half listening to him and now I completely changed the subject, "it sure is good to have you here. I felt mighty alone."

"Well, son, you got company now."

"Where's Tuck?"

"He stayed over on the Texas side in Del Rio. Tuck is by no means a coward, you must be aware of that, but he's no fool." He tucked his head down into the dewlap beneath his chin and cast a glance at me. "Waiting in a strange town in Mexico for armed men to come shoot at you strikes Tuck as foolish. Of course, Tuck is nothing but a poorly educated Indian who can barely read, so what does he know?" Calvin sought to conceal his grin.

I saw nothing funny in the situation. What Calvin couldn't know was how the anger kept simmering in me like water bubbling around the edges in a stew pan over a low fire. I kept thinking of things I wanted to share with my lost friends, and I knew I never would be able to. The worst thing was that I kept hearing the sounds of laughter. That sounds peculiar, but every time a person I have loved has died, for some reason I remember that particular thing.

Calvin pulled the bottle away from me when I reached for it, and drew it to his side of the table. "You're getting drunk as Cooter Brown," he said judgmentally, "and I am going to protect you from yourself. In a minute we'll eat some supper, and that will help you sober up. But in the meantime, we'll sit and visit. There is nothing that gives me greater pleasure."

Then a dam opened up and I found myself talking, and to my surprise, he listened. I told him about my dream, the nightmare I've had for so long where I face a man, go for my gun, but his comes up quicker, and I'm looking straight into the muzzle of a .45—I'm staring squarely into the face of death. I fell silent and he waited. Then I told him how it started when I was still seventeen and just a kid, after I had killed Jack Malone. The only solution I had ever found was practicing, and I told him about it. How I worked with the finely balanced six-gun Jason Field had given me —and how that old gunfighter had spent time teaching me. Later, after the bullet almost took off my right arm—while it healed—I worked fanatically with my left hand so I wouldn't be helpless. I finally found a matching .45, and in the course of time reached the point where my speed and accuracy with my left approached the level I had achieved with my right. I stopped speaking, for it bothered me that Calvin might think I was bragging. Boastful men put my teeth on edge. I explained that I worked so hard out of fear. To drive out the dream.

"For a good while," I said, "whiskey has helped a little, but the last few months I've found myself waking in the scary darkness, around three in the morning, with my heart pounding."

I felt the room roll ever so slightly and I grasped the edge of the table so I wouldn't get thrown from my chair. I said, "I've talked too much."

"There are times when it's good to get things out in the open where you can look at them."

"You may be right," I said. Then I added, "Since Ben Jordan was killed —and the Westbrooks—I've felt . . ." I stared at him, searching for the word. "Weak." I frowned. "I worry that I may have lost my *edge.*"

Calvin asked, "Edge?"

"The thing that a gunfighter has to have if he wants to stay alive. It's hard for me to explain." I thought about it and, in my condition, decided it was impossible.

Calvin began to talk, as much as anything, I suppose, to entertain me, to take my mind off my troubles. He also, it struck me, enjoyed listening to the sound of his own words.

"I have never, thank God, been forced into a gunfight," Calvin declared. "There are so many contrary young cowhands wearing guns these days, that it is a miracle that I've stayed out of serious difficulties. I dearly love to sit in a nice cantina, like this one, and have a friendly drink, and talk to folks who are of like minds. I really ought to avoid bars, as much as I like them, for when young men drink liquor some of them have a tendency to want to fight. Me, I've always turned friendlier as the evening wore along. And my size has helped me—together with a sense of humor. I've extricated myself from more than one tight spot with comical language. When people begin laughing they forget that they want to shoot you." Calvin grinned. "But once in a while I have run across a mean son of a bitch who has no sense of humor. When that happens, my salvation has been to do the unexpected."

"I recall 'The Great South Concho Fish Fight,' " I declared.

He chuckled. "In spite of the fact that I've been forced into occasional fits of violence, I go out of my way as a rule to avoid trouble."

I looked at him with faltering concentration. To my considerable surprise, I saw two of everything, and seeing two of Calvin Laudermilk left little room for anything else. I stared around both of him at the bartender and saw to my dismay that he also moved in tandem behind the bar. I closed my eyes, wrinkled my brow, and said, "I've got to have one more drink."

Grudgingly, Calvin poured a small one for me. Then he said, "I have suffered insults through the years because of my girth. You need to understand that fat people can be every bit as sensitive as thin people. What many don't realize—this is a special point I want to make—is that I have extremely delicate sensibilities." His face broke into a broad smile. "What the hell, if you don't have a good opinion of yourself, why should others?" Then he went on, "Let me tell you what I mean. I consider myself to be an exceptional man with unexpected gifts. Consider this: I am the only person I know who has ever heard a hummingbird break wind. I would tell you more, but you might not believe me."

"Calvin, that is about the most ridiculous thing I ever heard."

Through the wolfish bared teeth of his grin, he said, "Just wanted to see if you were listening to me."

My double vision cleared up and for a time I saw things as nature intended that I should. I noticed that Calvin sat very carefully at the table, both feet planted on the floor, and part of his weight supported by his elbows. He saw the direction of my glance and said, "I can't tell you how many chairs have collapsed under me. Aside from being a great embarrassment, it can hurt like thunder. So I make sure I'm well braced until I find by a process of careful testing that a chair is exceptionally well made."

The guitar player began to play with more energy than skill and the steel strings rattled and twanged against the flimsy wood of his instrument. The cowboys nodded and kicked their feet against the bar's rail in time to the Mexican tune, and one of them gave out with a high-pitched yell. The tempo in Antojitos Cantina picked up its pace. Calvin rose and ordered a concoction from the bartender, having spent some time eyeing one like it which had been mixed for a cowboy standing at the bar. The squat-looking man carefully poured liquid from four different bottles into a tall glass and then shoved it across the counter. Calvin tasted it very carefully, then pulled his head back, making a terrible face while the man next to him grinned. Calvin wanted to stir his drink, so in a loud voice he demanded what he thought was a spoon. He bellered out, *"Cuchillo."*

Well, even I know that is the word for "knife," and that the thing he should have said was *cuchara.* At Calvin's cried-out word, the guitar player abruptly stopped plucking at his strings, the hunched Mexicans along the bar stiffened, backing away from him, and on the instant the confusion of noises came to an abrupt stop, turning Antojitos Cantina into an expectant, threatening, theater of silence.

The dwarfish bartender slowly reached behind him to a scarred cutting board where he sliced limes and from beside it picked up a long, much-sharpened butcher knife. He handed this razor-edged stiletto hesitantly to the looming creature across the bar who had demanded it. Open-mouthed, wondering what was about to happen, nerves could be seen to twitch as mouths hung slackly, as hands slid slowly toward their own knives—and in a few cases—to their guns.

Calvin, as nonplussed as any one of them, nevertheless reacted with great flair. Seizing the long knife he raised it high, the light reflecting for an instant from its blade, then plunged it point down into his drink, stirred with vigor, then stabbed the *cuchillo* in the soft wood of the bar with a dramatic sweep of his great arm. It quivered at the spot, its wooden handle whipping back and forth. From the hush I heard an exultant voice come from the knot of men, crying out *"olé!"* as if a bull had gone down before a matador's curved sword.

Relieved laughter, together with more cries of *"olé!"* broke out, and leather-faced men crowded about Calvin, clapping him on the back. They saw the big man's head above them, beaming down benignly, and they suddenly accepted him. Or so it seemed to me.

I suppose the tedium of one more night just like all the others they had seen along those sun-baked streets had for once been broken. I can't explain it any other way. For after this they came in groups to sit with us, insisting that we drink together with them.

The girl brought us plates with slabs of cabrito—charred and crisp outside, surrounding hot tenderness within—that ran with juices. Frijoles swimming in their simmering pale brown liquor, cooked with curling slices of salt pork for days to reach this state of perfection, had been heaped beside the meat. A scattering of sliced green jalapeño peppers topped this feast; and at our elbows lay a steaming separate platter of soft, curled corn tortillas. I watched in growing amusement as my new friend devoured everything in sight.

"My system requires nourishment," remarked Calvin as he slid another pound or two of food upon his plate. Refilling his glass, he commented, "And it is a necessity that I replenish my vital bodily fluids."

He had several more helpings before his appetite waned. Holding out his arms and stretching, he commented, "A pious man once told me that we should treat our bodies as temples. I have never completely understood what he had in mind, but—having just swallowed the better part of a sacrificial goat—I do believe that I have done my utmost to comply with the mentioned mandate."

After the meal, I sat without moving for a long time, enjoying a warm sense of well-being. While watching Calvin, who stood at the bar beside the cowboys, a peculiar truth struck me: Under the right circumstances a few hours in a given place can make you feel as if it were a second home.

When I had first approached Antojitos Cantina it had seemed anything but homelike. In fact, it had looked downright sinister. I recalled standing across the way, hesitating, looking at it. On the other side of the street a blacksmith plied his trade. I had watched him pump his hand bellows as horseshoes turned almost cherry red. He took them from the fire with tongs and held them that way with one hand while with the other he handled a short but heavy hammer with ease and skill. Sparks flew as he shaped the heated iron upon his anvil. Then he trimmed the hooves of a nervous mare which stood nearby, tied to a hitching post. After this, the blacksmith shod her in a brisk and professional manner.

I had put off going into the cantina, and had stood there, watching the burly, bare-armed man who wore a heavy leather apron. When darkness fell he locked up his tools, then took a small length of metal pipe and rapped upon a big brass cowbell hanging by a twisted wire from a beam above the anvil. As the sharp, brazen tones of the bell rang out I heard the shouts of children. Two small, half-naked youngsters came running toward him, and he swept them from their feet and departed, laughing and talking to them. The father carried his children, one sitting on each arm, off to the haphazard line of shacks I could barely make out behind his shop.

Something bothered me about one of the Mexican men slouched at a table not far away, and this concern snapped me back to the present. I noticed him out of the corner of my eye—observing me—but when I turned he ducked his head and looked away. He glanced back up to find my eyes still fixed on him, and he frowned slightly.

"Do you know me?" I asked. He gave no sign of understanding what I'd said, so I asked, *"Me conoce?"* Still no answer. "Are you deaf? *Está sordo?"*

He rose slowly to his feet, his gaze locked on mine. I heard the clinking of oversized spur rowels. He stood taller than the other Mexicans in the place and was thin. He wore a sheath knife and his hand rested on the butt of his six-gun. The hair on the back of my neck bristled and I let my right hand fall off the table out of sight. But then, acting as if nothing had happened, he turned and walked away, threading his way through the men and out of the cantina.

My nerves, I decided, were a wreck. I had come within a hair's breadth of drawing on some stranger whose only offense had been that he had looked my way. Sighing deeply, and fighting off the fidgets, I poured myself a stiff drink of tequila and downed it.

When I poured a second drink Calvin showed up and took the bottle off the table. He said I'd sure as hell had more than my share of "the cup that cheers," at least for one night. He said he wanted to check on his horse, and explained that he'd ridden directly to Antojitos Cantina, stopping only for directions, when he got to town, and had hitched him right outside. Before going he told me that one of his new *compañeros* at the bar had lived for years in San Antonio, and he said that this fellow spoke very good English. In fact, it turned out he had at one time been a teacher. He told Calvin that the word *"antojitos"* means "little whims," and this struck Calvin as being a delightful name for a bar.

Calvin was in an expansive mood and like many talkative people he found it difficult to say goodbye, even when, as in this case, he would be absent for something like three or four minutes. He proceeded to expound on the fact that he believed that he had almost recovered the moisture he had lost on the long, dry trip to Mexico. Finding this bar, he declared, had been his salvation. As he left, he stated, "I rode down this dusty street and when I spied the Antojitos Cantina it was to me 'like the shadow of a rock in a weary land.' "

With that pronouncement, Calvin Laudermilk made his way, although with difficulty, first to the bar—where he set the bottle in front of the pleasantly surprised cowboys—and then down the narrow aisle left between the men and the wall as he went outside to check on Sully. It occurred to me that the locals must consider his horse to be a curiosity, for he was surely the first Percheron to walk the streets of Villa Acuña.

The trouble came, as it nearly always does, with a desperate suddenness. Two of the Mexican cowboys at my end of the bar had been quarreling. One of them must have said the wrong thing, because the other's face looked as though a quirt had lashed it; he jerked back, turning red with the seeming helplessness of his rage, and it looked as if the other had him buffaloed. He stood half a head shorter than the man who had insulted him. But then he saw the knife still in the bar where Calvin had stuck it, and he grabbed hold of the handle and pulled it free.

The advantage switched, and the bigger man who had, I guess, been bullying the smaller one, leaped about a foot in the air. The noise in the saloon had been like a smokey blanket piled on top of all of us, but in an instant it was as if a giant hand had ripped it off and left us in a deathly quietness. The small man's eyes began to glow as he advanced, the long, curved, gleaming knife blade waving about in small circles. The tables had turned, and now the weaker man had hold of the whiphand, or—more precisely—the knife. He savored his advantage to the full and snarled menacing Spanish curses as he backed his man before him.

The other Mexicans had moved away and pressed themselves to the side wall of the saloon, watching the drama with that excited fascination that men somehow have in the presence of a blood letting.

The unarmed cowboy who retreated, desperation in his eyes, slid sideways along the bar. All of a sudden he came upon the bottle Calvin had placed there. He seized its neck and smashed the bottle on the blunt edge of the pine counter top. Glass and tequila splattered in all directions as the man spun, all crouched over, holding the jagged, splintered weapon that the broken bottle had become.

The upper hand switched abruptly back to him, for the holder of the knife flinched backward, as though he could almost feel the thrusting spikes of glass. Seeing this, the larger man regained his confidence. He began telling the smaller one exactly what he meant to do to him, edging down the bar as the former attacker now retreated.

Then they joined in a flashing of arms before they fell back, both men bleeding, both screaming at each other. That was when the bar seemed to erupt. The other men couldn't stand not joining in, and all hell broke loose. Bottles and chairs flew through the air. Men who had been drinking together now clutched at one another's throats. Two or three fell, grappling to the floor. About that time the big mirror behind the bar descended with a crash, and I moved, I guess by levitation, and found myself sliding into the little patio out back where the terrified girl huddled in a corner made by the tall adobe walls. There was no chance of escape, for the riot in the narrow saloon had us trapped. The pandemonium inside began to spread. Some men fought on top of the serving bar, others fell behind it, then came up with bottles to throw.

Through the flailing arms and legs I saw an apparition in the dancing light. At the door of the saloon I saw Calvin Laudermilk come in leading Sully. Long ago I read that the so-called "great horse" had been bred for battle, and had a long history of selective breeding so that he could, with armor plate strapped to him, advance into melees, ignoring swords, arrows, axes, and pikes. After what I saw, I can well believe it. The blood of Sully's distinguished ancestors ran hot within him.

Calvin had him by the bridle bit, obviously having a good bit of trouble getting him through the saloon door, and once inside the Percheron broke free, for even Calvin's strength could not control him. Throwing his head high, he let out a whinny that sounded like a trumpet's blast, while at the same time he reared halfway up, throwing out those pie-plate hooves. When they came down they sounded like a thunderclap, and the men looked up—still holding their adversaries in their hands—with faces mute with horror. Rearing up again, the badly frightened warhorse must have looked to them like a fire-breathing dragon. About this time Calvin took off his hat and slapped it across Sully's majestic rear end with an energetic wallop, a blow which couldn't have hurt the horse, but it made a loud slapping noise and certainly startled the hell out of the animal. Then Calvin let out a wild-Indian holler that could be heard in Del Rio, and that was all it took.

Sully bolted forward, knocking men winding, flattening the cowboys who now sought, instead of combat, a place to run. The Percheron, in its panic, surrounded by howling madmen, trapped in a foul-smelling narrow stall, whipped in ever tighter circles, and then began to kick. The pine bar flew in pieces—splintered boards flew everywhere, looking like kindling wood. The wall came in line, and with a few more smashes of the massive horse's mighty hind quarters, boards crashed away, the ceiling sagged, lanterns fell from the wall—and flames splashed in all directions. Spilled tequila blazed white and ran swifter than a fuse on dynamite across the floor. The fire engulfed a rack of bottles which blew up, sounding like glassy shotgun shells exploding. Sully, his widened eyes rolling wildly as he shied away from the fire, saw the door. He broke for the opening, with Calvin trying his dead-level best to stop him. At the last instant, just before he got trampled into jelly, he stood aside and Sully burst out into the night, screaming like a wild mustang the first time he's been roped.

It ended as suddenly as it had started. Antojitos Cantina looked as if a meteor had fallen from the skies and crushed it. The crumpled figures on the floor struggled to their knees, trying to get away from leaping flames—and looking about frantically to make sure the demon beast had truly gone. Though the original contestants had bloody-looking arms, everyone had more or less survived the onslaught, although some of them obviously had broken arms, and maybe one or two would have a permanent limp. From the front door I heard Calvin's Comanche-style yell again. He must have learned it from Tuck Bowlegs.

I stumbled through the shambles, stepping over the stunned men who sat in bewilderment in the midst of shattered boards and broken bottles, and made my way outside. I would have expected the ruckus to have drawn a crowd, but only four or five men had come to see what all the noise had been about. Some of them went in the cantina to help the battered cowboys, and a few tried helplessly to put out the raging fire that the falling lanterns had started.

Calvin stood in the street, waiting for me with his fists planted on his hips. "By God," he cried out to me, "old Sully cleared the bar out for you, Tom. I suggest," he said, "that we find my horse and get the hell out of town before some of these men decide to get even."

My vision had fractured again and I looked at the left man and then the right, trying to decide which one was talking to me. Across the street I saw movement inside the blacksmith's shop as someone crouched behind the anvil. Even in my state I knew something was wrong. I felt the old prickling of nerves that sought to warn me.

Calvin borrowed a rope from a man's saddle, without asking permission, and headed down toward the center of the town, looking for his horse. I started to follow him but someone stepped from the shadows and blocked my way.

CHAPTER TEN

Calvin Laudermilk glanced back one last time before hurrying after his horse, grasping in his right hand the slightly greasy rope he had borrowed. He had leaned forward into his heavy stride but then he checked his steps, coming to a stop and turning. Later he wondered why. Had he sensed the threat of violence? By now flames had erupted from the roof of Antojitos Cantina, and immense waves of shadows and light washed over Tom English, making him stand out in relief in the powdery dust of the street, perhaps fifty feet away from the weathered wooden wall of a building next to the darkness of the blacksmith's shed.

A Mexican cowboy edged into the wavering firelight, his back to the wall, his eyes fixed on Tom. Calvin watched the man observe Tom, who staggered in the center of the street, half tripping on the ruts left by wagons.

The Mexican must have figured that Tom was too drunk to fight, for he called out a challenge. Calvin stood there, frozen, in spite of the gust of heat across his face that billowed from the blazing cantina.

The two men squared off, their hands hanging low. Tom stared through narrowed eyes at his adversary as reflections from the fire illuminated the lean form in front of him. Calvin heard Tom's slurred voice: "I saw you inside—looking at me." He seemed to collect his thoughts and then said with difficulty, pronouncing each word as precisely as he could, "I wonder if you own a brown mare, one with a blaze face and white socks on all except the left hind foot?"

If Calvin Laudermilk lived to be a hundred he would never forget what happened next. The Mexican lunged for his sidearm, but before his hand even touched it, two Colts flashed into the hands of Tom English and stitched a web of holes which chewed out chunks of wood a foot to the Mexican's right. By this time the Mexican's pistol cleared its scabbard and came up into the seeming stream of lead thrown by Tom's twin weapons. One or more bullets smashed squarely into the Mexican's gun and it literally exploded, as though it were a ball of fire or a small metal bomb bursting in his hand. It cartwheeled away as the man went down yowling like a mountain lion, holding his right hand with his left, rolling on the ground.

Behind Tom, Calvin heard a six-gun bark. He pulled his own weapon as the pistol fired again, a small flash spurting from its barrel. Someone hovered in the blacksmith's shed behind the anvil. Flames from the cantina built higher as the new assailant fired again. Tom spun down upon the dirt clumsily, and came up on his left elbow. His right gun fired and a bullet hit the anvil, striking sparks as its whining ricochet hit a cowbell hanging over it—making an ungodly clatter.

At that instant the fire in Antojitos Cantina must have hit some kegs of tequila, because it sounded as if a heavy artillery shell had gone off. In the brilliant, incendiary plumes Calvin could see clearly into the recesses of the blacksmith's shed. A young man had thrown himself in a corner and had his arms up instinctively, trying to protect himself. His six-gun had fallen where he dropped it.

The stunted bartender with his pitiful mustache and beard scurried into view, beckoning men behind him. He held his arm up before him as he ran, pointing at Calvin. He screamed out, *"El gordo lo hizo!*

Calvin saw a ragtag collection of Mexican soldiers, Federales, at the bobbing man's heels. Out of the corner of his eye he saw the man who had challenged Tom and then gone down hollering and holding his hand. He stood up and began to flee, all bent over, into the darkness. There's no time to waste on him, Calvin thought, directing his attention at an officer with a big gut, his shirt only half-buttoned, who led the soldiers. He clutched a small pistol in his hand, and the six men with him held rifles at the ready. The bartender rattled off Spanish, pointing at his burning place of business, and then at Calvin. But the soldiers had their eyes fixed on Tom English, who struggled to his feet and then stood there, weaving in the center of the scuffed road, two Colts in his hands.

The Federales raised their old rifles to their shoulders, and Tom stumbled as he backed toward the wall where the lean Mexican had stood. Calvin retreated down the line of frame, one-story buildings away from the trouble when he heard someone hissing at him. Looking around, he saw Tuck Bowlegs approaching down the edge of the street. He rode his long-eared mule, Cautious, and led Sully behind him.

"You found my horse!" Calvin exclaimed.

Tuck stared at Calvin a moment. He did not appear to feel that this obvious statement required a comment from him. "Things were too quiet in Del Rio," Tuck said without emotion. Without changing expressions, he added, "They look to be too lively here."

"Hard to find a place that's just right," Calvin grunted as he stepped into the creaking saddle on Sully. "By God, I'm glad to see you," he said with heartfelt emphasis as he took a quick dally around his saddlehorn with one end of the rope and pitched the other to Tuck, who did the same. Calvin rode down the right side of the street, going past Tom—who flattened himself against the wall as Sully plodded by. Tuck rode down the left side, and gradually the dragging rope skipped from the street between them as it tightened.

The Mexican soldiers had their rifles cocked and pointed at the man with two guns. They advanced uncertainly, their officer behind them now, crying out orders and encouragement in a high voice. They ignored the two riders who went down the edges of the street on either side of them, apparently trying to get out of the way.

As he drew even with the Federales, Tuck cut loose with his Comanche warcry, a bloodcurdling scream which was enough to make mothers for half a mile around grasp their babies with instinctive shudders. As it echoed, Calvin's wild hooping joined it. Both men drove spurs into their mounts, causing the enraged mule to bray with rage as they surged forward. The rope between them snapped into the shocked Mexican soldiers, whipping them down hard in a confusion of arms and legs. Coming to a stop beyond the struggling men, Calvin and Tuck flipped the rope loose, wheeled about, and thundered back down the street.

Calvin hauled back on his reins, bringing his Percheron to a jolting stop as he swung to one side, reached down with one huge arm, and wrapped it around Tom English. He swung the man off the ground as easily as if he'd grabbed a child, and spurred Sully into a high lope.

When he had passed the blacksmith's shed he looked inside, but the youngster who had dropped his gun must have run during the confusion.

They galloped around a store at a corner, scattering onlookers who had come out to watch the unexpected fireworks, then slowed to a walk. In the distance Calvin heard sharp, popping noises, and he didn't know if the Federales were shooting or if more bottles in Antojitos Cantina were exploding. And, he told himself, he didn't choose to go back to look into the matter. He pulled Tom up behind him before kicking Sully into a jarring trot.

He felt Tom holding to his back and heard him say indistinctly, "I don't want to hurt your feelings, Calvin, but I can't get my arms around your waist."

They went to the hotel for Tom's horse and bedroll, and then set out for the bridge that led to Texas out of Mexico, hurrying, trying to get there before the soldiers thought to block it. But when they galloped across the rickety bridge, their horses' hooves sounding like a cannonade as they beat out a rattling clatter on the loose, heavy planks, the border guards only laughed and waved. They were accustomed to Texas cowboys and their wild ways. They took the gunshots behind them to be signs that more *Tejanos* were having a wild night on the town in Villa Acuña.

When Sonny Cade finally arrived at the hideout ten miles up the Rio Grande, he was relieved to see Raul Ysleta's mare tied to a scrub cedar tree outside. Sonny had made his getaway, found his horse, and fled without a thought of his companion at first. Then he had begun to worry—what would the others say about his running off and leaving Raul behind?

All he could remember of the encounter in Villa Acuña was the way panic had damn near choked him. He wanted to explain to someone how it had built up until he could scarcely breathe. He had waited too long in the shed; it had made him so tense that he'd felt like screaming—but he had known he had to remain silent. It was as if he had a big spring inside and it kept winding tighter and tighter until the pressure reached a point where it had to be released or it would fly in pieces. Then the fat man and his uncle's killer came out. It was perfect! The fat man got out of the way and Sonny had his pistol out—everything was exactly as it had been a hundred times in his fantasies.

Then things went bad. Raul came from the darkness and faced English. Sonny had his gun leveled on the man while this happened. He balanced his arm on the anvil, hunching down behind it as he waited to get a shot off. The thing that broke his control, that seemed to set off that spring inside, was how English reacted: the way his left and right hands flashed up, guns erupting, *both of them at once,* and how Raul went down, yelling but not dead.

His nerves still prickled when he thought about it. He felt the coldness of the anvil's steel as he leaned on it and tried to still the desperate shaking of his hand, making himself take the time to aim. Sonny recalled the sensation of his six-gun jerking as he fired it, missing each time he shot. And he relived the sudden numbing flicker of horror as Tom English dove into the dirt and rolled up, looking at him, pointing his big pistol directly at his face. He felt the contractions as his muscles spasmed, as he looked into the muzzle and as he thought: *I'm dead.* He saw the flare of light, heard the awful shriek of the ricochet, and the incredible crash of metal somewhere above him. He didn't remember dropping his pistol, though that must have been when he lost it.

And then there had been the explosion across the way in the fire that had gone out of control at the cantina. He remembered huddling down, curled in a corner, holding both arms over his head, doubled up, expecting the hot tearing lead of a bullet any second—shuddering—crying.

There had been yelling in the street—a crowd of people there—Mexican soldiers. He saw Raul pulling up on his knees, preparing to run for it. Choking back his desperate sobs, he scrambled to a low back window and fell through it with a thud. Then he ran as if possessed until he found his horse. He didn't think of Raul at all for quite a while. He had ridden hard, feeling the wind rush against the wetness of his eyes. He kept thinking— I'm alive.

Now, after tethering his horse, he walked hesitantly toward the adobe house. Soft lantern light illuminated the windows.

"No te mueves, amigo. Manos arriba," a soft voice said.

Sonny didn't understand a word of his instructions, but he instinctively obeyed them to the letter. He didn't move and he raised his hands.

Two Mexicans, pistols held before them, pushed him roughly toward the front door of the house, calling out to the people inside. He stumbled into the room and saw Raul, sitting in a chair without his shirt. A silent Mexican came from the shadows, black eyes locked on Sonny with rattlesnake intensity. Another man emerged from behind a flimsy curtain which shielded a bed in the corner. He had a frizzy black beard and an aquiline nose, and in his hand he held an old long-barreled Navy Colt.

"I was here before . . ." Sonny began to say, but faltered.

A skinny Mexican woman came in from outside. She carried a pan of water which had been heating on a fire behind the house where, it appeared, she cooked for the men. Wearing a worn, cotton dress of faded red she knelt by the chair where Raul sat and gently took his hand. With care she began to clean it while he clinched his teeth and closed his eyes.

Raul said to Sonny, "Relax. They know who you are."

"I'm sorry about what happened in town," Sonny said. After waiting for an answer that didn't come, he added, "I missed him when I shot." Then, speaking in a rush: "A bunch of men watching the fire that broke out in the cantina got in the way—then some Mexican soldiers came running up."

"Where's your gun?" Raul interrupted him, disregarding the empty excuses.

Sonny said foolishly, "I guess I lost it."

He walked closer, morbidly curious, looking at the quivering fingers the woman had been washing. Raul's badly swollen right hand looked purple and red. Black powder burns formed an angry crust that ran in streaks up from it, and between the thumb and forefinger a deep unnatural split appeared, exposing raw, seeping flesh and the whiteness of bone.

"Tenga cuidado," Raul snapped, jerking slightly in his chair. He scowled at the woman as he demanded that she be careful. She ignored him and continued bathing the hand patiently.

"Nothing is broken," she said to him in Spanish. "Your hand is fine."

"Idiota," Raul snarled.

The man with the frizzy black beard that grew almost to his eyes, completely obscuring the lower part of his face, took Sonny's arm and led him to a table which sat against the side wall.

"I've been hunting many times," the man said in English, "and have come back home empty-handed. These things happen."

Sonny sat at the bench and ate the beans and rice offered to him, rolling them in tortillas. As he did so he listened to the man he'd first met earlier that day when he and Raul had forded the Rio Grande above Del Rio. He remembered the things Raul had told him: These men were like family to him. Raul had lived with them ever since Tom English had killed his father and brothers on that black day long ago across from Langtry.

While he ate, suddenly ravenously hungry, Sonny listened to the man who acted as his host. His name, he reminded Sonny with pride in his voice, was Paco Cruz. He claimed that his great grandfather had been a Sephardic Jew from Spain. Or maybe he had been a Jesuit priest. He wasn't sure. But he carried the proof of his superior bloodline on his face; his was a Spanish heritage. "Indians don't have beards like this," he boasted.

Paco enjoyed practicing his rusty English, and explained that as a child he had lived with his mother in Matamoros, across the river from Brownsville, Texas.

"After I grew up, I traveled north to the place in Mexico where my family had lived. Later I came across the border to Langtry," Paco said. "My friends and I worked for Judge Roy Bean. Didn't make much money

—but we got along. Every now and then we hanged a horse thief or a rustler for the judge. He didn't pay us any extra for that, though." Paco laughed. "We sure weren't getting rich. So we moved down here and went into the rustling business ourselves. The Federales leave us alone as long as we steal in Texas, and the Rangers don't like to cross into Mexico. The U.S. Cavalry sends out patrols at times, but we stay clear of them—just as we do with the judge and his men. For some years we been taking steers from Minor Cain's ranch and selling them to ranchers in Chihuahua. Those damned *ladrones* don't pay us what they're worth, though," he said, wrinkling his forehead as he discussed the thieving tendencies of his customers.

Paco said to Sonny, "You see that quiet man over in the corner? That's Loco Elizondo. You need to be careful around him, he's crazy. Loco carries a garrote—you know, a piece of wire with wooden handles on each end. He is the coldest and the cruelest man I've ever known." He smiled at Sonny as though sealing in that way their new friendship.

"Gitano," Paco commented, nodding his head at one of the other men in the room, "works as a cowboy on the Cain ranch and has for years. Right now he's out here looking for the rustlers." Paco began laughing. "They trust him since he has worked for them so long, and every time they lose some steers they ask him to try to track them. Sometimes we let him have a few to take back to them. We know when Minor Cain has guards on his herd and when he doesn't. Gitano gets paid cowboy wages and he gets paid by me, so he has a good job. Besides, I'm married to his sister." He lazily pointed at the bone-thin woman who was carefully tying the bandage she had wrapped around Raul's hand.

Paco acted immensely pleased with himself. He looked like a man who had found his life's work, Sonny decided.

Raul got up from the chair and walked over to the table. "We're going to need some help," he said in rapid Spanish to Paco.

He held his hand up and looked at it. "In a few days I'll be able to handle a knife and maybe a rifle, but the others aren't worth anything." He glanced scornfully at Sonny and said, "This kid is useless. The big man from Colorado, Walden Doggett, is wounded, but strong. I don't know about the other two—they're fairly old. Both have broken ribs; one of them is in bad shape."

"Raul, old friend, you're like a brother to us. But this is not our fight. Besides, I've heard of this dangerous man you're after. Judge Bean has talked about him ever since he passed through Langtry. Did you know he sent the judge a colt from that ranch he owns on the border? Anyway, why should we go look for the gunfighter?"

"Money," Raul answered softly.

Paco Cruz raised his eyebrows. "How much?"

"Five hundred dollars, U.S., for you, a hundred for each of your men after we kill him."

"That's a lot of money. More than you ever had in all your life. Besides, we got nothing against Tom English."

"Walden Doggett has a fat wallet. Koestler, one of the old ones with broken ribs, told me how much I could pay for men willing to join us. This was the plan he gave me to use in case I couldn't get a bullet in that *sinvergüenza,*" he said coldly, referring to Tom English.

Paco Cruz scratched his stomach thoughtfully. He said, "It all gets paid to me; I'll give them later what I decide they're worth." He belched contentedly and stated, "I hanged at least six horse thieves I wasn't mad at. I guess I can help you shoot this gringo."

"Why we stopping? This must be the tenth time," Tuck Bowlegs said querulously.

"Are you blind?" Calvin Laudermilk demanded. "He's sick again."

Tom rose from behind the prickly pair and the red-flowered claret cup cactus, brushing his hands against his knees to knock the dirt and fine rocks from them. After rejoining his companions, he mounted and they rode without comment for several miles. Finally Tom asked, "Did I have a good time last night?"

"Not so far as I could see," Calvin replied. "Nearly getting yourself killed is not the thing you do for fun."

Tuck had fallen behind but now, having cut a long switch from a mesquite tree, he used it as a quirt on his reluctant mule and caught up.

"I don't know why I do it," Tom said. "Men drink to feel *better,* but the first thing you know you're feeling worse, so you think you have to get hold of the bottle so you can at least get back up to how you felt before you started . . ." He seemed to search for a phrase to conclude his thought, but gave it up as a lost cause.

Tom reached back into his saddlebag and took out a pint of yellowish liquid. He took a small, tentative swallow and screwed up his face.

"Hair of the dog that bit you?" Calvin inquired.

Tom nodded. "Only thing that seems to make me feel human on mornings like this," he said.

"We should be thankful that we live in such an enlightened age," Calvin remarked. "Just think, a thousand years ago, long before they invented whiskey, what did humans drink so that they could feel like themselves?"

"Don't confuse me, Calvin. You know what I meant."

Calvin chuckled.

"Besides, my nerves are far from steady. I needed that to get calmed down."

"Well," Calvin said. The single word spoke volumes in his opinion. It could be interpreted any way the listener might choose, but since he had really not said anything, he could not be called to account.

His skepticism, however, had been apparent, and Tom looked offended. "You'd feel shaky, too, if some stranger had called you out. And there was a second man aiming at my back all along. Damn it, Calvin, of course it shook me. Particularly when I looked at that Mexican in the firelight and saw two of him. I shot at the one closest to me—and it was like shooting at a ghost. Here I was, pumping bullets in his gut, going for kill shots, and he kept coming up with his gun."

"In all earnestness," Calvin stated, "I must say that I never saw anything in my life like your draw—your left hand as quick as your right. It made me think of something completely different—I don't know if I can explain it to you—but I'll try. It reminded me of the times I've been certain I could win my bet against those sharpies who run shell games. I've stood while they shuffled a pea from under one walnut shell to another, then moved all three shells around. I have placed my wager after being certain that I knew which shell covered the pea—damn it, my eyes don't lie and I had *seen* where it ended up—but invariably I would lose that bet. The moral to the story is this: Do not bet against those fellers. Their hand is quicker than your eye. And if I was a fighting man—which I'm not—I'd tell myself: Do not bet on yourself against Tom English. Which is the long way around to say that *your* hands are most certainly quicker than anyone's eye. Remarkable," he said as if to himself, and then said again, shaking his head, "truly remarkable." His eyes widened as a new thought struck him. He added, "God knows how fast you are when you're sober."

Tuck's mule, Cautious, flattened his long hairy ears. Tuck must have known what was coming for he raised the slender mesquite branch he was using as a switch high in anticipation. The mule darted his head back, trying to get his teeth locked on his tormentor's leg, but Tuck banged him on the nose as hard as he could. The mule tried to buck for a minute, but abandoned the idea as a waste of energy, and settled into a more or less normal trot, although he did cock his eye from time to time, sending baleful glances back toward Tuck as though to say, "Just wait, I'll get you yet."

"The wild reports and rumors were buzzing when we left Del Rio this morning," Calvin advised. "They were to the effect that Tom English shot a gun out of a man's hand. The individual who told me this claimed to have seen it with his very eyes, although, between the two of us—he was not present. He said that this extraordinary shot spared the life of the man who'd been fool enough to draw on 'the most dangerous man alive.' He said he read that about Tom English in a book, and that it is gospel truth. Anyway, he went on then to relate how a scoundrel lay in wait and fired upon the exposed back of this 'dangerous man,' but that Tom then dove headlong, firing in midair, and banging a bullet right smack into a cowbell hanging over the attacker's dastardly head. Well, that scared the bushwhacker so bad he was put to flight." Calvin rared back a bit in his saddle and peered at the pale, sick man riding beside him. "What do you think about that?"

"My God," was all that Tom could say at first. He commented dryly, "From what I recall—and the things you've been telling me the last few hours—I knocked the hell out a wall, hit a gun by accident, and then managed to level down on an anvil and a cowbell."

Calvin said in a comforting tone, "Don't fret about your aim, Tom. Ain't too many can hit an anvil and a cowbell with one shot."

CHAPTER ELEVEN

The tired men who worked for Hester Trace, the neighbor of Tom English, straggled into the bunkhouse of the Bar T ranch after unsaddling their horses and currying them. Severn Laycon flopped down on his cot and groaned, "Seven more days to payday, and I'm flat busted. However, if I had money in my pocket I'd likely ride into Villa Plata and get drunk, it being Saturday night, so maybe it's just as well that I'm slap out of cash."

Asa Coltrane, called "Pretty Boy" because of his chiseled features and curly black hair when he'd first gone to work for Roy Trace years before, limped to the next bunk and sat down wearily upon it. He was proud of his reputation as a bronc buster, but stated soberly that they had busted him considerably more than he had them. Though still a fine-looking man, the years had hardened his face to the point that, even behind his back, no one called him by his old nickname. He grinned at Severn, who was his best friend, and told him to be patient, that the booze in Villa Plata could stand to age for seven more days.

Milo Studly, the touchy new cowboy, was talking to the others. He had just said, "How about a friendly game of cards?" when Blue began making his nightly infernal racket outside. An eruption of clanging vibrated through the open windows as the cook clattered a two-foot length of pipe on the inner three sides of an iron triangle. Jagged metal sounds assaulted their eardrums as the triangle danced upon its twisted wire, which dangled from the limb of a sturdy liveoak tree.

Cowboys stepped awkwardly in their worn, high-heeled boots through the door and down the single step to hard, bare earth outside. Then they stumbled in the twilight, cursing, walking stiffly after ten hours in the saddle. They waited their turn beside the chuck wagon for cups of coffee, slabs of stringy beef and a splat of undercooked frijole beans in battered, pewter-colored, tin plates. This evening they had sourdough biscuits as well. The blackened, greasy grille and heavy cast-iron pot with a black crust on its bottom sat in the hot gray smoke that rose from a mesquite-wood fire which snapped sparks when flames hit a sap pocket.

The first in line as usual was young Charley Pettigrew. The broad-shouldered, perpetually hungry kid had ridden a walleyed paint into roundup camp the previous spring, traveling light. All he carried was his bedroll and a happy-go-lucky, devil-take-the-hindmost grin.

While the silent cowboys bent over their plates the bright flames died down and the logs crumbled into white ashes with dark flakes. The smell of smoke, boiled coffee, and seared beef swept across the men who ate under the gunmetal sky, which turned light lavender with pink and orange streaks in the west.

The cook, a former slave with a creased, ebony-colored face whose name was Blue, always did his work outside except during the coldest months of winter. The widow of Roy Trace—who owned the ranch—scolded him for this, saying there was a perfectly good fireplace inside the bunkhouse, that he ought to cook indoors like civilized folks; but whenever she said that to him Blue would purse his mouth and shake his head. He liked being in the out-of-doors. Besides, working over a fire in a furnace-hot room made no sense.

After supper Milo Studly managed to talk several of the men into joining him. They returned to the bunkhouse and sat at the table. Milo had his back toward the corner, and ranged about him sat Ira Turnbull, Charley Pettigrew, and Turner Hopewell, the foreman.

Asa Coltrane declined. He avoided Milo Studly; he couldn't stand him and considered the man nothing more than a poor-white-trash drifter. For one thing, Milo kept making suggestive remarks about Hester Trace, the widow with the funny English accent who owned the Bar T. He made himself out to be quite a man with the ladies. Asa had been raised to respect all of womankind, and remarks of this nature offended him mortally. Around seven or eight months before, Milo had been with a group of cowboys from the Bar T who had worked with the Mexican cowboys from the Lazy E spread to the southeast that Tom English owned. A fence had gone down and the stock had mixed, so the men saddled their best cutting horses and worked with some pleasure, dividing the cattle by brands. Afterward they had been rewarded with a fine meal at the Lazy E headquarters. English had still been in Montana at the time and Milo had the gall to go up to the big ranch house to see if he could start a conversation with the owner's wife, Sally English. Asa recalled seeing Sally, red in the face and angry, showing Milo Studly out the door. But Milo had strolled up to the perplexed Bar T cowboys, telling lies about what had, in his words, "really gone on in yonder." Asa flopped down on his bunk in the shadows and pushed his hat over his eyes, trying to think of something else.

Severn Laycon talked Blue into loaning him four dollars and then, with a flush of enthusiasm, pulled up a chair at the table where the men prepared to play poker, saying, "Count me in. Once I've cleaned you boys out I'm heading for Villa Plata."

"I don't wonder that Milo always wants to play since he invariably wins," Ira Turnbull grumbled. But he took his usual place and waited expectantly.

Turner Hopewell served as banker. He adjusted the wick in the lamp which hung above them and then with heavy deliberation and seriousness of purpose he put a cigar box at his elbow in which dried, uncooked frijole beans rattled. Turner counted out ten beans in exchange for each dollar given him, and in moments each man had an irregular circle of frijoles in front of him. They drew for high card to see who would deal first. With each subsequent hand the cards would be handled by the man to the left of the former dealer. Then they began their standard game, which was five card draw poker with no cards wild.

Milo's queen of spades was high, and he began to shuffle the worn deck.

While the dog-eared, crumpled cards made slapping sounds against each other Severn said, "Milo, I'm certainly glad you came up with this idea, for I am going to give you boys a lesson. You are about to see a master at work."

Ira Turnbull, a taciturn man, cut the cards, shoved them back to Milo, and said, "Deal."

However, a count showed that one man had forgotten to "ante up" his frijole bean; only four sat in the center of the table. Embarrassed and mumbling excuses, Severn pushed his missing bet in front of him with his blunt forefinger. Milo then dealt each man five cards and the game began. A pair of jacks or better were required to open the betting, so Milo dealt two more hands, with a fresh "ante" each time, before this condition had been met.

Severn studied his hand long and hard. He had opened with a pair of jacks, drawn three cards, and one of these was a third jack. He didn't want to make a bet which might drive the others out, so he only pushed three frijoles out on the table. Ira and Charley threw in their hands, but the foreman, Turner Hopewell, said, "I'll see your bet and raise you two."

Milo Studly met Turner's bet, silently sliding five beans out, then announced a ten frijole raise.

Severn Laycon drew back as if he'd been slapped. "My God," he blurted out, "I thought you said you wanted a *friendly* game." Then he made a bold move. He decided Milo must be bluffing. Bluffers always make the mistake, he said to himself, of tipping their hand by betting too much. Well, he decided, I'll call the bet and then some. With that Severn raised Milo's bet by a dollar, a full ten beans.

Charley Pettigrew leaned back in his chair to watch, his brown eyes shining. He said to Turner Hopewell, "My daddy always warned me to avoid the company of gamblers, and I believe you might want to consider his advice."

Turner glowered at the kid before saying, "I'm out." He tossed his cards down where the others had thrown their discards. When he did this, Severn saw that Milo pulled them over to him absently and blended them with the deck.

Milo stared at Severn for several minutes after he'd had his raise come back at him. Milo's eyes were large and they protruded slightly from their sockets. Another thing that made him stand apart from others was his hair. No matter how much water he put on it, his straw-colored, bristly hair stood up in spikes all over his head. His bushy eyebrows stuck out in matching tufts over his eternally surprised-looking eyes. Without changing expressions he began separating beans, counting them out loud as he did. He reached thirty, and shoved this little pile out beside the larger one. A full three-dollar raise!

Severn pulled on one side of his long mustache. Offhand he didn't know how many years he had been playing poker in this bunkhouse, but it had been a considerable period of time. Up until tonight—in all those years—he did not recall more than once or twice when a raise had been for as much as one dollar, much less three. He screwed up his forehead, trying to remember how many cards Milo had drawn. One. Milo had made a point of speaking out—of saying, "The dealer takes one."

Severn craftily analyzed the situation. Milo had been trying for a straight. Or a flush. Or maybe he had two pairs and was trying for a full house. Hell, he thought, the odds against his drawing to any of those were high. The sonofabitch is trying to buy the pot, he said to himself. Or maybe he *did* fill his straight or flush or full house. On the other hand, Severn argued internally, it seemed more likely that Milo had kept four meaningless cards on the first go-round in order to draw only one—with the express purpose of running his bluff before anyone had adjusted mentally to the game. He would know that most amateur card players start off conservatively. I'll bet that's it, he almost breathed aloud.

Severn complained that he didn't have enough money to meet the bet, and said that they had always played "table stakes," to keep things fair. He grumbled that they usually bet two or three beans at the most, that four dollars' worth should last him all night and not just one hand.

"See the bet or get out," Milo said in that flat way of his.

Ira Turnbull and Turner Hopewell both began talking at once, explaining to Milo that Severn was right, that they'd never gone in for cutthroat poker. Milo pulled back his raise of thirty, and put in enough so Severn would have to bet all he had if he chose to stay.

"You got to do something sooner or later," Turner drawled as Severn sat, staring dumbly from his cards to the table and back again.

"I'm just studying the situation," Severn flared. "Damn it, this is the *first* hand. I borrowed four dollars from Blue, and if I lose it that means four days' work to pay him back." He began worrying his mustache some more with his callused fingers. Then with a sigh, he scraped his remaining stake into the pot.

"Let's see what you got," Severn said.

"First, let me take a look at your openers," Milo said in his breathy, soft voice. It sounded as if he had a leak in his windpipe.

"You think I'd cheat?"

"I wasn't the one who held out my ante when this thing started," Milo rasped.

Without a word Severn whipped his hand down. "Three jacks," he said angrily.

Milo turned up his hand saying, "Four tens." A wide grin spread across his face and he reached out his hand to rake in the pot, but Severn barked out, "Hold on a minute."

The men looked at him. "I discarded three cards," Severn said. "One of them was a ten."

"You're mistaken," Milo said, his face suddenly looking drained of blood.

"I don't think so."

Milo jerked his chair back and rose to his feet, his big frog eyes fixed on Severn. Then he strode across the room to his cot, undid his bedroll, and took from it a cartridge belt and holster. He strapped it on, slid a bone-handled .45 in it after checking the cylinder, and turned to the table where the other men sat in stunned disbelief.

"Go get your gun," Milo said.

Severn's jaw hung open. "Wait a minute . . ." he started to say.

"Don't be a fool," Turner Hopewell barked, rising to his feet. "Take that damn thing off right now." His voice had an iron edge to it.

Milo said, "I been insulted the last time by this cowboy. This is no affair of yours, Hopewell, so stay clear of it."

Severn's hands felt clammy. He tried to swallow and couldn't. All of a sudden he felt the urgent need to go outside and relieve himself. But all he did was sit and stare at the threatening figure before him.

"You cowardly son of a bitch, you called me a cardsharp just now. I've put up with your sneaky ways long enough, so go put on your gun."

"Hell," Severn managed to say weakly, "I don't even have one."

"I do," said a voice from the darkness toward the far end of the bunkhouse. Asa Coltrane stepped into the light, his head down, buckling on his cartridge belt.

Milo Studly's hand had his Colt out as he spun toward the man behind him. It roared out a split second later, hurling Coltrane backward. The entire bunkhouse shook from the impact made when Asa's body thudded into the wood floor.

The men around the table leaped back in astonishment and fear. Severn Laycon felt his equilibrium almost go, and he grasped the back of a chair to support himself for he could feel himself swaying. "Jesus Christ!" he said, thinking, *I don't believe this is happening.*

"Are you going to get your gun?" Milo asked, turning back to him and speaking as though nothing had happened.

Turner Hopewell threw a chair sideways and it crashed into the wall. "You'll have to kill us all, Milo," he said, advancing on the young man holding the bone-handled six-gun. "And that will be murder. They'll hang you for certain."

Milo brought the heavy Colt up high and cracked Turner on the side of the head. The foreman dropped to one knee, a hand on his head.

"You know you're fired, Milo. Get your tail out of here," Turner managed to say through gritted teeth.

Milo Studly walked to the table and cleaned out the cigar box that held the money the "banker" had collected from the players. He said, "You owe me twenty-three days' pay, but I'll take this, and after trading my mare for your night horse, we'll call it even."

With that he picked up his bedroll and backed from the room.

Turner staggered to his cot, groping for a gun, but Severn caught him and said, "Don't do anything. For God's sake, let him go."

Severn called to the other men, saying, "Help me with Asa."

Big Lucy, Blue's wife who worked in the main house for Mrs. Trace, brought a tray with a big pot of coffee and cups on it into the parlor where she had herded the nervous cowboys. "Watch them spurs," she said imperiously as she placed the tray on a sideboard. "Don't go nickin' the furniture." It did not appear that Lucy had a high regard for cowboys. They fidgeted as they sat in the formal room after she took her departure, switching her well-rounded rear indignantly. Turner Hopewell had a bandage on his head, and he leaned back in a rocking chair gingerly. He touched the bandage and said, "I got a lump above my ear the size of a Georgia peach."

Just then Blue walked down the stairs. He went to the sideboard with the coffee, and poured a cup for himself.

"Well?" Severn inquired.

"He ain't dead," Blue responded. Eight candles in the brass candelabra painted one side of his face with fluttered light and shadow. The cowboys waited, their attention centered on the slightly bent form of the old black man before them. He reached into his pocket and withdrew a handkerchief stained red with blood. He unfolded it and withdrew a slightly flattened hunk of lead, the slug from a .45. "I got the bullet out of him. It broke his left collarbone half in two, and one rib below it. This here was lodged in deep, back by his shoulder blade. That might be cracked—no way to know."

"Is Asa going to make it?" Severn Laycon asked.

"Oh yes," Blue replied with a positive shake of his head. "I've tended to many a hurt man in my time, though this is the first gunshot wound I've doctored. I had to use a pair of those long tweezers you boys carry when you work on wormy cattle. He bled aplenty, but we got that stopped. Lucy says tomorrow she's going to start putting her special poultice on to take the swelling down. But he's resting easy enough, all things considered."

"Is he conscious?" Turner asked. "Can he talk?"

"Course he can," Blue replied. "He didn't say much at first except to tell Miz Hester he was sorry to be bleeding all over her nice bed. Then, while I was probing for the bullet he groaned a little, then fixed his eye on me and said he surely wouldn't have complained about my cooking if he'd known

I'd take it so hard." Blue cackled with laughter, and the men, feeling a gust of relief sweep through them, roared with him.

Hester Trace, her green eyes shimmering with indignation behind their long black lashes, threw her head as she talked, tossing the sun-streaked, light blond hair tied loosely behind her neck. She sat with Sally English on the porch of the main house at the Lazy E headquarters ranch on the Concho River, talking about the one she termed "that scoundrel, Milo Studly."

Hester paused, trying to calm herself, and deliberately changed the subject. Then she said, "I knew that Doc Starret was due here for your checkup this week, so Big Lucy and I bundled up our patient and put him in the buckboard." She spoke rapidly, retelling events of their short trip, of Asa's rising fever, and of her concern.

Hester had just returned from settling Asa in the spare bedroom in Benito Acosta's small neat house which nestled in trees a few hundred yards away. She said, "We had to get him to a doctor, Sally."

Hester told how the men had to go out on foot into the horse trap at the Bar T at the break of day since Milo Studly had taken the horse held overnight for the wrangler's use. After almost two hours of unaccustomed running—waving their arms and yelling much of this time—they had finally herded most of the remuda into the corral; and then caught their horses for the trip.

Blue had driven the buggy with Lucy along to tend to Asa Coltrane. Hester had ridden her mare, Missy, which accounted for her long riding skirt. She still rode sidesaddle, her right knee hooked around the curving leather that rose from the front swell of the flat saddle. She had given up many of the practices she had brought with her from England, but not this one. Years had passed since Hester St. Claire had arrived in Texas with her father, Joseph, to inspect their landholdings. He had returned without her when she married the widower, Roy Trace, whose ranch lay near theirs. Six months after her wedding Roy died in a freak accident when his horse threw him into a tree. Hester had been the one to find him and she could never forget the way he hung with his head caught in the fork of a large mesquite tree, his neck broken.

Hester looked at Sally with concern, noting her friend's paleness. She had on a shapeless gray dress which her advanced pregnancy distended in front of her. When they had first met she had been immediately attracted to the friendly young woman who stood perhaps an inch over five feet. She had been struck by Sally's large brown eyes, by her quietly confident air. At that time she had been as slender as a boy, could even wear a boy's trousers, although she had an undeniably feminine figure. Sally had been raised on the Clark ranch, which she and Tom had inherited, and took pride in roping and saddling her own mounts. She had been so active all her life—and now sat helplessly, gripped by pain.

"I know Milo Studly," Sally said, her eyes darkening. Then Sally told briefly of Milo's forcing his way into her house, acting strangely—as if she might welcome his intrusion—and how she'd shown him out. "He frightened me," Sally said.

"Why didn't you tell me?"

"I couldn't talk to anyone about it; I didn't want Tom to find out. He can be so jealous and—well, he's had enough trouble. I thought I ought to forget it." She seemed uncharacteristically nervous, not completely coherent, and Hester had difficulty following her meaning as Sally continued. She changed the subject several times, but always came back to the thing that troubled her.

"I worry so about Tom. If I should die, I don't know how he'd get along." Sally made an effort to control her emotions. She brushed her eyes with her hands, then looked at Hester.

"Doc Starret warned me I couldn't have another baby. He's worried—so am I. If something happens . . ." Her voice broke off again. Then taking a deep breath, she said, "Tom likes you. If things don't go well with me, would you take care of him? Do you understand what I'm asking?"

Hester's eyes filled with tears. She knelt beside her friend's chair and said, "Don't talk like that. You're going to be fine."

They sat together for an hour, talking softly to one another.

"Where is he now?" asked Hester.

"I don't know," Sally responded. She looked toward the south, a worried frown on her face.

CHAPTER TWELVE

Calvin and I finally made it back to Santa Rita by Tuesday in the early afternoon. Judge and Sully walked as though they had aged ten years as we rode from the bank toward the wool warehouse, and I felt a little frazzled myself.

"Looks like rain," I said with a hopeful note in my voice.

The clouds in the west mounted high and in some of them lightning flickered.

"You're being tested," Calvin said. "It will rain right up to your property line and then stop. The Lord moves in mysterious ways, and has done things like this since Old Testament days." Calvin added, "Naturally, if He happens to be listening, I don't want Him to think I'm being critical."

A brisk wind whipped by and tree tops tossed as we urged our tired horses into a trot. A short time later we entered the oversized tin barn.

There could be no mistaking that we had stepped into a wool warehouse —a blind man would have known it instantly. The natural oil in wool, we used to call it wool fat though its correct name is lanolin, has an odor that is not unpleasant, but is definitely distinctive. The large, high-ceilinged building had a good many empty aisles now since shearing season is in the spring; but there were still seventy or eighty of the great brown burlap bags stuffed tight with the fleece of Rambouillet and other breeds of sheep. Each bag measured around nine feet long and maybe four feet in diameter, and we held them pending instructions for their shipment to Boston, where most of the woolen mills are located. Four sweat-slick Mexicans without their shirts were moving some of the bags, using steel hooks to drag them, and our bookkeeper came by us, carrying some papers up some rickety steps to a storage loft. Calvin and I walked past him with a nod, and stepped into the office where there was a table with a wooden swivel chair and two bentwood chairs clustered around it.

Earlier, when I had dropped by the bank, Max Hall had leaped to his feet and abandoned the young man who sat with him. Max had rushed up to me demanding, "Where in the Sam Hill have you been? You've had us worried sick." He told me that Sally had been fit to be tied. After a few days she got to feeling bad, so Doc Starret took her in his buggy back to the ranch, and was with her now. He saw my expression and rushed to reassure me, saying that she was probably just upset and, besides, she had been concerned about Rebecca staying alone at the Lazy E even though she knew Lupe Acosta was taking good care of our daughter.

Then Max had led me back to his desk and introduced me to a fine-looking young man with an easy smile. "This is Aaron Harris," Max had said. He hastened to explain that he was no relation to Pete Harris, an old enemy of mine. "Aaron has made arrangements with us to buy out Harper Dent. He's also going to take over Jim Boy Irons's place, which lies out from Water Valley not that far from your home place."

I liked young Harris instantly. He seemed a little shy and didn't say a lot, but that appealed to me. There is something that puts me off men, young or old, who act as if they have all the answers.

I invited Aaron Harris to bring his wife and come to the ranch to meet Sally and Rebecca, and I promised to help him any way I could, since I certainly knew how much work lay ahead of him. Then I couldn't help but remark that I was surprised that Harper Dent would even consider parting with his property, but Max straightened me out by saying that Harper had no choice in the matter.

I had a special reason for talking privately with Max Hall, but he needed to conclude his deal with Harris, so I told him I'd meet him at the wool warehouse in an hour. Max and I owned that operation as partners, and it had grown faster than I would have imagined. It wasn't business that made me need to talk to him, and he gathered that by my tone. About then Calvin Laudermilk came in the bank and I introduced him to both men. The sight of my new friend put Harris back on his heels, for the bank somehow seemed to fill up when Calvin entered.

Later, walking into the office of the warehouse, I smiled at the recollection. Calvin selected the swivel chair, since it looked particularly sturdy, and lowered himself into it with a sigh. "I am going to have to renege on my agreement to accompany you to your ranch since to do so would without much doubt kill me," Calvin said. He went on to state that he had found that the Taylor Hotel in Santa Rita had a bathtub in which he was able to fit. "They charge fifty cents for its use, which is a small price to pay for new life."

He fixed his eyes on mine. "If you should ever find me and I appear to be dead, do not let them bury me without first giving me a bath. That usually brings me back to the land of the living. If it works, I'll pay you back the fifty cents."

I had learned that time never hung heavy on my hands when I passed it with Calvin. He moved from one topic to another as we waited for Max. Calvin began to talk about his Percheron. "Sully has had few friends outside of me. It may be that his size makes other horses shy away from him —and I can sympathize with his problem. However, there *was* the time when he struck up an acquaintance with a boar hog I had at the ranch out by Fort McKavett. I know that sounds peculiar but it's true. The pig and Sully often lazed around the lot together. In apparent harmony, I'd say, but it was too good to last."

"What happened?" I had to ask when he did not continue.

"Well, one day Sully woke to find a chill in the air. He breathed clouds from his nostrils, and he became frisky. He ran this way and that. I left the house when I heard the noise he was making, and I paused near the pens for it gave me pleasure to observe him. Then he collided with the pig.

"Now, a pig is a bulky creature with a very low center of gravity. In spite of the great difference in their sizes, Sully went down. Of course, that squashed the pig, but worse than that, it killed what I had thought to be a perfect friendship."

I burst into surprised laughter. "That's a terrible story, Calvin. And probably a lie as well."

"No, it's a good story, it just has a tragic ending. If I were to lie, I'd make it come out with all creatures in it happy. But life," said Calvin Laudermilk, "baffles seekers after happiness, be they horses or men or, for that matter, pigs."

Fortunately Max Hall showed up then, and I wasted no time telling him briefly all the things that had occurred since I'd left town the week before. Calvin interrupted my narration at one point to say that the tale deserved a proper telling, for the one I was spinning had no color to it at all. I told him it had not been my purpose to entertain Max; that I was leading up to the question I needed to ask him. Then I picked up where I'd been, with Calvin and Tuck and me on our way back from Villa Acuña on our way to Santa Rita.

I told Max how we stopped once again at Tuck's cabin, and before daylight the next day we had gone to the ranch near Knickerbocker. This was the same place where Tuck had tracked the men who attacked us the week before when we'd been seining for fish in the South Concho. We had crept up as silently as we could, but found the place to be empty. There was not a sign of life. Later we went into Knickerbocker, inquired around, and discovered that a contrary old bachelor named Jason Quest owned the place.

"I've heard the name," I said, "but I can't place him, and that's why I wanted to find out if you could tell me anything about Jason Quest—and why he might want to kill me."

Max looked at me thoughtfully. "He's related to the Phillips family who lived to the north of you, up around Villa Plata." He ruminated awhile and then said, "Jason's mother was a Phillips—so the Phillips boys were his first cousins."

I had thought that Max would know a considerable amount about the man. A great part of a banker's stock in trade is to have an encyclopedic knowledge of the people in business in his trade area. Gossip is the staff of life to them, and bankers collect information with the single-minded concentration of a file of ants going to and from a pile of spilled sugar.

"Jason Quest," Max said, "is a strange person. For some years he came to town on a regular basis, but as time went on he stayed more and more by himself. We had reports that he fired his rifle at people who came up his road, so after that everyone left him strictly alone."

Max had sat in one of the chairs, and he tipped it back against the wall. Like all the Hall men, he had a remarkable talent for conversation, which he dearly loved to exercise. He said, "Quest bought his ranch from Jimson Weed Pike, a man with a serious religious problem—he gave up working to sit by the road. He said if he sat there long enough everyone he ever knew would sooner or later walk or ride by. It was his plan to preach to them about salvation when they should arrive. But he neglected to earn a living, so he had to move on, and eventually he and his brood moved back to Arkansas. During the many years he lived out by Knickerbocker," Max related, "Pike built a big rambling house, for he had a wife and eight children. I suppose that Jason Quest rattles around in it, being there alone." After a moment he concluded, "He and his brother, Leroy, were partners for a while but I understand they don't speak to each other now."

Max took out his pipe and inspected it. He reached into his pocket and removed a small knife with which he began to scrape what looked like black carbon out of the pipe's bowl. Then he spent more time fiddling with it, tamping tobacco down and trying to get it lit. It takes a man of great patience, it struck me, to smoke a pipe.

As I watched Max I thought of the things he wasn't saying. I suppose I had blocked out the memory of the cousins of Jason Quest, the Phillips brothers; it was not a happy one. There had been a fight. The youngest of the three Phillips boys, Ike, had gone down under my six-gun. Two others, Orrin and Lute, had come after me together with Joe Slade, the one people once called "the meanest man in West Texas." Some used to say that his draw was fast as a rattlesnake in midstrike, but I guess I was lucky. Or he was unlucky, for I killed Slade. That's when the other two Phillips brothers cut down on me, and bullets hit my back and arm. I felt again the whiplash kick of pain from that day, and recalled the way I managed to roll over and get off two shots which dropped Orrin and Lute. Ever since that day people have called me by the tag they'd used before as a label for Joe Slade.

"No use to say more; I know why Jason Quest might take an interest in me."

"Thought you might," Max mumbled with the pipe stem firmly between his teeth.

"What happened to Leroy?" I asked.

"All I know is that he and Jason had a falling out, and he lives in town now. Has a little shack not far from the river. Goes around grumbling that Jason cheated him. However, my information is that his brother bought out his interest in the ranch, which leaves Leroy with enough money to live on—but not much to do except grouse about things he doesn't like. One of which is his brother."

Max told us that a Texas Ranger, John Robert Hale, had sent word that he was on his way from Austin. Max asked me to stay around to tell my story to him, but I asked him to do that, explaining that I needed to see about Sally, that I'd be riding on that night.

The news that at last we'd have some law again made me feel relieved. With luck the Ranger would roust out my enemies and we'd know some peace again. At least for a while.

The reason Calvin had been so quiet, I noted, was that he seemed to have fallen asleep, and his head, supported by a succession of swelling chins, tipped gently forward. A resounding clap of thunder roused him from his slumber, and he looked around, trying to get his bearings for a few seconds. Then a scattering of rain drops thudded in a whipped line across the tin roof, pinging on it like two-dozen ball-peen hammers pounding. Wind-hurled raindrops splattered against the windows by us, and looking out, we saw the day turn dark. Then the barn sounded as though we were seated inside a snare drum played by a furiously energetic drummer. We stood in the unholy racket, seized by the storm's excitement.

Through the windows I saw bent trees looking like umbrellas turned inside out and held out sideways in the horizontal sheets of rain.

"I'd suggest you put off that ride to the Lazy E till morning." Calvin said in a loud voice so I could hear him as he labored to his feet. He stood with his back to a window and in the flash of lightning outside it looked for a brief instant that his head was surrounded by a bright halo. It struck a discordant note, I thought, noting his roguish smile.

"I suppose we do have time for a drink while this blows over," I commented.

The three of us left in a rush, getting on our horses and galloping in the driving rain until we reached the Lost Hope Saloon. We ran inside, laughing and ringing wet and heaving for breath. I looked up and saw John Hope standing behind the bar, inspecting us suspiciously. Though we were his only customers I couldn't get over the feeling that he considered us to be intruders. With a sigh, he put a bottle and some glasses on the bar.

The bartender didn't speak to my two companions, but he did make one comment to me, which strengthened my conviction that he was, in his own way, a friend.

"Figgered you was dead," said John Hope.

On the last day of her stay at the Lazy E, Hester Trace walked beside Rebecca, the tomboy daughter of Tom and Sally English. Rebecca, wearing denim pants and a red-checked shirt, strode full of purpose in the lead. Hester smiled as she looked at her, thinking the girl would be a heart breaker in a few more years. She will definitely get the boys' attention, Hester said to herself, noting Rebecca's curly, golden brown hair and that devilish look she had—a dimpled grin and dancing brown eyes which looked so much like her mother's.

"Hurry," Rebecca called back over her shoulder as she ran toward the corral. In the distance Hester heard the rumbling made by the hoofbeats of seventy horses as they galloped toward the immense corral with its long gate thrown wide open.

As the wrangler penned the remuda and closed the gate securely behind the excited horses, Hester and Rebecca climbed up to the topmost rail of the sturdy rail fence which surrounded the corral. Rebecca straddled it while Hester managed to sit sideways, smoothing her long gray skirt with one hand while holding to a tall cedar post beside her with the other. She wore the same skirt and the same dusty-rose-colored blouse that she'd had on when she arrived three days before. She had packed her other clothing in the bag she'd put in the buggy which Blue and Big Lucy had driven back to the Bar T. Hester had waited an extra day to make sure that Asa Coltrane would be all right. But after Doc Starret, who had remained at the ranch owned by Tom and Sally, assured her that Asa would soon be able to travel, she had made her plans to depart. After the men left today, she and Rebecca would ride back to her own ranch. She'd had no difficulty in convincing Sally and Tom of the wisdom of allowing the child to visit her during this difficult stage of her mother's pregnancy.

After her talk earlier with Sally she felt awkward around Tom. They had always had an easy, informal friendship, and these new feelings concerned her. She couldn't help being attracted to him. That morning at breakfast she had observed him without his knowledge. He'd been staring out the window, thinking about something that must have bothered him. She had never known a man with eyes like his—as blue and cold as reflections of a winter sky in an icy stream.

The laughing cries of the Lazy E Mexican cowboys brought her back to the present. The cowboys dragged their smooth, worn saddles, saddle blankets, and bridles with them toward the big circular corral with the snubbing post set in its center which rarely had to be used except when catching raw broncs to be broken, or when they brought in wild cows with screw worms to be doctored. They dropped their gear and climbed up on the weathered wood of the corral's fence beside Hester and Rebecca. Hester thought they looked like gangly crows on a telegraph wire, balancing without thinking of it, all in a line.

She watched Tom walk out alone into the whirling, milling horses. Sharp, high squeals came from them as several, caught up by their fresh, early morning enthusiasm, whirled and kicked the nearest animal to them, hind feet landing with sharp thuds. "Catch *Viejo* for me," old Benito Acosta called to Tom. The other men shouted out their preferences, trying to be heard over the muffled rumble made by so many horses moving in a brisk circle, hundreds of sharp hooves striking deep crescents into the powdered earth.

Tom English walked slowly, holding himself with careless, slim grace, the lariat's coil in his left hand. He shook out a three-foot loop with his right. He didn't twirl it overhead as a man might on horseback, but rather swung it in what some call a figure eight, slowly revolving the rope low around his right side, then in front of his body and across his left side, then back again. Out of the corner of his eye he must have noticed Hester, for he seemed to lose his concentration briefly, glancing her way with a quick

smile before addressing himself once more to his task. He focused his
attention on the horses rushing past him. They began to gallop, heads
high, snorting and whinnying as they scrambled in a crowded, dirt-kicked,
counterclockwise arc. Tom whipped his loop in a backhanded throw from
left to right over a horse's head then, lowering the tough hemp strand
behind his hips, both hands holding firm—about butt high—he "sat on the
rope," and an instant later the horse hit the end of the lariat's length and
jerked around. Tom skidded as he leaned back while the taut rope dragged
him, his high boot heels digging furrows. Then the horse turned, head
down, facing him.

One by one he caught the other cowboys' mounts. A rangy sorrel called
Red for Pepe Moya, a rawboned gray named Chopo for Luis Batalla. Then
he roped a paint for Santiago, Benito's son. After that he caught a *grulla*
with a stripe running down his back from his dark mane to his matching
tail for Juan Suarez. He roped a wild-eyed dun for himself.

The cowboys led their horses from the corral and saddled them outside.
But Tom's, a half-broken bronc that Rebecca told Hester bore the name of
Deuce, stood in the center of the pen, firmly snubbed to the hitching post.
The young gelding fought the rope in vain since the pulling almost choked
him.

"This is the fun part," Rebecca said to Hester, her eyes shining in anticipation of what was about to happen.

With Santiago's help Tom managed to get his saddle and bridle on the
dun. Then they removed the rope. Santiago had the horse's head down and
an ear clamped between his teeth—"earing him down" was the expression
Hester had heard which described this barbaric sight—as Tom, reins held
short, got his left foot in the stirrup. The second he put his weight on it the
bronc reacted as if a string of fire crackers had gone off beneath him.
Deuce spun free from Santiago, dumping the cowboy on his back, and
Tom grabbed for the saddlehorn with his right hand while with his left,
which clutched the reins, he seized the horse's mane. He swung his right
leg over the saddle, but before he found the other stirrup the dun wrenched
his head down between his front legs and began to buck in bounding,
forward motions, coming down each time on four stiff legs, jarring the
helpless rider.

Hester, eyes wide, *knew* he'd be thrown. She could see him coming off,
losing his precarious balance. Clear daylight showed between him and the
saddle. His left foot flared out in its stirrup and he seemed to be sailing off
on the other side, but then the crazy bronc sunfished—curving in midair

like a perch out of water—and twisted under him. Tom clung to the saddlehorn with all his strength and managed to jam his right foot into its
stirrup, then at last found his seat. Releasing the horn, he brought both
legs up and began to rake the bronc's shoulders with his spurs, punishing
him. The dun's breath screamed out in strange, hoarse whistles each time
he struck the ground. Weakening, he slammed sideways into the corral's
rails, bounced off, then fell into a rocking lope, giving up. Tom pulled
Deuce's head up, he had it almost in his lap, and Hester could see him
trying to catch his breath. The heaving animal came to a stop, legs braced
and trembling. Only then did Hester hear the raucous cheering all around
her. The good-natured cries from the men kept up as she fought to calm
herself. Tom nodded at the cowboys and, seeing her wave, answered it
with a broad smile.

She walked with Rebecca toward a series of pens and chutes behind the
corral. Next to one fence, Hester's mount, Missy, tugged backward against
her tied reins, obviously alarmed by all the confusion. However, Rebecca's
fat and sleepy little sorrel mare, Skeeter, stood patiently, waiting for her
rider. Both had been kept up in the pens and the wrangler, a boy named
Manuelito, had saddled them before going out into the horsetrap for the
remuda.

Tom rode with them part of the way, then made his farewell, thanking
Hester for helping with Rebecca. He threw his daughter a kiss as he struggled with Deuce, trying to teach him to neck-rein, and turned about.

Hester urged her delicate-looking mare up beside Tom's horse. Leaning
to one side, she put her hand upon his arm without thinking, speaking the
conventional words of parting while hardly thinking of them, her mind
caught in a strange confusion which made her suddenly feel very young.
Her long skirt billowed up against Tom's leg and she saw what seemed to
be a sudden blush upon his face. Then Deuce got nervous, began to crow
hop, and Tom sat—straight-backed, legs braced forward in the stirrups—
getting him under control. With a final wave, he rode off to join his men.

Hester Trace sat with her right knee curled high on her sidesaddle,
feeling the dry wind blow across her face. Then she and Rebecca rode
toward the Bar T, talking about the freak rainstorm that had struck Santa
Rita. Not a drop of water had fallen on the English or the Trace ranches.
Even the pads of the prickly pear cactus looked shriveled.

"God a'mighty *damn*," Rebecca said, "I wish they'd let girls ride
broncs."

"If you get in the habit of speaking like that," Hester admonished her young charge, "your parents won't let you stay with me."

"I'm sorry," Rebecca apologized. Then she added, "But have you ever seen anyone like my dad?"

"No," Hester Trace said. "I can honestly say I never have."

Deuce danced sideways underneath me, still brimming with energy. The strain from holding him in check began to tell, and my left arm felt weaker by the minute. I turned him toward the house, vowing to change to a gentler horse, but knowing that when I got there I'd go inside and rest. Why I'd picked a day like this one to show off was beyond me.

I made a solemn vow to find someone else to work with all our rank and ornery horses in the future. My head felt as if someone had slammed it with an axe handle from the roughhouse ride I'd had, and my every bone cried out. I could only take shallow breaths, for a deep one slipped a knife point toward my lungs. Could be a broken or a cracked rib. My tailbone protested with every step that Deuce took; and my left knee, which that idiot bronc had banged against the corral fence trying to dislodge me, hurt like bloody hell. After a while I quit making the sad list of aches and pains. All I could think of was getting Sally to rub my back a little, and make soothing noises. In times past that had proven to be my best medicine.

By the time I got near the corral I knew I wouldn't change horses and go out with the men to spend a full day in the saddle. I'd be little help, I rationalized, and besides, I'd been away—I needed to spend a little time with Sally. Manuelito had seen me from a distance, and he took the reins when I stepped off Deuce and told him to put up my gear. Then I headed for the house.

The minute I went in the back way I heard voices and laughter coming from the front porch. I went through the kitchen and big dining area and up the long narrow hall which led to the front door. Then I went out on the sheltered veranda to find Sally near Calvin Laudermilk, leaning forward in fascination as he spoke to her.

"If I were pressed to give my opinion of the Creator's greatest achievement," Calvin pronounced in a self-important way, "it would be something closer at hand than galaxies and more substantial than atoms. It would relate to something I can more or less understand and genuinely appreciate. I am speaking of flesh." He patted the deep swell of his stomach, then looked up to find me approaching.

"Howdy, Tom, I'm getting acquainted with your wife."

Sally broke into peals of laughter—a sound which filled me with warmth. I can't think how long it has been since she's felt good enough to give way completely to her sense of humor—which in the old days was always bubbling just below the surface.

"Did I hear you judging the Almighty?" I asked.

"It's not as though I'd presume to give Him a report card or anything like that. But surely, a word or two of appreciation can't be out of line," Calvin stated.

I kissed Sally on the cheek and sat next to her in the porch swing, lowering myself as carefully as if I were made of fragile, easily breakable crystal.

"Did you hurt yourself?" she asked, instantly concerned. Sally is a nurturing, caring person, and she will leap from her own sickbed to tend to someone else.

I fell into my accustomed way with her, telling a little about riding Deuce before describing the smallest of my symptoms at some length.

"Spare us these graphic details," Calvin demanded. "I had remarked upon my appreciation of the flesh as you arrived, but no rational creature wants to think of all the squirmy things that lie beneath it—of blood and nerve systems and things like brains and bones and organs. I'm content with the idea that we are packaged neatly with flesh and, over that, by the ultimate kiss of genius, skin. I don't like to contemplate the balance of our makeup."

Then he warned me against riding broncs. He said, "I see no harm in old sayings, even though some of them are tired and worn from use. The very fact that they have lasted is often due to their timeless wisdom. The maxim to which I wish to direct your attention is one which relates to getting thrown off bucking horses. It ain't the fall that's so bothersome, it's the sudden stop at the end of it."

Sally's amusement stopped abruptly. A spasm hit her swollen body and she clutched herself, face going dead white in an instant. I saw a look of instant, horrified surprise in her eyes, and her mouth opened a little. "Oh," was all she could manage.

"What is it?" I held her as best I could, feeling rigors ripple through her.

"Where's Doc Starret?" I asked, and Calvin said, "She told me he was out back in the little house with Asa Coltrane. I'll get him," he added, on his feet and moving quickly.

I heard Sally cry out, and then in a choked whisper say, "I'm in labor."

"You can't be," I said, holding her tightly to me. "You're just past seven months . . ."

"Help me," she said, and her eyes mirrored the unbearably sharp pain that stabbed her.

CHAPTER THIRTEEN

The afternoon sun shone upon the loneliness of Tarpley's Gulch. Sonny Cade decided he had never in all his life been in such a godforsaken place. He walked behind the miserable shanty and kicked at the dry ground. A horned toad scuttled away in alarm and Sonny watched, bemused. The little creature, with its ferocious, multipointed crown, looked like a tiny throwback to the days of dinosaurs. In fact its flat, oval back and short tail also had a protective cover of sharp spines. What a place, Sonny sighed. Goat horn sticker patches on the ground, poisonous thorns on mesquite trees, prickly pear cactus everywhere, spear grass and needle grass—and even the frogs have horns. He felt a sudden surge of homesickness for Montana.

Sonny saw Walden Doggett emerge from the shack, squinting his eyes against the brightness, and then walk forward, testing his leg. He had bandaged and rebandaged it, and kept limping around as though he could make his injury get well if he worked on it. The late sun made his shadow grotesquely long, throwing it at least twenty yards until it straggled across the side of the shack and up the angled roof to the rusted stovepipe that protruded from it.

A dry breeze made the tree limbs wave, and the canvas strung between two liveoaks flapped about because one corner had come untied. Beneath it Sonny and Raul had their bedrolls. Walden, Koestler, and Jason Quest crowded at night into the delapidated house.

Raul stood by the scarred chopping log, making the time pass by throwing a long, thin knife with his left hand. His bandaged right hung by his side. Sonny saw the blade glitter as it twirled in a swift blur, then stuck in the open-grained unpainted wood of the shack, quivering.

He's good, Sonny thought to himself, impressed. Even with his left hand, he is very good with that knife. He felt a shiver go up his back. Something about Raul Ysleta made him uneasy. For some reason even the silvery jingle of the Mexican's big roweled spurs caused Sonny to become tense and nervous.

Jason Quest sat outside in a chair which once boasted woven wicker, but which now had strips of leather crudely in place to form a seat and back. He wore, as always, his pants legs tucked inside his tall boots. These boots had what some called "shotgun tops," for they were cut straight across, not rounded; and they had flop-eared, pull-on loops drooping down on the outside. He took shallow breaths, Sonny noted, and his skin had taken on a sallow cast since that scary fat man had grabbed him from behind in the river and almost squeezed him to death. Sonny ambled over to him to ask how he felt, but Quest glared at him, so he went back to his bedroll and sat down.

Sonny often wondered what he was doing in Texas, spending all his time with these strange people, trying to find a way to kill a man he really didn't know. He'd been in awe of his uncle, J. K. Cade, and jealous of his step-brother, Jodie, who'd been his uncle's favorite. The terrible shock of learning that a notorious gunman had slaughtered his uncle had shaken him to his very roots. He had to *do* something, he kept thinking. The death of Jodie hadn't bothered him, and he felt guilty about that until he had heard a man say, "By God, if Jodie was still alive *he'd* revenge the death of J. K. Cade." He couldn't help it, he'd always resented Jodie.

When he heard that Walden Doggett planned to go after Tom English, he had reached an instant decision: He would be a part of the crusade.

Sonny had second thoughts now; he wanted to go home.

Carl Koestler rode up and took his horse to the little rail corral out back. After he had put his horse in with the others, he unsaddled him and then stumped around to the front of the shack where the others awaited his report.

"I've got interesting news," Koestler said. Jason Quest leaned forward to listen, and Walden Doggett limped closer. Raul Ysleta pulled his knife from the wall and slid it in its sheath at his belt. Sonny stayed on his bedroll, listening intently.

"Jason," Koestler began, "I went into town and found your brother Leroy. He may hate your guts, but he hates Tom English more. And Leroy has picked up some information that we can use."

"Did anyone see you?" Doggett interrupted.

"No one seemed to pay any mind to me," Koestler said. "Naturally, I took care not to ride through the main part of town." He looked at the men's faces around him as he continued. "Leroy told me he was down by the livery stable this morning and he heard Max Hall say he was going to have to spend half the night on paperwork at the wool warehouse tonight. I'd say that opens the door for us to put our plan into operation."

Sonny watched Raul Ysleta's face while Koestler talked. No flicker of any emotion at all crossed it.

Walden Doggett winced as he moved in front of the men. "We have a collection of walking wounded here. Jason is useless, with all them busted ribs. The kid," he said, glancing at Sonny, "is the only one of us who has no injuries, but he don't have the stomach for what we plan to do."

Sonny felt his face burn with shame and anger. But what the man said was certainly true.

Walden had taken the sticking plaster from his ear and the chunk which had been torn from it by the Indian's arrow made it look grotesque. He put his fingers to the red scabs that had formed around the jagged gap as he said, "We have to move fast. English and the fat man and that Indian can identify us. We have to get to them before the law shows up. That means we go after another of the friends of Tom English. It worked before, and there's no reason why it shouldn't again. But this time when we cut Tom English out of that herd of gunhands he has hired, we won't fool around the way we did before."

Koestler said dryly, "The shape this crew is in, we'll need some help." He turned toward Raul Ysleta and spoke to him, "Tell us about those three Mexicans you hired."

"I rode with Paco Cruz for a good many years and I can vouch for him. He is the hook-nosed one you met, the one with the beard that grows clear up to his eyes. Paco is the one we'll pay."

Raul continued, "His wife's brother, the one called Gitano, is dependable. Not too smart, but he does what Paco tells him. I don't know the third man well. They call him Loco—Loco Elizondo. He acts a little crazy, but maybe that's what we need."

Raul said, "They've been camping a few miles from here, over by the river. I had to promise them extra money for having to wait around."

"How much?" Jason Quest asked, but Walden told him it didn't matter.

Koestler said, "Raul, you know what has to be done. How about taking those three in to do it. It will be a good test. Besides, this sounds like something you might get a kick out of."

Sonny saw a light shine for a moment in the Mexican's eyes before it went out. Raul didn't answer, simply nodding, and then he buckled on the new six-gun he had bought in Del Rio. After that he went to the corral for his horse.

Koestler said, "They don't know their way around Santa Rita the way I do—I better go with them."

"I want you to prepare yourself, Tom. Things aren't going well." Doc Starret turned and bustled back to the bedroom where Lupe was helping him with Sally.

He left me alone, standing on the front porch where I'd been most of the day. A chill of fear numbed me as the meaning of his words sank in. A single dull protest formed in my mind: *This can't be true.* I stared out through the scary twilight and watched the amber light fade as shadows changed the nature of the yard from a familiar place to one that seemed completely foreign. Ordinary sounds intruded on this strangeness: Two of the dogs shot around the corner and tumbled in the bushes in a growling, play-like fight; and out toward the bunkhouse I could hear the noises the men made coming in from the corral.

Calvin Laudermilk clumped out from the front hall carrying a bottle and two glasses and filled one for me.

"I don't think so, Calvin. Sally's been after me to quit."

"I have had a long experience with decision making," he said. "You are fortunate to have me with you tonight as you face this situation, for I will tell you an iron rule which has never failed me. I'm speaking, of course, of moments when you're faced with a hard choice as you are now. The element in this which is critically important is the *timing.* All too many of us live only for today. Surely you have heard people complain of that. We don't even think of the future. Bearing that in mind, here is Laudermilk's law: *Make all important decisions tomorrow.*"

I accepted the drink. If the truth were known, I didn't need all that much encouragement. "Doc came out to see me a minute ago."

"I know. He told me."

Silence fell as the new moon rose, orange and oversized, across the valley where it hung above the low hills on the east side of the Lazy E. I drank and stared and waited until it gradually got high enough to look the way it should. Toward midnight Doc came back to the porch, carrying a coal oil lamp that flickered on the blood that covered his hands and arms clear up to his elbows. He had rolled his sleeves up out of the way. He said, "You have a son."

I stood up. "I need to see Sally," I said, starting into the house.

"Don't go in for a minute, Tom. I need to talk to you first," Doc turned away from Calvin and me and said, "Let me clean up. Pour me a drink—I'll be right back."

I stayed on my feet. "What's wrong?" I asked, but Calvin sat without moving, without speaking.

"We've wanted another child for a long time," I said. "Rebecca will be so pleased to have a baby brother—we need to send someone over to the Trace ranch to bring her home." My comments weren't connected. "I've thought about names. Sally and I felt we'd name a boy Ben Westbrook—Ben Westbrook English. That would be for Ben Jordan and for Betsy and Lewis Westbrook." Calvin made no comment.

I paced back and forth until Doc came back.

"The baby is mighty small, Tom. I'd guess him to weigh between four and five pounds, about what you'd expect for one this premature. The big problem is with his breathing—a baby's lungs aren't fully developed when his mother has only carried him seven and a half months."

"There is something you aren't telling me." Then a dreadful thought struck me: Doc hadn't mentioned Sally—he had only spoken of the baby. Did that mean that she had died? My mouth went dry as I forced myself to ask him the question.

"No, she's still alive, but she has lost a lot of blood. Sally's barely conscious." Doc put his hand on my arm as he said, "You can go in to see her and the baby—but you need to know that neither of them has more than a fifty-fifty chance. The next twenty-four hours are critical."

The five riders had no difficulty seeing the dusty, rutted trail called the Knickerbocker Road because the white light streaming down from the new moon clearly illuminated it. Carl Koestler led the way. Raul Ysleta and the three men he'd hired as mercenaries in Mexico followed in single file. They rode silently past the shacks of camp followers and washer women which clustered near the fort. Veering to the west they rode through a mesquite flat that lay on the ill-defined outskirts of Santa Rita. Koestler held up his hand as a command to stop, then all of them stepped down from their horses and tied them in a stand of pin oak trees.

"We'll walk the last half mile," Koestler said to Raul. "Tell them that Hall will be inside the wool warehouse by himself except for the hired hand who stays there all the time to look after the place."

Raul Ysleta spoke rapidly in Spanish to Paco Cruz, Gitano, and Loco Elizondo. The last named held a length of wire with wooden handles at each end of it, a garrote, in his hands.

The eerie sound of a coyote toward the west howling at the moon quavered in the air as they made their way silently, avoiding the few darkened dwellings that lay in their path.

The large metal-clad building loomed in the sky, its tin roof shining in the moonlight as if made of purest silver. The land on which the warehouse had been built slanted, and on the low side it had been built up and had a wooden dock so wagons could more easily unload their great bags of wool. A man sat on a crate out on the covered dock, smoking a cigarette. He started to turn his head as a board behind him creaked, but he was too late.

Loco Elizondo slipped the wire of his garrote over the unsuspecting man's head and hauled back on it violently, holding the wooden handles firmly in each hand. The wire instantly slit through the man's windpipe and jugular vein. A spray of blood shot out as the man arced backward, hands helplessly clutching at the slippery wire. But by that time he lost consciousness and fell, kicking grotesquely as he died.

Swiftly Paco Mendez, Gitano, and Loco Elizondo ran to the dock, climbed the steps, and rushed into the cavernous building. Raul Ysleta joined them, his knife held low in his left hand. Carl Koestler waited outside.

The four men edged down dark aisles past stacked woolsacks. They reached a wall and followed along it, bodies bent forward. Then they saw a pool of light upon the floor beside an open door that led to a small room. Raul pointed to it and then motioned toward a long, heavy sack which had several steel hooks protruding from it. Gitano and Loco Elizondo pulled these curved wool hooks from the bag, and fixed their fingers around the handles. They followed Raul as he crept toward the office door.

Outside the building Carl Koestler carved a chew of tobacco from a hard plug of tobacco which he carried in his pants pocket. He bit into the corner of the plug and tasted the hot bitter sweetness, the distinctive liquid taste of tobacco. With relish he let a rivulet creep into the back of his mouth, then collected it and spat it out. At that moment a high-pitched shriek rang out, seeming to vibrate with a metal hollowness from the center of the tin warehouse. Other screams followed, dreadful hoarse cries, and then Koestler heard only silence. He ejected a long spurt of brown liquid from his mouth and struggled up from his haunches as he made his way to the warehouse.

The last thing they did was to hang the coal oil lantern by a nail in the pine stud that ran up the wall. The light disclosed Max Hall's body suspended from ropes that hung from rafters. The ropes ran through the bent handles of three steel hooks which had been sunk deep into him. One pierced his upper leg, another buried itself in his stomach, the third stuck out of his armpit. Blood ran down from these upon the grimy floor.

Carl Koestler carefully put a piece of paper on the blood-slick shirt which covered Max's chest. On it he had written these words:

To Tom English—
I told you to come alone to Mexico. This will teach you to follow instructions.
You know where to find me—I'll be waiting for you. Come by yourself or the rest of your family and friends will die like this.

CHAPTER FOURTEEN

"I can't go," I said when riders arrived at the Lazy E at dawn with the news. I held the note in my hand and read it again.

"Of course not," Doc Starret agreed. "It's out of the question. You have to stay with Sally. In the meantime the Ranger ought to be in Santa Rita any day now—and when he gets there he can get up a posse and go after those men."

The messengers, Junior Sims from the livery stable and his uncle, Amos Potts, informed us that by a miracle Max Hall had not died yet, but that he was barely holding on. Amos had to do all the talking since his nephew, Junior, stammered so badly when he got excited that no one could understand a word he said.

Doc Starret grabbed his bag and began putting all his equipment back in it while he told me that he had done all he could for Sally and the baby, that he was sorry as hell to have to leave us now, but that he had no choice. He emphasized once more that he felt it to be important that I should remain with Sally and the baby.

The boys had hitched Doc's horse to his buckboard and before I knew it he had left in a cloud of dust, rushing to Santa Rita to see if Max might be saved.

Calvin Laudermilk said he'd best be on his way, acting unusually quiet, and a little later I heard him ride out.

Sally lay on her back, her eyes closed. I tiptoed into the room and glanced inquiringly at Lupe, who sat beside the bed with the baby in her arms. Lupe shook her head to indicate, I suppose, that nothing had changed. The baby had hardly any hair and looked wrinkled and red. The incredible thing was his unbelievably small size—only fourteen inches long, I judged. He curled his tiny hands by his face and lay there. I stood for a very long time, looking at him. Earlier in the day he had been almost blue but now his color had improved. Or at least that's what I told myself.

A low fire built within me as I went out of the room and down to the lot. I knew that only a matter of time remained until I found myself on the hunt. The men who had killed Ben Jordan and the Westbrooks—who had put Max Hall at death's door—would have to be tracked down.

I raised both hands and held them before my eyes. Not a tremor. I could hear a ringing in my ears that seemed to drown everything else out. One of the cowboys spoke to me but I had passed him before the sound of his voice registered. I kept on walking without turning back.

Manuelito had saddled Dan for me earlier, and he stood beside a hitching post next to the bunkhouse. Dan must be at least seventeen years old now, and for a long time I'd thought of him as the best stallion in our part of the state. One of his offspring, Joe, by my favorite mare, Bess, had carried me to Montana. I had left Joe and another good stud, Ross, up in that mountainous country on the ranch I owned in partnership with Jeff Cunningham, the son of my old friend, Hap. Jeff had inherited his father's interest last year—and I had gone after the Bull Doggett gang in order to revenge Hap Cunningham's death.

I mounted Dan and rode out in the pasture, trying to concentrate. When too many things happen at once, it seems that the shock can keep a man's brain from functioning normally, or at least that's the case with me. I couldn't seem to think straight. I pondered the strange emotion which afflicts men, demanding revenge, for I knew that is what had set Walden Doggett and his pack on me. The cycle of death and vengeance seems to have no end. At the moment I didn't want it to, for a single-minded intensity swept over me. I would have to seek them out.

I wondered if I would still feel this way if Sally and the new baby, Ben, died. I knew I would. Maybe it would be best if I *were* killed—and got it over. Most gunfighters go down sooner or later, and maybe that would be best. I'd rather lose my life knowing I was going into a fight than have some trigger-happy stranger gun me down from ambush so he could build his reputation. I told myself that didn't seem fair to Rebecca, but then I made myself forget that, telling myself that there would be nothing fair for her about my being bushwhacked later on either.

I was tired. With a shrug I turned Dan and headed for the arroyo where I practice with my guns just about every day. I hated to go so far from the house, but I didn't want Sally to hear the sounds my six-guns make. In a few hours I'd be beside her bed to take up my vigil.

Later, riding back, the idea I'd had earlier began to take hold. Why *not* force the issue? If I got killed, at least my enemies would stop tracking down my friends while they tried to get back at me. And these men had threatened to take the lives of my family! While my remaining at the ranch might give Sally moral support, my doing so more than likely was setting the stage for Walden Doggett to send his men out to try to kill her. I sat in the saddle, thinking these thoughts and not where I was going, and all of a sudden I realized that old Dan had stopped and started eating grass.

I pulled his head up and headed him for the house. And all at once a breath of freedom seemed to blow across my face. Caught up by a sense of recklessness, little explosions in my brain blew away the caution and, for that matter, all the fear. I'd take what came, and if it meant my life, so be it.

The next morning I sent for Scott Baker, the manager for all my ranches, and while I waited for him I sat down at my desk in the cluttered space that served me for an office.

On one wall a map hung showing our land holdings on the Concho. It had lots of marks we'd drawn showing the fence line around each ranch and where the gates were located. Later, after we had put down water wells and installed windmills, we cross-fenced every ranch we owned. The map helped me visualize how we stocked the place. With all fences drawn with ink, we could mark in pencil the count we had on cattle and sheep for each pasture, and could rotate the stock so as to give the range a rest on a regular basis. I have observed land that has been overgrazed, and it looks like talcum powder when there is a long dry spell. Some ranchers must not worry about things like that, but I had resolved that the place I'd leave behind would be improved by my time on it, be that long or short.

Standing before the map I touched the little narrow spread that was the original Lazy E. Not more than ten sections, it went along both sides of the North Concho. With the help of Jason Field and Mr. Clarke, Sally's father, I'd bought what I now termed the East and West Ranches from neighbors who had turned into enemies. Then as the years passed, we inherited the Field and Clarke ranches. Counting the distant Circle X out past Langtry on the border, we had 381,440 acres, which comes to 596 sections. It takes a man a considerable amount of time to ride over range of this size, even if he averages twenty or thirty miles a day, for we're talking about *596 square miles.*

In addition, I own an undivided half interest with Jeff Cunningham in the ranch north of Black Horse, Montana. We didn't have a good survey on that property, but Hap Cunningham and I had estimated it to be in the neighborhood of sixty sections. A section has 640 acres in it, and that figures out at 38,400 acres. You still can't buy land in the Montana territory, although we expect to be able to do so one of these days. In the meantime we have to live with the uncertainty of what is called "Montana's Law of Customary Range," which my banker in Black Horse assured me has been recognized by the authorities there since 1877.

Today I wouldn't bother Scott Baker with instructions about Montana, or for that matter about the Circle X, since I had no debts associated with either of them.

Scott Baker came in from the kitchen carrying a cup of coffee. After we exchanged greetings he sat down and shoved back his hat. One of the many things I like about Scott is that he is a worrier. I don't have to fret about things for I can rest assured he has already done so. His forehead is so corrugated by wrinkles that it looks like a washboard, and he constantly checks on matters to make sure he hasn't forgotten anything. I used to wonder why things always went so smoothly at the big Clarke ranch when he ran it for Mr. Sam Clarke, Sally's father. Then it struck me: Scott does something few managers consider. It sounds simple when you say it, but in practice it requires great discipline. Scott follows through. Most bosses give instructions, and raise hell if it turns out someone didn't follow them. But by that time the damage has been done. Scott gives instructions and then, by God, he follows up to make *sure* that those instructions have been carried out. I learned that this makes all the difference. When I went to Montana and changed my name, trying to get away from my past, I had put him in charge of everything I had in Texas, and on my return I saw no reason to change it.

Scott had made Jim Farr foreman on the Clarke part of our spread, and we sent Joe Burnett out to head up the Circle X and get it fenced. Even as late as 1886 it amazed me how few men had been willing to enclose their ranches, for old habits die hard. But times were changing.

Ted Carrothers served as foreman on the West Ranch, and Osie Black ran things on the East. Of course, old Benito Acosta had his hands on the reins at the original Lazy E, although we certainly didn't have much stock there. His son, Santiago, and my Mexican cavalry spent most of their time making damn sure that some bushwhacker didn't creep up on me. It sounds like a waste, but when Ben Jordan set up the system it had seemed to make sense.

"Some unpleasantness has been going on," I remarked.

"Heard a little about it," Scott replied. "You'll be happy to know that Max Hall is still alive, although the fellow who rode through the ranch on his way out from Santa Rita didn't know much more than that."

We talked for a time about Max. Then I told Scott that I had determined to get out of debt. While I was alive, I had no concern about my ability to talk bankers into going along with me, but if something happened . . . I didn't have to finish my thought, for it became clear enough.

"Are you about to do something foolish?" Scott asked me.

"Not by my standards," I answered.

"That ain't saying a hell of a lot," Scott countered.

In an hour he had my letter giving him full authority to sell off all the cattle and sheep he had to, regardless of the prices he got, in order to pay off every debt I owed. In the letter I gave him a careful list of these, including the note still due the Trimingham boys. I'd signed the main note with the Fort Worth National Bank, and I had a few notes at Max's bank in Santa Rita as well.

"You know that prices for beef have been falling?"

"I wouldn't be surprised to see them go lower," I answered.

"Well, then," Scott said, getting up. He folded the letter and stuck it in his shirt pocket and muttered, "I'll do my best." He stared at me a good long time, then said, "You might want me to ride along with you, Tom."

"No, Scott, someone's got to be sensible. There's no question in my mind that you fit that description better than I do."

He left abruptly, saying, "Take care of yourself, you hear me?"

I nodded. After he had gone I decided that I had put my affairs in order as well as I could in the short time I had. I put the new will I'd drawn in an envelope addressed to Sally or Jedediah Jackson in the center of my desk and put a brass cigar humidor which I had never used on one corner of it as a paperweight.

"He didn't come," Walden Doggett said at the end of the third day after Raul's mercenaries had left the note on Max Hall's chest in the wool warehouse.

"Reckon Tom English lost his nerve?" Jason Quest asked.

"I wouldn't bank on it," Carl Koestler said. "He's bound to know that the law will be coming to Santa Rita and that time is on his side. We can't wait around here any longer. We have to go after him; he won't expect that."

"What about those gunhands of his?"

"We'll hit while they're asleep. Here's the plan: We'll set fire to the bunkhouse and in the confusion we'll lay in wait. When Tom English steps out to see what's going on, we'll drop him in his tracks. You could almost read a newspaper by the light of the moon last night—we won't have any trouble at all in getting our sights on him."

The men stared at Koestler without speaking at first. Then Jason Quest said, "You always make these things sound so damn easy." He started to say more, but Walden Doggett broke in.

"I'll go along with Koestler. We've run out of time. After we kill English we'll find the fat man and the Indian and shut their mouths too."

Koestler rubbed his hand over his bristled, unshaven chin. "None of us wants to hang. We have no choice about making sure there will be no man who can ever testify against us."

"No use your trying to ride with us, for your ribs won't stand it—you'd only slow us down," Koestler said to Jason Quest. "You should go back to your ranch house and wait for us. Take the kid with you."

Koestler continued speaking to Quest, ignoring the scowl leveled at him by Sonny Cade. "When we see you the next time it will all be over. We'll tell you what happened—we owe you that—and then we'll pay off Raul's Mexican friends and split up."

"I'm going with you," Sonny Cade said unconvincingly.

"No, kid, you ain't going to do that," Walden Doggett growled. "Someone has to look after Jason. Besides, this is something for men to do."

Calvin Laudermilk waited impatiently for a rattling wagon to pass by and then strode through the dust thrown out by its wheels until he reached the plank sidewalk. He stepped up on it and then shouldered his way through the two swinging doors of the Lost Hope Saloon.

"By God," he said, sitting at a table by the window, "the crush of life in the city is enough to compress a man's spirit into odd shapes." He saw Jimmie, Tuck's woman, waiting to take his order at the bar. This must be the time of day when John Hope takes his nap, he decided.

"No one," Calvin said darkly, "can get into heaven with a pinched, compacted soul. City folks don't have the foggiest chance of talking their way past the gatekeeper, sly and slick as they may be."

Jimmie made no response. Her black eyes fixed themselves on him, staring from her mahogany face. Calvin met her gaze. She was, he thought, a cushiony-looking woman, not one of those bony, decrepit creatures who resembled spavined, starving mares. No, this woman had substance to her. Tuck Bowlegs, Calvin decided, was a lucky man.

He ordered a bottle and, since he hadn't eaten for several hours, asked for an overcooked sirloin steak, even though he suspected that as far as

Jimmie was concerned, one cut of meat was like another. His eyes adjusted to the gloom inside and he saw a man at a table in the back.

Calvin felt like talking so he took his bottle and glass and joined the other patron, walking to his table and sitting down. He looked at the man a moment, trying to see who he might be. The reason he had difficulty was that his companion had his head down on his arms, almost lying on the table.

"Howdy," Calvin said. "Might I offer you a drink?"

Harper Dent raised his bloodshot eyes and slowly leaned back in his seat. "Go to hell," he responded.

"I'm getting what I deserve," Calvin stated, "for mingling with the swinish multitude."

"What?" Harper asked, his eyes narrowing.

"I came to town to find some riders who would be willing to join me and Tom English. We are going to form a posse to go out after the men who have been committing these atrocities."

Harper put his head back on his arms. His voice, sounding muffled, said, "Don't look for me to help Tom English. I can't stand the son of a bitch. You ought to go across the road to the Concho Street Saloon to look for volunteers."

"I have just come from there," Calvin said. "I talked to a surveyer, a man thinking about putting in another wagon yard, and a salesman who wanted me to look at his pictures of windmills. None of them seemed any more interested in joining with me than you do."

"English is rich. Let him hire people to do his fighting for him."

"What on earth is bothering you, Harper? I've known you for some years, and have never seen you acting in this poisonous way. My Lord, if a rattler had as much venom as you, no snakebite victim would have a hope in hell of surviving."

"Goddamn it, Laudermilk, leave me alone. The bank has foreclosed on my ranch—I'm wiped out. Max Hall got what he deserved the other night. As for English, why should I help him? *No one* gets that rich by honest means," Harper Dent flared, rising to his feet. He picked up his hat and strode out of the bar.

Calvin returned to his table and seated himself. He savored his drink and decided that he preferred being alone to passing his time with men of small and mean minds. Nevertheless, when Jimmie brought his meal to him he said, "We must forgive Harper. Bastards can suffer with just as much sensitivity as saints. It's a mark of the world's unfairness that they don't receive the same degree of sympathy."

Jimmie did not reply.

An hour later Tom English came in the saloon looking haggard. He joined Calvin, poured himself a drink, and downed it.

Calvin said, "I certainly didn't expect to see you this soon. How are your wife and new baby?"

"They both seem a little better." He splashed out another drink but stopped himself. Very carefully he poured the whiskey from his glass back into the bottle, spilling a little which ran down on the table.

"I'm through waiting, Calvin. I've got to *do* something. But first I had to see about Max Hall." Tom shook his head. "I've just spent the most godawful time over at his house."

"Tell me about it."

"I only looked in a minute. He's in terrible pain—as you might imagine —and looks like death warmed over. Cele, his wife, is distraught and won't leave him for a minute. I did talk to Doc Starret, who said something I'm still trying to understand. He said, 'Sometimes a man can clamber out to the other side of his problems, and I think Max may do that.' "

Calvin said, "That sounds encouraging, although not real scientific. I prefer doctors who look at me with sympathetic eyes while they speak Latin."

Tom looked at him seriously. "Do you take everything lightly, Calvin? I love to hear you talk, but you usually just touch the surfaces—you never seem to let yourself go deeper than that."

"I'm sorry, Tom. Men get into habits, usually bad ones." He stopped, struck suddenly by a thought. "I never once have fallen by accident into a *good* habit." He mused a moment, then went on. "Anyway, my way with words is an example of the type of tendency which is my curse. Generally, I find most situations where mankind is involved to be humorous. However, the things that have happened to your friends have a totally different character.

"I am convinced," Calvin Laudermilk continued, "that man by nature is a mess. Since that, by definition, is 'natural,' it doesn't overly concern me. But all have within them a darkness that can surface, that can take over. Those who give in to that—pass beyond being mere pests. There is one thing which I cannot and will not forgive: deliberate cruelty—particularly when it's directed at me. These scoundrels are guilty as sin of carrying meanness a step too far," Calvin huffed.

Calvin proceeded to tell the story of his fruitless efforts to find men willing to join in a posse. "I knew you'd show up, planning to go after them, and I figured you might need help. But since the town folks prefer to sit tight while they nurse their indignation, what would you say to my going out to talk to the commander at the fort? We'll get the U.S. Cavalry to lend us a hand."

"They don't like to get involved in local affairs, and you can't blame them. They maintain it's up to the towns and the counties and the state to maintain the peace."

"Speaking of that, I don't suppose you've heard when the Ranger might come to town?" Calvin inquired.

"None," Tom responded. Then he said, "I'm heading out to Knicker-bocker tonight."

"Might just join you." Calvin sighed. "From the looks of things I'm wearing out my welcome here. Folks won't forgive you for asking them to do something they know they ought to do when they are determined not to do it."

"No need for you to go to the trouble of going with me," Tom said, "for to tell the truth I prefer to ride alone."

"Do you often get these suicidal urges? Have you taken up some new religion that clamors for self-sacrifice? My God," grumbled Calvin, "how is it possible that someone with no more horse sense than you has managed to live to be a grown-up?"

Tom didn't reply.

"And another thing, here I've been trying to enlist support from some less than enthusiastic townspeople, while you have in your employ some men who have long carried weapons in your defense. Why in bloody hell have you not brought your Mexican gunhands along if you're headed for a showdown?"

"Calvin, you know they threatened my family. I had to leave them well protected."

"If that's the case you're stuck with having me tag along. And I'll see if I can't locate Tuck Bowlegs, although he more than likely will have too much sense to join us."

Tom looked relieved, although he didn't comment on it directly. After a minute he said, "A cousin of Lewis Westbrook's has taken over the hardware store. I need to drop by to pay my respects and, while I'm there, pick up some ammunition." Tom rose and prepared to leave the Lost Hope Saloon. "Meet me there in twenty minutes," he said to Calvin.

CHAPTER FIFTEEN

Gitano rode up to the pens where the Lazy E cowboys stood, watching his approach. He pulled his horse to a stop and sat, waiting for an invitation to join them.

An older man, Mexican like the others, walked up to him. Speaking Spanish, the man on foot asked, "Who are you?"

"My name is Gitano Gutierrez."

"Gitano?" The name meant gypsy.

"That's what I'm called, but my real name is Dagoberto. I'm looking for work. I've been a *vaquero* for Minor Cain on his ranch near the border."

"Why did you leave?"

"It was time to go." He knew this would not be questioned. Most cowboys tended to move from ranch to ranch, drifting as the inclination struck them.

"We don't have a job for you, but you're welcome to pass the night," Benito Acosta said.

That evening he sat in the bunkhouse with the others. Pepe Moya volunteered that perhaps Gitano might find a job at the Trace ranch, explaining that a cowboy named Milo Studly had left not long before. Pepe, using "Tex-Mex" words blended with his Spanish, stated they might find themselves short-handed.

"Juan Suarez is going from here in the morning to the Trace ranch with a message. You can ride with him if you like." Pepe explained that the owner of the Lazy E, Tom English, had left today for Santa Rita. His wife had recently had a baby, Pepe went on, and the daughter of English had been staying with a neighbor lady, one Señora Trace. Suarez would leave at daybreak to tell them of the birth, and to ask them both to come to the Lazy E to help Benito's wife, Lupe, with Señora English and the new baby.

Gitano digested this information without comment. He said he'd like to ride with Suarez the next morning, then excused himself and left the bunkhouse. He followed a footpath, clearly visible in the moonlight, and reached a privy seventy yards down the slope. But instead of stopping there, he went past it to a draw that meandered toward the river.

In moments he found Raul Ysleta and Carl Koestler at the agreed-upon rendezvous, and related without fanfare the things he had learned. He reached no conclusions, but rather let the facts speak for themselves. Their quarry had escaped. They would have to change their plan.

Raul Ysleta asked, "How many of them did you see?"

"Four at the bunkhouse, including a kid who is their horse wrangler. The foreman's wife is at the main house with the woman and baby. Two more men are up there, guarding the place."

"Are they armed?"

"Yes, all of them wear sidearms. The two guards took turns coming down for supper. They carried rifles and wore six-guns."

Raul talked to Koestler, translating the things he'd heard while Koestler nodded his head impatiently.

Raul asked, "Do you want me to slip by the guards and kill the English woman and her baby?"

"No," Koestler said. "I've got a better idea."

The midday sun showed three riders heading south on the Bar T Ranch owned by Hester Trace. Below a ridge behind them a fourth man rode, taking care not to be seen.

Juan Suarez said, "Señora Trace, the man called Gitano who went with me to your ranch is following us." He took his rifle from its saddle scabbard and levered a cartridge into the firing chamber. He reined his horse around, using his right hand to hold the rifle butt on his upper leg, the barrel pointing up. "I'll see what he wants."

Hester Trace lengthened her reins, allowing her mare to graze on the random patches of dry weeds it could find. The mare tore these with a bobbing motion of her head, making a rough, tearing sound. Hester wore a light green skirt and matching long-sleeved blouse. It brought out the vivid greenness of her eyes, which looked on her young friend, Rebecca English.

"Aren't you excited about going home to the Lazy E? Just think, you'll see your new baby brother!"

Before the child could answer they heard in the distance the unmistakable crack of a rifle firing, and both of them whirled about. They saw Juan's horse go down, and saw Juan push off, landing heavily on his side. He came up on his knees and then pitched forward headlong—landing on his face—seconds before the sound of the second shot traveled through the tingling air and exploded about their ears.

The killer could be seen, walking his horse forward carefully, holding his rifle on the still figure.

"Quick, Rebecca," Hester Trace cried out, whipping her mount's rump with the leather riding crop she carried. Her lithe mare, probably more surprised than hurt by the slapping blow, lunged, taking short steps as she pranced sideways, and then broke into a gallop that lengthened into a run. Skittering behind her, short legs flashing, ran Rebecca's fat pony. Hester pulled on the reins, slowing her mount so that Rebecca might keep up with her.

Hester looked over her shoulder and saw the Mexican named Gitano spurring his horse in pursuit. She leaned forward, almost choking with a desperate fear, and urged her mare up a rocky trail toward the crest of a hill. On the other side, she knew, there lay a scattering of broken hills and brush-choked trails. Her cowboys complained of this pasture, for they had difficulty locating stock in it. She held her mare in check so she wouldn't get too far ahead of Rebecca, and halfway up the incline she turned awkwardly, trying to look behind her, and almost lost her seat. She swayed precariously to her right for she had nothing on that side to use as support. Her left foot slid in the sidesaddle's only stirrup, and her right knee, hooked around the curved leather in front of her, slipped loose. She clutched the knee brace with both hands as she might have a saddle horn and found her balance. The wind whipped tears in her widened eyes, and snapped her long green skirt behind her. Looking around again she caught a glimpse of their pursuer, closing the gap between them. Dry-mouthed, heart pounding, she forced herself to wait for the stocky pony carrying Rebecca.

She yelled out, "When we get over that hill and start down, follow me. I'll find a hiding place."

We're nearly there, she thought as Missy, her excited mount, plunged up the steep, stone-littered ground in muscular bounds. She heard rocks fly behind her as Skeeter, Rebecca's pony, scampered furiously, trying to keep up.

When she reached the top of the hill she took a deep breath and swept a glance about, looking for the best place to hide. As she hesitated, a broad-bodied man with a heavy, wheat-colored mustache pulled his horse out squarely in front of her from behind a stand of scrawny trees.

Hester, her heart almost stopping, hauled back on her reins, and Missy reared straight up, front hooves pawing and eyes rolling. The mare came down, neck bowed and backing owing to the pressure of the bit in her mouth, as four more men rode out of the thickets and moved in a swift crescent around Hester and Rebecca.

The swarthy Mexican called Loco Elizondo flicked his rope over Rebecca and hauled her backward from her horse. She struck the ground with a thud, then rolled over, hands on the dirt, trying to breathe. Loco backed up his horse and dragged her along the graveled soil and across the dry points of a yucca cactus. When he stopped, the girl struggled to her feet, blood showing on her hands and arms and through the torn knees of her denim pants. She fought vainly to pull free of the rope, but every time she'd loosen it, her tormentor with a shrill laugh would jerk it tight.

When Gitano reached them he saw a scene that made him roar with laughter. On one side he saw Loco playing with his catch as if he had a big fish out of water at the end of his lariat. Fifty yards away he saw the woman lashing out with her flexible riding crop at Raul Ysleta, who had caught her horse and now leaned forward, holding her bridle bit in his hand. Raul, angered by the stinging slaps, clubbed at the woman with the back of his hand and smacked her almost off her horse's back.

On the other side Paco Cruz rode up close beside her. With his free hand he grasped Hester's long blond hair and yanked her head back painfully, revealing the long, white curve of her throat. She grasped his arm with both hands, struggling in his grasp and sobbing.

Speaking English he said, "I get excited when a woman fights me. Do you want that?" He held her head back and to one side, twisting it powerfully as he spoke. He poked his bristly, bearded face close to hers, grinning as she flinched away from him.

"Leave her alone," Walden Doggett said harshly. "When we get to where we're going, I won't give a damn what you do to her or, for that matter, to the girl. But right now we've got some riding to do."

Sonny Cade and Jason Quest sat in the front hall of Jason's house on his ranch. Sonny felt miserable. When he and Walden Doggett had come to Texas they had caught one train and then another. The older man had made all the travel plans and the younger had simply followed when the time came to move on. They had finally ended up in El Paso after riding a stage coach for what seemed an eternity to him. They had bought horses there, and then the ride to Santa Rita had lasted a hard ten days. After stopping only long enough to find the general direction of the little community of Knickerbocker, they had ridden on until they had at last made contact with Jason Quest. The vindictive Quest had read the magazine articles about Tom English and had written a letter to Walden Doggett, mentioned in the *Chicago Weekly* as the brother of Bull Doggett, who had been killed by Tom English in an epic battle.

The more Sonny thought about it, the more he realized that he didn't have a clear idea how to get home to Montana—even if he had the money for the trip. However, he had recently heard that some new stretches of railroad had opened, and some said if he got to Fort Worth that he could easily get by rail to Chicago, and then from there to Helena or some other stop in Montana. That certainly sounded more straightforward than trying to backtrack by the tortuous way which had brought him from the rockies to the flatland of Texas.

"I would surely like to go home," he said to Jason Quest.

"Well, then, go."

"The truth is, I need some traveling money."

Jason gritted his teeth, and Sonny observed him carefully. He had noticed that the owner of the ranch had been having difficulty breathing. His skin looked like dried parchment on his skeletal face, and his eyes glowed with fever. "Do you take me for a fool? Hey?" Jason asked.

Outside, the night wind shoved its unseen back against the limbs of an elm tree so that they made moaning noises as they rubbed against each other.

Sonny began to pace. He changed the subject. "Koestler says that we might all get hanged for what has happened, but *I* haven't done anything. Raul killed the sheriff, and Walden shot those two people."

"It would almost be worth the money if you *did* go to Montana," Jason muttered, shifting positions in the rocking chair, trying to get comfortable.

"If you'll loan me a hundred dollars, I'll sign a note for two hundred with whatever interest you like."

"Boy, why talk like an idiot? Just hush your mouth so I can rest," Jason Quest said querulously.

"Oh," Sonny Cade said, his voice quavering.

The front door had swung open and the gargantuan frame of Calvin Laudermilk filled it. He held a Colt .45 leveled on Sonny's nose.

"Oh, my," Sonny groaned.

Jason Quest, his eyes squinched shut against the pain of his broken ribs, sighed heavily as he wheezed out, "What are you cryin' about now?" He snorted in disgust. "Didn't you hear me tell you to hold your peace?"

He opened his eyes with a glare to underscore his irritation. When he did he saw Sonny backing away from the fat man who held a six-gun in his face. Behind him Jason saw Tom English, a Winchester in his left hand, his right hovering near one of his twin Colts.

"*Jesus Christ,*" Jason Quest croaked out. He sat up straight, his mouth working, before he managed to hiss, "God a'mighty!"

"Brother," Calvin Laudermilk said, "it makes my heart sing to know that you have finally found the Lord. But," he cautioned, waggling his pistol loosely in his hand, "don't assume I'm equal to you in piety." His eyebrows rose and lowered theatrically as he shoved Sonny Cade before him and walked closer to Jason's chair.

"I have cleaned out their larder," Calvin Laudermilk announced in grave tones as he walked into the chair-strewn front hall of Jason Quest's house. "If they don't get here soon my disposition is going to sour. If there is one thing I cannot stand it is the idea of a prolonged fast. The very word makes me ravenously hungry."

"The Cade youngster told us six men went out to the Lazy E after me day before yesterday," Tom English said. "He expected them back by last night, about the time that you and I showed up."

"What do you think happened?"

"Lord knows," English replied. "Benito and the boys knew to be on guard, and I have to think that they'd be able to fight them off."

"Don't go getting the fidgets, Tom. If you left here right now and rode full tilt, you still couldn't get to your ranch by day before yesterday."

Tom frowned. "I know you're right, but staying here—waiting all this time—is the hardest thing I've ever done in all my life. If something has happened to Sally . . ." He couldn't bring himself to finish the sentence.

Sonny Cade sat in a chair near them, tied hand and foot with stiff *mecate,* a rope made from the fibers of the maguey cactus. Jason Quest, similarly bound, had been bundled up and placed on the couch. Calvin Laudermilk, when carrying him to it, had said, "I have a sudden, overpouring urge to give you one last, good squeeze. However, you're looking a mite fragile today—not to say puny—and I fear you might break all over the floor." He shook his head in mock horror as he placed his burden gently down upon the dried leather.

The eyes of Jason Quest mirrored the horror in those of Calvin Laudermilk, but in Jason's case the emotion shown was quite real. In his worst nightmare he could not have envisioned himself as being carried about in the monstrous arms which had already snapped so many of his ribs.

"Did you hear something?" Calvin asked.

Tom rose and went to the partially open front door. He held his Winchester in both hands. Cocking it, he said, "They're coming."

Calvin picked up his own rifle, which he had taken from his saddle when they had hidden their horses the night before. He went into the small parlor which adjoined the hall and propped it against the wall next to the rifle he had taken from its rack over the chimney. On the floor between the weapons he had set an open box of cartridges. He took off his hat and, drawing his revolver, sank to one knee at an open window.

Things are going just as we planned, Calvin was thinking as he inched his head up, preparing to peek out the window. At the first glance he said to himself, "No, by God, they're not!"

In the distance he saw two men leading Sully, his dappled gray Percheron, and Tom's horse from the trees where they had been hidden. Immediately in front of the house he saw a woman on foot. She had on a torn shirt and a long, very dusty green skirt. She stood under the large oak tree that shaded the front of the house. Her hands were tied behind her back, and a rope went from the noose around her throat over a gnarled, horizontal limb. Calvin could barely make out two men trying to conceal themselves behind the tree trunk. They held the rope so tightly that the woman had to tiptoe.

From another tree off to Calvin's right a deep voice bellowed, "Tom English—you and the fat man take off your guns and come out with your hands up."

In spite of the situation in which he found himself, Calvin felt a flash of irritation. He never characterized underfed people by a word that described their skinny, undernourished condition. It would never have occurred to him to say, "Look at that *thin* man," for example. Yet the world at large seemed content to put him in a category of fatness, as though the shape of a man's body reflected anything of significance. Without thinking he ripped three shots out the window, knocking hunks of bark from the oak tree.

Instantly the rope drew taut and the woman's feet left the ground. She writhed and jerked an instant before the rope's tension eased and she touched her feet on ground again.

Someone called out, "She's choking, give her some slack." In response to the command, enough play was given to the rope to permit her to fall in a heap upon the ground. Calvin peered over the window sill and saw the woman moving her head, straining to breathe.

"I'm going to tell you one more time," the deep voice off to the right bellowed once again. "Take off your guns and come outside or we'll hang the woman right before your eyes."

"Great God!" Calvin whispered, staring out the window, spellbound. He knew the voice—it came from the thick-bodied man, Walden Doggett, who had led the villains who trapped them at the river.

"There's one other reason to do what I'm telling you," the same voice rang out. "Take a look and you'll see what I'm talking about." Doggett yelled, "Raul, tell Loco to take the kid out where they can see her."

Then Calvin saw a sight that made his blood run cold. From behind another tree a man emerged, pushing a little girl before him. He recognized Rebecca, Tom's ten-year-old daughter. The man called Loco crouched down, using her as a shield, and he held the two wooden handles of a garrote firmly in his hands. The wire between them strained into the child's neck. She stumbled forward as he pushed her, eyes wide and glazed by terror.

Calvin saw Tom English now—walking from the house—no guns in his hands though he had not taken them off. "Let her go," Tom called, stopping some twenty feet in front of his daughter.

The wire bit into the child's neck and she gasped. In that split second a six-gun flashed into the hand of Tom English and a bullet exploded into Loco's right elbow. The Mexican arched up and back in agony, surging above the shield provided by the young girl, and a second bullet, fired as the first still echoed, splintered through the center of his forehead.

Calvin grasped his rifle and opened up a withering fire, shooting as fast as he could lever shells and pull the trigger. Under the cover, Tom ran forward, picked up his child, and began his retreat toward the house. Calvin threw the empty weapon down, grasped the second rifle, and renewed his cannonade.

The front door slammed, and Tom hurled himself to the floor with Rebecca in his arms as a hailstorm of bullets swept in a swathe across the front of the house, thudding and tearing. Holes the size of a man's fist blew inward from the door behind them as he pressed the little girl in his arms, feeling her tenseness as his hands held the smallness of her arms. He pushed her into a corner and looked into her eyes. She was in shock, sitting as rigidly as a wooden doll. The wire of the garrote had cut a thin red gash that made a trickling necklace around her throat, yet she didn't seem conscious of it.

"Stay here," Tom said, starting to move from her side.

"Don't leave me," she whispered.

He met her eyes an instant, then said, "I'll be back."

Tom stood with his back to the wall beside the door. Cautiously he opened it and peered through the crack. Behind and slightly to one side of the oak tree he made out two men leaning back with all their weight and strength, hauling on the rope. *They were hanging Hester Trace,* and her swinging feet flicked helplessly as they left the ground. As he tensed to make his charge he saw one of the two executioners stagger away from the rope, both hands flying out before him. The other let go of the rope, dove for cover—and Hester plunged back down into a heap. The firing from the trees stopped as all eyes centered on the astounding drama taking place before them.

The man Tom had seen stagger now swayed out in clear view. An arrow penetrated completely through his throat, its feathered shaft on one side, the glistening barbed head protruding from the other. A wide, sprayed stream of blood shot in the air before the victim, who slowly spun about in wordless agony before toppling facedown upon the rock-hard soil.

In the confusion Tom burst from the house, diving to the earth and rolling behind a small bush. Coming up to one knee he fired at the other man who had held to the rope around Hester's neck. The bullet punched into the man's chest and slammed him violently backward.

Tom saw Walden Doggett retreating in some trees to his right and he fired too late, for Walden had disappeared.

Behind him he heard Calvin's rifle cracking out shot after shot. He saw a man go down, start to rise, and then the rifle exploded again and an unseen force knocked him flailing and kicking. He shrieked wildly, doubled in a curled-up knot, and then lay still in crumpled silence.

Tom rolled onto his feet, running awkwardly in his high-heeled boots. Walden Doggett had a horse's reins in his hands and was jerking his mount from the tree where he'd been tied. The animal shied back, half rearing, but Doggett forced him down, caught the saddle horn, and began pulling up. Tom braced himself, raising his six-gun. A second horseman came between him and his target. Tom saw a bearded man holding a pistol toward him, saw a flash at its muzzle at the same instant that a wind-shocked whine spat past his ear. His left and right guns went off at once and the bearded man went backward off his horse, landing on the base of his skull with a cracking noise.

Tom fired helplessly after the fleeing figure of Walden Doggett. From the corner of his eye he saw Tuck Bowlegs vault into a saddle and careen off in pursuit, shrilling out a high Comanche scream.

Tom stood still, momentarily paralyzed, two smoking pistols hanging from his hands. The ringing in his ears shrilled monotonously, sounding almost like cicadas, like a host of locusts in some Old Testament plague.

He heard Calvin calling him, and he turned to help take the rope from Hester's throat. Her eyelids fluttered as she saw him. For an instant he thought he saw a hint of recognition in her eyes and a half-smile of greeting, but then she fainted.

CHAPTER SIXTEEN

Calvin helped me carry Hester into the house. We put her on a Navajo rug in the parlor that had some rusty-looking stains on it. When I straightened I saw Rebecca at the door looking in.

"There isn't anyone out there now, honey. You're safe," I said to her.

Rebecca knelt beside the unconscious woman and touched her cheek. I saw an awful torn redness the rope had made around Hester's neck, and heard her ragged breathing. "She fainted," I said. "Stay with her while we check things outside."

"I don't want to be alone."

"It won't take us long." She sat beside Hester on the floor, face pale, her hands shaking as she stroked the long blond hair of the woman who lay so still upon the rug.

I had to ask the question. "Rebecca, did those men—well—did they hurt you?"

She stared at me with eyes that looked thirty years old out of her child's face while touching the circled cut in her neck. "How bad is this?" she asked.

"It isn't deep," I said. "You'll be fine," I added lamely as I sank to the floor beside her.

Then she said, "One of them roped me off my horse." She held up her raw, bloody palms and examined them, then turned over her arms, looking at the dried blood on her elbows. Leaning back she scooted up her feet and showed me the bloody torn places on the knees of her pants. Then she straightened out her legs and said, "I know that isn't the kind of hurting you're talking about." Her voice faltered, "They talked about what they planned to do to Hester and to me. They laughed a lot, as if they were having fun, but what they said wasn't funny at all." She looked vacantly in front of her. "They could see how afraid we were—and they seemed to enjoy that. It made them act so—excited, so crazy."

I could barely hear her words for she spoke in a very low tone, her head down, eyes turned away. Then she looked up and said, "But you were here, waiting for them."

For an instant the black taste of bile surged in my throat, and the trembling insanity of rage circled close. It is one thing when men take after me, but when they threaten someone like this, in all her innocence and youth, it is quite another. Gradually the spasm of hatred left, and in its place I had an empty, helpless feeling.

I looked down at Rebecca's stricken face, and my heart went out to her. I didn't know what else to do except fold my arms around her. I felt her within them, holding back tensely, and then it seemed that she dissolved and pressed her face hard against my chest. There are times when touching works when all words fail.

I backed away and held her out before me. She looked so small and vulnerable and stunned by all that had occurred. Her spirit had been badly bruised and I didn't know how to kiss that to make it well.

I stared at the woman who had almost died, and at my daughter. Anger mixed with sadness, and these held off the total sickness that I knew would come. I had sworn vengeance and had carried it out, but these are surface things men do, as if these actions might erase past wrongs, as if they weren't evil in themselves. I surely knew that killing didn't change any-thing—except, perhaps, the man who did the killing. Underneath lay the absolute conviction that I had done something terrible that day. I had killed again. Three more men lay dead because of me. The count had grown to thirty-three.

A preacher's voice droned in the back of my mind, a hazy childhood memory. I even felt the hardness of the pew as I listened. He had spoken of sins that could never be forgiven.

I rose and strode from the parlor to the wide, central hall with Calvin at my heels. We untied Sonny Cade, and when he began to cry, Calvin said, "Calm down, boy, I'm too much of a sportsman to shoot even a dove or quail on the ground, so surely you must know I'd take no pleasure in felling a blubbering boy. Now if you was able to *fly* I might get a kick out of trying to hit you on the rise, but as things stand I'd take no pleasure out of gunning you. Besides, unless I'm mistaken, we've already shot our limit. Proper hunters always leave some game for the next time out."

"There won't be no next time," the Cade boy whimpered. "If you'll just let me go—I promise you'll never see me again. I'll head straight for home in Montana."

Jason Quest snorted from where he lay, all trussed up on the couch. "I can't stand a weakling, never could. Doggett was right to send you off to tend to me. Like he said, you have no stomach for the things that needed to be done."

He glowered at Sonny Cade, then turned his attention on me. "I swore to get you for murdering the Phillips boys. They were more than cousins and blood kin to me, you son of a bitch, they were good friends and had no chance against you. Well, you have the upper hand for now, but sooner or later you'll get your comeuppance, you hear me?" He half raised but fell back.

I saw a bubbling, a pink froth, around his mouth. The sight surprised me. Walking to him, I touched his forehead. "You're burning up with fever," I said, sinking to one knee and untying him.

Jason Quest closed his eyes as I pulled his bonds off. "Don't do me no favors," he rasped huskily.

"That man has his own distinctive way with words," Calvin Laudermilk remarked. "Take note of the understated manner he employs to express his gratitude to you for your kindness in untying him."

"I think some of those broken ribs may have punctured a lung," I said to him out of Jason's hearing. "I don't know if that is the only complication—for he looks like an old timer I once saw who suffered from the last stages of pneumonia. Whatever the trouble is, he needs a doctor."

"Tom," Calvin said as though trying to reason with a youngster, "this is a man who, if he recovers, will—as surely as the earth is flat—try to shoot you in the back."

"Flat?"

"Exactly," he replied. "I once rode right up to the edge and looked over. It was a fearsome sight."

Calvin took Sonny Cade by the arm and marched him outside. "We are going to inspect the carnage," he announced cheerfully, "and you are to identify the villains."

The three of us walked out to the tree where they had tried to hang Hester Trace. Beneath it lay a man with his eyes and mouth wide open, looking desperately surprised. An arrow ran through his throat, and blood had stained him scarlet as though he'd been dipped in a vat at a slaughterhouse.

"That's Carl Koestler," Sonny said, averting his eyes and gagging.

We went a little farther and came upon the man who had held the steel wire around Rebecca's neck. His shattered right elbow lay unnaturally to one side, and he had no forehead at all. "They called him Loco Elizondo. Raul Ysleta hired him and two others in Mexico."

In short order Sonny Cade pointed out the other two mercenaries hired to shoot me. One called Gitano lay where Calvin's rifle had flattened him. Another, a bearded man named Paco Cruz, sprawled on his back. My six-guns knocked him from his horse when he rode between me and Walden Doggett.

We retraced out steps to the oak tree, where the hanging rope still hung slackly. At one end of it, not far from the dark trunk, we came to Raul Ysleta. Remembered images, like fluttered shadows made by firelight on a wall, reminded me that this was another man who had fallen before my gun. I had never spoken to this man or to Loco Elizondo or to Paco Cruz. The last two had tried to kill me to earn some dollars. This one came to revenge himself for something that happened so long ago that it seemed like a story I had read about, although the truth is that I'd forced myself not to think about the past.

"Raul Ysleta is the man who killed Ben Jordan," Sonny volunteered.

"It's hard to know why he would do such a thing," I said. "He had no grudge against Ben; they'd never met. I know they did it to get at me; I got the note they sent, but who could have come up with a twisted plan like that? Why did he use *acid* when he murdered him?" Anguish hammered at my temples. Knowing the answers to these questions couldn't help anything, but I felt I had to ask.

"Carl Koestler made all the plans. It was his idea for Raul to do what he did. When I heard about it I decided I couldn't help them—even though I had dreamed of killing you. I've wanted to get back at you for a long time."

I looked at him. "Do you hate me so much?"

"I don't know what to think," he replied. "I thought I did. My uncle meant a lot to me."

"He was J. K. Cade," I said.

"Yes."

"You haven't mentioned Jodie Cade. What kin was he to you?"

Sonny hesitated. "A step-brother. I'll be honest—we didn't get on that well. But anyway, your friend shot him, not you."

"Thatcher Stone shot Jodie Cade," I said. "I thought at the time that Thatcher was a friend. When he tried to kill me, I decided I was mistaken."

"What?"

"It doesn't matter," I sighed. "There's no need to dredge all that up."

"Who murdered Betsy and Lewis Westbrook?" Calvin asked.

Sonny said, "Walden Doggett did that all by himself. Nobody went with him."

"What about Max Hall?" I demanded, trying to keep control as I thought of what they had done, sinking steel hooks in him and hanging him by them to the rafters. When I saw he didn't seem to know the name, I said coldly, "That's the name of the man who got caught by some of your friends at the wool warehouse. Did you take any part in that?"

His eyes looked terrified. "I swear I didn't have anything to do with it. Carl Koestler went with the men Raul hired in Mexico—Paco Cruz and Loco and Gitano—to town to do that so they could lure you into a trap. When it didn't work, they sent me here with Jason, and then they went out to get you at your ranch. They said they were going to set fire to the bunkhouse, then shoot you as you came out of your house."

My blood ran cold as his words sank in, as I thought of all the things that might have happened at my home. I had to get there as quickly as I could.

"Maybe we ought to ride out to see if we can help Tuck," Calvin said. "The last I saw of him he was chasing the ringleader of all these scoundrels. If we're to settle this thing, we have to catch Doggett."

"I've got to take Rebecca home," I said. "And we need to see about Hester too. Besides, which direction would you go?"

"That is a good question," Calvin said, turning in a circle. "I've always liked having freedom of choice, but we've got every mark of the compass open to us."

At that minute I saw movement in the distance. "You won't have to worry about it," I told Calvin. "There comes Tuck yonder—and he's on foot."

Tuck Bowlegs joined us, scraped and scratched and fuming. "I nearly caught him," he announced.

"I've heard those exact words pronounced many times by men holding cane poles at fishing holes," Calvin said.

Tuck ignored him. "He took cover in some brush near the river and waited for me. It never occurred to me that he would stop running. But he did and he shot my horse out from under me when I came near. He came after me but I managed to double back and get away. I could have been killed!" he added.

"Well, of course you could," Calvin said. "Your tone of voice intimates that you feel Doggett didn't play fair, but fairness is not at issue in games which have no rules."

"Fat man," Tuck said, "do you think anyone listens to those noises you make?"

"Noises!" Calvin looked as though he had been truly hurt.

We went back to the house with Calvin telling Tuck that at least the horse which Doggett shot belonged to one of the "blackguards," as he put it, and he pointed out that four more of these horses now stood tied to trees, waiting to be claimed. But Tuck merely grunted and said he'd stay with his mules.

A short time later I found myself with Rebecca and Hester, who had recovered consciousness. We sat in the parlor for a time, while Calvin prowled through the kitchen, complaining about the sparseness of provisions there. He and Tuck sent the young man, Sonny Cade, out with a shovel and instructions to dig five graves. After he left they passed the time with the only thing they could find in the house of real interest to them, the stock of whiskey Jason Quest maintained.

Calvin Laudermilk came to the front of the house, bottle in hand, to see how Hester was doing. He also insisted that I join him in a drink, but for once I managed to refuse. I told him, "Whiskey has caused me more pain than pleasure, all things considered. I may not be able to give up drinking altogether, but I plan to do my damnedest not to take that first drink each day. That seems an easier task, simply concentrating on one single drink, rather than all of those that would surely follow it."

"Monks who wear hair shirts and scourge themselves, and others who embrace a philosophy of self-denial totally mystify me," Calvin said. "Would you be part of such an unsavory group? Besides, just think how *dull* your life will be."

"I suppose there must be a *few* happy people who are sober," I insisted.

"Drab souls, all of them. They are like artists whose palettes limit them to painting in shades of gray."

"Calvin, I've never known a drunk who didn't try to force whoever might be close at hand to drink with him. Isn't that what all your confused talk boils down to?"

He looked offended and did not reply at first. But a moment later he said, "A man has to be small-minded to content himself with reality, for when you're stone-cold sober that's all there is to life."

From the depths of the house we heard a bizarre howling which could only be Tuck Bowlegs, who had, as all Indians do, a very low tolerance for alcohol.

"Sounds like one of your large-minded friends," I observed.

Calvin chuckled. "I offer Tuck as proof of the value of the consumption of spirits. The world knows that Tuck, sober, is a social bankrupt. But you can hear for yourself how convivial he becomes after tasting from the cup which warms." With that he left us.

An hour later Hester felt well enough to travel. We hid the bottles from Tuck, and Calvin walked him up and down in front of the house, trying to sober him up a little. He told him that we had to go, but that Tuck was to remain behind with Jason Quest.

"Did he understand you?" I asked.

"I think so," Calvin replied.

I gave Sonny Cade all the money I was carrying, which might be enough for him to get most of the way home. However, I asked him not to leave until he had finished burying the dead, and until Tuck seemed sober enough to know what we expected of him. We planned to send Doc Starret out from town to see about Jason Quest, but we realized someone had to tend to Quest, for he was far too sick to be left alone.

Sonny looked at me in amazement. I don't know what he thought we planned to do to him, but he certainly didn't believe he would be free to leave—or that we'd give him traveling money. His eyes filled with tears all of a sudden and he said, "Damn, I'm sorry I ever got involved in any of this, Mr. English."

A short time later the four of us rode toward Santa Rita. Calvin lagged behind with Hester Trace, who still seemed groggy and unsure of herself, while Rebecca and I forged ahead of them.

We rode in silence for quite a time, then Rebecca said, "For years I've heard people talk about you and the things you've done. I didn't really know what to think about most of it—you know, the fights you've had and all of that." She stopped speaking for a moment, looking at me to see if she might have hurt my feelings. Then she went on, "Once you and Mama and I went to town and stayed with the Halls. There was a book there about you, telling awful things, but it made you sound so strong." She wrinkled her brow a little. "I don't know why, but it made me proud. And when we'd go into town I would see how all the men looked as if they were in awe of you, and I liked that—you seemed so important."

We rode past clumps of soapweed yucca and a scattering of prickly pear. Rebecca spoke again, "Until today I'd never seen a man shot down. I hadn't seen what dead bodies looked like." She seemed to choke and couldn't continue.

"I hope you never see anything like that again," I said.

"I do too." She hadn't cried very much before, but now tears slid down her cheeks past her mouth, and she looked so pale that the dusting of fine freckles across the bridge of her nose stood out.

Through her tears she said, "I don't want you to do that anymore."

I understood exactly what she meant.

Rebecca looked at me with a deep urgency in her eyes. "Will you promise me you won't ever kill another man?"

I pulled my horse to a stop and she did too.

"Will you?"

I nodded.

"Say it."

Softly I said, "I promise."

Rebecca scrubbed the back of one hand across her face, trying to clear the tears away. She leaned forward and touched my hand, and then she smiled.

CHAPTER SEVENTEEN

We went first to Max Hall's house where his wife, Cele, took us in as if we were her long-lost children. She had the welcome news that there had been no trouble at the Lazy E. Sally had sent Santiago to town to find out if anyone had heard anything about me—for she had been worried—and also to see how Max was faring. When Santiago came to the house, he told Cele that our new baby and Sally were, in his words, "right as rain," and in our part of the country there is no better condition.

Cele bustled about, preparing guest bedrooms, and sent for Doc Starret to tend to Hester and Rebecca. I was amazed at how well both of them seemed to be holding up, and I talked to Doc after he had seen them. He stressed that their wounds were only superficial—that they looked a lot worse than they were. His concern related to the things you couldn't see, for each of them had gone through a terrible ordeal. I slipped upstairs to check on them and found each had fallen into an exhausted sleep. So I went back down to visit some more with Doc before he had to leave to see about Jason Quest. I told him briefly of the events at the Quest ranch; and he reassured me about Sally's condition. After this I found it difficult to hold my eyes open.

"I'm bone tired, Doc."

"I can tell that by looking at you. Your friend, Calvin Laudermilk, on the other hand, appears to be as fresh as a daisy. I saw him a short time ago headed for John Hope's saloon."

"Though I'm younger than Calvin by a good many years," I said remorsefully, "I will have to confess that I can't keep up with him. He has an iron constitution and the energy of a man half his age."

"There are those who are born strong," Doc admitted. Then he said, "That reminds me. The Texas Rangers have arrived in force, at least for them. Two showed up. One is none other than Captain John Robert Hale from Waco. I think you'll like him, Tom. He doesn't say much, but he doesn't have to—his actions speak for him. I'm sure you've heard the same stories that I have. I've spent some time with him and so have Jedediah Jackson and several others, so he has an idea what's been going on."

"You say two are here now?"

"Yes. The second is an interesting character named Teddie Jakes. He is said to have fallen from a tree as a kid, and he broke his left arm. It wasn't set properly and is as crooked as a dog's hind leg. But it doesn't seem to slow him down. He's an easy going type of man, and the captain says his only fault is that he's so blame proud of his horse. He rides a chestnut mare which he advised me is named Epiphany. I told him that sounded sacrilegious, but he said he had no part in naming her, and only the vaguest idea what the word means anyway. But he maintains that she is the fastest at the quarter mile of any horse in the history of the Western world. He says he holds as proof of this a fine black saddle with silver conchos on it which he won in a race against strong competition in Austin last summer."

We sipped our coffee and talked while sitting in Cele Hall's friendly kitchen, surrounded by the odors of the wood fire in her stove and the fresh bread baking in its oven. A sense of safety crept through me and for the first time in weeks my tension eased.

Before he left, Doc Starret said that when he had been talking to Captain Hale he learned that the military may be moving out in a few more years—that they plan to close Fort Concho, and in time all the Texas frontier forts.

"The hell you say!"

"My reaction exactly. It's enough to make your skin crawl, but Hale says that with proper organization the Rangers and local law enforcement officers will be able to maintain the peace. Right now our concern is Tom Green County, where we're fresh out of lawmen, and Hale has taken it on himself to do something about that. While we look around for an experienced sheriff he has hired Jim Boy Irons, who ranched near Water Valley until he went broke. Jim Boy says the idea of bustin' men instead of broncs sounds fine to him, and besides he needs the work. The upshot is, Santa Rita has a new deputy, and his first job is to make certain that all men who enter town check their weapons at his office. From now on no one will be allowed to carry a six-gun or rifle or shotgun while inside the city limits— which is a system that has worked well in other places."

I suppose my skepticism must have shown for he said, "Anything is better than having armed men drinking in the saloons, Tom. My God, that's an open invitation for trouble." He examined me a moment, and then said, "I spoke to Captain Hale about all the men who have threatened you—and he understands your predicament. But he says that the rule has to apply to everyone without exception or it won't work at all. That means you will hang up your Colts at the deputy's office just like anybody else." He said forcefully, "Now don't start frowning, Tom, there's no call to look defensive. If all men in town are unarmed you'll be a hell of a lot better off than in the past. Has wearing guns kept you out of gunfights up till now?"

He knew damn well it hadn't, of course, so I didn't feel I needed to answer him.

After Doc left I stretched out on the daybed in the upstairs hall to rest a few minutes. It felt as though I'd only closed my eyes, but when I came to my senses, it was dark and I had been asleep for more than three hours. When I made my way downstairs I found Hester and Rebecca in the kitchen with Cele. They said they had tiptoed past me as I slept, taking care not to wake me.

"I don't make a practice of taking a nap in the daytime," I apologized, but they hushed me, and all three of them seemed amused at my embarrassment. Cele told me that Max wanted to see me, so I went to his room. His appearance shocked me, for he must have lost thirty pounds, or it looked to me as if he had. I sat beside his bed and we talked about the things that had happened.

"How many men did this to me?" Max asked.

"Four," I replied. Then I said, "All of them are dead."

"How many did *you* kill?"

"Three," I answered shortly.

After a moment of silence Max said, "I'm sorry, Tom," as though having them on my conscience were in some way a fault of his.

I left him a little later, feeling as though a cloud had lifted, for I'd been sick with worry about Max. A man doesn't have that many good friends, and I had already lost too many. When I came back to the living room where the people had assembled, I found the Ranger captain waiting for me.

On rare occasions you meet a person for whom you feel an instant sense of trust and sympathy. I recalled the easy friendship I developed with Cully Clarke, Sally's brother, and now I had the same relaxed sensation with this man; and I suspected that John Robert Hale shared this attitude.

No one could be around Hale and not be aware of his strength, although this in no way came from his appearance. On first meeting the man, you would never think that he had fought Indians on the warpath, or that he had once gone out alone against a mob upon the rampage, as he did one time in Galveston. The Captain stands around five feet nine, I guess, and probably weighs no more than a hundred and sixty or so. He has a hawk nose and strong features. A fan of fine wrinkles spread at the outside corners of his eyes and these laugh lines crinkle up when he smiles. He has hazel, troubled-looking eyes, and a voice so soft you have to listen carefully to what he says or you'll miss it altogether. He looks perfectly ordinary, but when you talk to him you quickly realize that just below the surface he is as hard as flint.

We excused ourselves and went alone into the small office Max has at his house. When we had seated ourselves the captain offered me a drink from one of Max's bottles which sat on a sideboard, but I said, "Not today." He looked at me and asked, "You sure?" and I said, "Well—" And then, before I changed my mind, I said, "Yes I am. I've had my quota and then some." And he laughed.

"I understand you're a man with enemies," Captain Hale said out of the blue.

That put me back on my heels for an instant, for none of us likes to think he can be summed up in a single phrase. Most of us resist the idea of being put into a category, but then it struck me as being a most accurate description. "I am," I answered. "One in particular is on my mind right now." Then I gave him a rough outline of all the things that had happened, from the death of Ben Jordan up to the events at Jason Quest's ranch.

"The enemy I mentioned is the one who got away, of course, Walden Doggett."

"And you figure he's not the kind to run?" John Robert Hale said.

"I know it," I answered. "It was my bad luck to get crossways with his brother, Bull Doggett, who led a gang of outlaws in Montana. Both of the Doggetts have a crazy streak in them, a meanness and cruelty that can't be explained by logic." I hesitated before continuing. "I'm not an authority on many things, but I have been exposed to situations like this more times than I care to recall."

I stopped for a moment, thinking, and then I said, "There have been quite a few men who have wanted to kill me: some to make a reputation, some for revenge, and a few who I can't really understand—maybe they were raised at Lucifer's knee. I'd like to tell you something that happened a long time ago. It will sound as though I'm clear off the track, but it's connected with the way I feel about Walden Doggett. Once when I was no more than fourteen or so I took shelter in a cave. I dove into it to get out of a sandstorm, and because there was no room to stand up, I had to crawl. When I got in out of the wind it was dark and there was a funny smell, but I felt safe. I edged a little farther, and suddenly, *fell,* though only for a few feet before I caught the edge and hung on for dear life. It turned out there was a pit inside the entrance and I had almost slid down in it. My boot caught the edge when I pulled myself up and it broke loose, and some dirt and rocks tumbled down. I caught myself and lay there, when all at once I heard the most godawful noises. I had some matches and lit a torch, and then I leaned over the side and looked down and saw dozens of rattlesnakes all coiled up and writhing around, hissing and striking up at my arm. It scared me so bad I ran for a quarter mile through a driving wind which made the sand completely cover the sky—you couldn't see ten feet in it. You're probably asking, what in the hell does this have to do with the Doggetts, and I'm taking the long way round to tell you. You see there are, in my opinion, certain men who have a part of their brain that is like a reptile's in some ways, and it controls them. I would no more put out my hand in friendship to one of these men than I would stick it down into a pit full of rattlers. The only protection you've got against snakes and blood-crazed men is this: You know about their nature, and you can predict that they are going to come after you given the chance."

"So you figure you haven't seen the last of Walden Doggett."

"I won't be free of him till one of us is dead."

"That," John Robert Hale said thoughtfully, "is one hell of a note."

I agreed with him. Then he said he would be going out toward Knickerbocker to question Jason Quest, and we agreed to meet the following week after I'd had time to go to my home to see about my wife and the baby.

"By the way," the captain said, "you have a mighty pretty daughter." I thanked him and he said, "I couldn't help but notice that both she and Mrs. Trace wore scarves about their necks."

I hadn't had the heart to go into all the things that had happened at Jason Quest's ranch, but now I explained this to him. "Those scarves belong to Cele. They cover the bandages Doc Starret put on their necks."

"What?"

Then I explained that Hester had been strung up by men trying to hang her, while another man held a garrote around Rebecca's throat. I concluded, "They both were hurt before we could get them loose."

"Damn!" Hale said, his eyes snapping sparks. He rose to his feet and began to pace back and forth energetically. Then he sat back down and talked to me briefly about himself. His family had moved to Texas from South Carolina in 1869. As a young man he had married a girl named Anne, but she had died some years ago of consumption. He seemed uncommonly interested in Hester Trace, I noticed with some amusement, especially when he learned that she was a widow.

When we rejoined the ladies, Rebecca had gone to bed, but Hester and Cele were still in the living room. I announced my plans for leaving with Rebecca for the ranch the next morning, assuming that Hester Trace would be going with us. But Captain Hale said that he and Teddie Jakes would need to make a trip to Villa Plata after they had talked to Jason Quest, and since they were going that direction anyway, he hoped that Mrs. Trace would permit them to accompany her. I saw her vivid green eyes fix on him a moment and then, lowering her long lashes, she said in her clipped, British way, "Why Captain, that would be very nice of you."

The next morning Rebecca and I left the general store with several packages. We had bought a present for Sally—a sky blue dress with what the lady said was Belgian lace around the neck—and in addition we found a silver spoon for the baby and had it wrapped in tissue paper with a bright red ribbon around it. As I put these in my saddlebags, a man I'd never seen before came up. He stood patiently while I finished buckling up and then said:

"I heard you were in town."

I looked at him with curiosity but not alarm. Neither of us were armed since Jim Boy Irons, true to his pledge to John Robert Hale, had zealously required all who rode into the downtown area to check their weapons. He took the responsibilities of his office with seriousness.

"Do I know you?"

The stranger replied, "No, we haven't met, but I've been waiting for you."

I didn't like the sound of that. I stared at him. He had corn-yellow hair sticking out under his hat over his ears, and heavy eyebrows of the same color. His eyes were quite large and stood out as though he were startled. He said in an unemotional way, "I'm here to call you out."

It took a second for that to sink in. I stood there, dumbly, looking at him.

"We'll walk over to the deputy's office and pick up our guns, and then go out of town where no one will interrupt us," he said.

"I don't know you, and I sure as hell don't know where you came up with such peculiar ideas, but as you can see, my little girl is coming out of that store and I aim to ride with her to my home."

He came up closer. "I *thought* you might be afraid. The word is that you've lost your nerve."

My hackles began to rise in spite of myself. "It's a wonder to me that you have lived this long. I'm going to ask you to stand aside now, for as I said, I'm leaving town."

"My name is Milo Studly," the peculiar-looking stranger said. "I plan to drop by the Lazy E one of these days. I spent quite a bit of time there when I cowboyed at the Trace ranch."

Rebecca was still in the store talking to the lady who tended to things there for the Westbrook estate. After all that I'd been through lately I could feel my patience growing thin, but still I really couldn't feel too alarmed. Just sick at heart. It had happened so often before: a young gunsel who decided that the way to fame for him was to be known as the man who shot and killed Tom English. I saw the Ranger captain, John Robert Hale, riding up on his way out to the Quest ranch, and this made me feel a little better.

"Don't bother," I said shortly. "You won't be welcome at the Lazy E." Hale hitched his horse not far away and stood there, looking curious. But the stranger ignored him.

"Oh, I believe you're wrong there. I'll be welcome, all right. You see, I want to go see my new son."

"What did you say?" I could feel my cheeks grow hot.

The stranger with the bushy eyebrows grinned. "Why, hell," he said, "he *has* to be my son, because nine months ago I was there on the Lazy E, but you was off somewheres in Montana. So I reckon the kid is mine." He kept his big bug eyes fixed on me while he spoke.

Blood rushed to my head and I could feel my face twitch as he kept talking. "The name's Milo Studly, although a few of the gals like to call me Stud."

I tried to keep my voice from shaking but couldn't. "I know the only reason you've come up with lies like that is to get me into a gunfight with you. Now, I told you I was taking my daughter out of town. But I'll be back, and when I do, you had better be nowhere around."

My temper got hold of me then and I began walking toward him. But Captain Hale stepped between us. He said to the stranger, "Mister, you can get out of this town on your own or you're going to get drug out on the end of my rope. I don't particularly care which you choose."

The one called Milo Studly stared at me, widening his pop eyes, then turned away and left.

An hour later, with Rebecca riding at my side, I thought about Milo Studly. The wind had switched to the north and the first hint of winter breathed about my face.

CHAPTER EIGHTEEN

"There's no doubt in my mind," said Teddie Jakes. "My little chestnut, Epiphany, can run rings around that bay of yours." He and the Ranger captain had ridden to the Lazy E from Villa Plata the day before after escorting Hester Trace to her ranch earlier in the week. From the moment that Tom had shown him his prize horse, Jakes had been leading up to this challenge.

Tom English looked, with some question in his eyes, at the stocky, short-backed mare. She had thick, upright pasterns, very heavy shoulders, and a bulky, muscular neck. "Well," he said doubtfully.

"You don't believe me?" Jakes demanded, fire in his eyes.

"I'm sure you have a fine horse," Tom answered.

Teddie Jakes took off his hat indignantly and slapped it against his leg, making a small puff of dust fly from it. They stood at the corral at the headquarters of the Lazy E. Epiphany had been unsaddled and until that moment Jakes had been scraping her back with a curry comb. Now he bowed his neck and glowered at his host.

Tom said, "You've never seen Sam run, and of course, I've not had the pleasure of seeing Epiphany in action."

"That's not the point," Jakes said patiently. "You don't seem to understand that Epiphany is the fastest quarter horse that ever lived."

Guardedly Tom observed, "That's a fairly broad claim."

"Nonetheless, it's true, and I'll tell you what I say to all the doubting Thomases that come down the pike: The only way to settle a matter like this is with a stake race." A confident but grim smile creased his face. "I'll put up all the money I've got, which is twenty-two dollars, and we'll settle this thing in the next hour."

Tom couldn't help but smile back at him, for Teddie Jake's sudden grin became contagious. "Let me make a suggestion," he said. "Some friends of mine in Santa Rita have in mind putting on a stock show which is to start in exactly two weeks. One of the organizers has gone so far as to suggest that it be called a *'fat* stock show,' but unless their cattle are in better shape than mine that may be stretching the truth a mite. But be that as it may, Leighton Howell has dedicated a pasture of his just north of town as our fairgrounds, and there is a good bit of interest developing. I've been asked to serve on their committee to help get the thing started although I tried to get out of it. But it might stir up interest to stage this race you're talking about. And if you're all that sure of your horse, you'll find plenty of men who'll give you odds, for they know that Sam traces his line back to a thoroughbred stallion we brought all the way from Kentucky. We crossed him with our best mares, and have developed what I consider to be an unusually fine line of horseflesh. We have around fifty of these colts and Sam looks to be the best of the lot."

"I don't have but *one* horse," Jakes said a bit defensively, "but I'll tell you what I'll do: I'll bet you all my money and in addition, I'll bet Epiphany against Sam—winner take all!" He put his hat back on his head and bobbed his chin down aggressively, as if to demand, "Now, what do you say about that?"

"I'm not going to take your horse . . ." Tom started to say when Teddie Jakes interrupted him.

"Hell no you ain't. You're going to lose the race."

"What I mean," Tom said, laughing by now, "is that even if by some miracle that little overmuscled mare . . ."

Teddie Jakes howled in protest over this description, but Tom's voice overrode his.

"If Sam manages to come in ahead, I'll be damned if I'll take your mare, for I know how it is to get attached to an animal. But let me make you a counterproposal: If you lose, then Epiphany stays here and we'll breed her to our best thoroughbred, and I'll buy her colt. We'll give you the loan of a good cowpony during the time you're without her. On the other hand, if you win, you can take Sam with my blessing. But there's a catch." His eyes shone as he spoke, and he regarded his friendly adversary with intensity. Few things engaged him more than bargaining.

"What is the catch?" Jakes asked suspiciously.

"The racecourse is to be laid out and carefully measured by the surveyor they have in town who is platting the property that Max Hall owns. The track will be straight, no curves at all, and on dead-level ground over a distance of one mile."

"Jesus *Christ,*" Teddie Jakes exploded.

"All right," Tom said, "I was just testing you. What would you say to three quarters of a mile?"

"Hell no, this is a quarter-horse race."

"Now, hold on a minute. We never said any such thing. You challenged me to a stake race between your mare and my bay stud, and there has been no agreement as to the length of it."

They wrangled heatedly for several minutes. The Ranger captain, John Robert Hale, strolled up and asked, "What on earth is all the caterwauling about? You sound like a couple of tomcats that are all bowed up before a fight."

"Nothing like that in prospect, John Robert," Tom said with a grin. "Merely a bit of earnest negotiation going on."

With an injured expression on his face, Teddie Jakes said, "Thank God you're here, Captain, this man is determined to fleece me."

"We need to get on up to the house; supper must be ready," Tom said. "Here's my last offer: we'll hold the race over a course of six hundred yards."

Reluctantly, Jakes agreed. Next they debated over who would ride Tom's horse. Learning that Tom's wrangler, Manuelito, who weighed 120 pounds, would be his jockey, Jakes insisted upon adding ten pounds in Manuelito's saddlebags to make up the difference in his weight and that of the boy. With this last obstacle behind them, he shook hands with Tom and cackled, "There, you've shook on it and can't back out now. I think I need to warn you that Epiphany has been in four stake races since I've owned her, and though they were each held over a course of a quarter mile, she looked stronger at the finish than at the start. In fact I've had to haul back with might and main to stop her." Shaking his head with mirth, he added, "Captain, I'm going to need to float a loan from you. The folks in Santa Rita are going to be looking at my little mare and his big bay stallion, and I'll be asking not less than four-to-one odds!"

Sally English leaned back in a heavy red oak rocking chair in what she and Tom called the "East" room for want of a better designation. The big house, built on a knoll not a quarter of a mile from a bend in the North Concho River, sat on the site of a former Comanche campsite. Evidently the Indians had returned there repeatedly from their hunting forays, for anyone could walk for a few minutes, kicking at the ground, and turn up evidence of their past habitation. Tom and his cowboys had found dozens of small flint arrowheads used by children, and occasionally the larger ones used by men. Rebecca had even found a very old flint knife blade in a depression not fifty yards from their fenced yard. The attraction of the site to the Indians must have been the ready availability of water, and the small hill put them in a position to see enemies who might try to slip up on them.

Sally looked through the windows, thinking vaguely of the Indians who had lived there. Then returning to the present, she gazed down with tenderness at the tiny bundle in her arms, wrapped in his soft wool blanket. She could see signs each day of Ben's growing strength—and certainly of his appetite. He had cried before the sun came up but after being fed he slept contentedly while she rocked rythmically, creaking back and forth.

A rooster crowed, and then Sally heard Lupe come in the back door, letting it slam behind her. Birds outside were singing, and through the room's high windows she watched them in the trees. Mockingbirds and a host of sparrows greeted the day.

The tall, multipaned windows on her left flooded the room with clear, early morning light. A houseplant sat in a dull-orange clay pot on her right, and sunshine threw its shadow sharply upon the off-white painted wall behind it. Every leaf and slender branch showed as precisely as if it had been etched in black ink with a sharp steel pen upon white paper.

I wonder, Sally thought, have I ever been this happy? The idea troubled her, and she remembered her father's quoting once—during a similarly contented period—that he should "cast a wreath to the gods lest they be jealous." She shrugged off her concern, determining to follow Tom's advice to concentrate on that day—and be thankful for it.

Cradling the baby in her arms, she walked up to her bedroom and put him gently face down in his crib, taking great care not to wake him.

Tom, as usual, had risen early and left at first light. Today he said he wanted to work some more with Deuce, a young horse he was breaking. Sally pulled off her cotton nightgown and sat on their bed. She rolled up in the warm covers and pressed her face in the sunken place in Tom's feather pillow. Closing her eyes, she detected his scent, and she smiled. Then she stood up energetically, and began to dress. For the first time since the baby had come, she felt good.

Sally rushed down the steps, one hand gliding along the top of the polished banister rail, and burst into the kitchen. Lupe looked up, startled, then spoke to her in Spanish, complimenting her on her appearance. Sally beamed with pleasure at the unexpected remarks, then she plunged into her daily routine. As her strength increased she found genuine pleasure in simple things that she had previously taken for granted. Humming to herself, she set the table and then arranged a centerpiece of dried thistles in a cut glass vase which had belonged to her mother.

Sally walked through the screened back porch and went outside, shivering in the unexpected coolness. She strode down the path to the smokehouse where she intended to get a fresh side of bacon. When she reached the low door of the squat stone building she could smell the smoke and salt and the musky odor of the meat hanging from the walls and rafters inside. Then she saw Santiago walking very slowly beside Tom, heading from the corral toward the house.

Sally's heart stopped at the sight: Blood ran down Tom's face and he walked with great difficulty, not moving his arms and shoulders at all, holding himself carefully, stiffly. Even at this distance she could make out the pallor of his face.

"Not again," she moaned. Then she ran toward him.

An hour later she had him propped up in bed, his eyes closed against the pain. "I've broken this collarbone before," he said between gritted teeth. "I'm pretty sure that's what happened. The aggravating thing is that some of my nerves seem to be involved—I can't raise my right arm."

Sally sat by the side of the bed in a straight-backed chair. She leaned forward and touched his badly swollen and discolored left wrist, which he had placed on a pillow beside him. "What about this?" she asked.

"I think it's no more than a sprain," Tom said, "but for all I know I may have broken something in my wrist. It hurts like bloody hell," he complained. Then he burst out in exasperation, "Damn!"

Sally's laugh, low and vibrant, sounded in the morning air. She couldn't help it, for she felt so relieved. She had thought he might be more seriously hurt. "I have you and Ben in the same room where I can tend to both of you. People have been looking out for me long enough—it's my turn. Besides, I'm a good nurse; you know how much I like taking care of you." A glance at his face showed her that he didn't share her enthusiasm.

Tom winced and closed his eyes. Without opening them he said, "It's my own fault. I wasn't looking where I was going and I rode Deuce right over some loose barbed wire that had been left over when we fenced the horse trap. The wire shouldn't have been there, of course, but I ought to have seen it. Anyway, even a well-trained horse will panic when he gets caught by a coil of wire, and Deuce is far from that stage. When his hooves hung up he went wild. As the saying goes, he broke in two, and threw me before I ever caught my balance." Tom's mortification showed in his face. "I must have hit on my left hand," he said, looking at the damaged wrist, "and then he bucked right over me. And that's the last thing I remember. When I came to, Santiago was there helping me get up—and I had a terrible ringing in my ears. A hoof must have hit me here," he said, tenderly touching a large lump above the hairline at his forehead, "and another caught the collarbone." He lay on his plumped-up pillows, sighing, and obviously feeling very sorry for himself.

Tom said, "I don't know if you can appreciate how helpless I feel—not being able to use either hand. When the men get back this evening I want you to talk to Benito. He's to make sure that word of this doesn't get out."

"Did you hear what happened to Tom English?" Chesley Upshaw asked Calvin Laudermilk. Chesley served as the new bartender at the Concho Street Saloon now that Joe Case had moved to El Paso.

Calvin stood heavily at the bar, feet planted solidly as he hoisted a large glass of warm beer with a thin head of foam. Upshaw had his attention. "No," he said, "but I expect you plan to tell me."

"Keep this under your hat," Upshaw said. "My wife heard it from Martha Sue Lockhart, who had been by to see Doc Starret. Well, she heard him talking to his wife about English."

"Is he hurt? Get to the point, damn it," Calvin expostulated.

Feelings bruised, Chesley Upshaw said bruskly, "Bide your time, and you'll hear." He waited a full minute as punishment, then continued. "The thing is, he got throwed off his horse. Broke his right collarbone and some bones in his left wrist, and now can't use either hand. Furthermore, he's coming to town tomorrow for the big race. You might know he wouldn't miss seeing that."

"Don't discuss this," Calvin warned.

"I don't see why not. Everybody I know is excited about that race," Upshaw said. "I wouldn't be surprised to see a hundred people come to Santa Rita. The wagon yard is already full, and so is the livery stable. A good many folks are making camp out at the new fairgrounds, and you can see how things are in here."

"I mean, there is no need to talk about Tom English being hurt. There are people who might want to take advantage of his condition."

"You're right," Upshaw said. "I never thought of that." He swabbed the bar dry with a moist rag, then adjusted the apron he normally wore. "They say that English used to come in here a lot, but since I've had this job he hasn't crossed the doorstep."

"He had a bad experience in this saloon," Calvin said. "I suppose he doesn't like to be reminded of it."

"Guess you're right," Chesley Upshaw said, and he turned away to wait upon another customer.

Neither man noticed Leroy Quest, who sat with his back to them at a nearby table. He rose and walked out through the swinging doors to the echoing plank sidewalk. Stepping down from it, he untied his horse, mounted, and rode off to the south.

Walden Doggett wore a long canvas duster as protection against the wind as he rode up to the front of the Quest ranch. He saw a man, hat pulled down to shield his eyes from the late sun, sitting tilted back in a chair, protected from the brisk north breeze by a fleece-lined coat which had its collar turned up. The man paused in his whittling, allowing the stick and knife to rest in his lap as he stared at his visitor.

Doggett swept his gaze around and noted six graves under some trees about sixty yards away. One of them was new with a mound of loosely packed fresh soil on top of it. He pulled his horse to a stop in front of Leroy Quest. "I see you already buried your brother."

"Yep. Jason has gone to his reward, the son of a bitch."

"And you have yours, it looks like to me."

"You're damn right I do. This ranch was as much mine as his—but he got the title put in his name." Leroy Quest's face twisted with emotion, and he snarled, "Now it's mine. Jason left no will and I'm his only kin. They tell me there is some legal mumbo jumbo to go through, but the long and short of it is that this here is my ranch now."

Doggett did not reply. He dismounted, tied his horse, and said, "Let's get inside out of the weather."

When they reached the kitchen, Leroy poured coffee from the blackened metal pot that simmered at the back of the cast-iron stove. The smells of coffee, woodsmoke, and then whiskey, as this splashed in the two cups, blended in the air. They sat, warming their hands on the thick mugs.

"I want to thank you for sending me supplies while I was out at Tarpley's Gulch," Doggett said.

Leroy did not reply.

"Your Meskin said you had news for me."

"I do." With no change of expression Leroy Quest told Doggett exactly what he had heard the bartender say to Calvin Laudermilk in the Concho

Street Saloon. He concluded, "English will be in town for the race tomorrow, and he won't be able to defend himself."

"Well I'll be damned," Walden Doggett said, staring out the window.

Leroy Quest poured more whiskey in his mug.

CHAPTER NINETEEN

Under leaden, overcast skies the first real norther of the season swept an icy, constant wind which swirled around the crush of wagons, buggies, horsemen, and pedestrians who crowded with holiday intensity into the unprepared town. Cowboys on horseback fought to control mounts which crowhopped and danced sideways as they coped with the unexpected sights and sounds of teamsters snapping long bullwhips over teams of bellowing oxen, while draymen slapped reins on draught horses tugging their low, heavily laden carts. Excited dogs spurted through the crowd, snapping at one another and barking incessantly, intoxicated by all the activity. A single drunken Mexican reeled as he progressed down the raised wooden sidewalk, bumping into three offended cavalrymen. The few soldiers who had been able to get away from Fort Concho on passes sauntered jauntily in their vivid blue uniforms, wide-brimmed hats cocked forward on their foreheads. Down an alley which ran beside George Henry's café a group of men on foot stood in a long oval while two drunks stood toe to toe, bashing at each other's faces with wild, roundhouse punches until they got so tired they had to quit and sit down in the two-inch-deep dust, stupefied by exhaustion but still glaring. The disappointed crowd tried to encourage them to get up and fight some more, but the combatants had by now lost interest. Besides, they no longer remembered what had started the trouble. The long-expected day of the first annual fat stock show had arrived.

Santa Rita townspeople, with considerable gusto, had decided to create a tradition. For weeks the word had gone out concerning the event—a combination county fair and stock show where respected judges from as far off as Fort Worth would award ribbons for the best animals in each category. At the fairgrounds, north of the village, pens had been constructed for the livestock: boar hogs and sows, rams and ewes, bulls, cows, calves, and an assortment of horses. There were even cages for roosters and chickens. Off to one side, away from the pens, a collection of haphazard tents stood, canvas billowing as gusts of wind struck them. The ropes which held the canvas strained against tent pegs. Inside the flapping protection, under the watchful eye of Santa Rita's self-appointed mayor, Joe Y. Poteet, housewives set out preserves and cakes and other goods on rickety bare pine tables for their own best-of-show competition.

Hammers rang out nearby as half a dozen amateur carpenters bent nails and banged their fingers in the effort to complete the judge's stand at the finish of the racecourse. Flags had been staked out on both sides of the six-hundred-yard track, and whitewash had been liberally slathered over the hard prairie dirt to set out the finish line clearly. This race between the celebrated chestnut mare owned by the Ranger, Teddie Jakes, and the three-quarter-Thoroughbred stallion which belonged to Tom English was the centerpiece of the day's activities. For days men had been arriving from distant points just to see this race. Men from Pecos and Laredo whose horses had been consistently victimized by those owned by Tom English had come prepared to bet on Tom's stallion in order to recoup their losses. Others who had seen their best horseflesh left far behind by Epiphany, Teddie Jakes's squat powerful mare, had traveled all the way from small towns like Bandera and Boerne with full wallets and the sense that they could not lose if they backed the mare. Newspapers from far and near had written glowing stories concerning the matchup, and interest had grown out of all proportion to the importance of the event.

Amazed saloon owners soon realized that they would run short of the fluids needed to aid the celebration, and sent out frantic riders to nearby communities who bought replacement supplies at cutthroat prices. Gamblers had rolled into town in surreys or on the regular stagecoach which came through from Brownwood; and money which had been stuffed in socks or under mattresses had seen the light of day for the first time in years as the owners of these guarded caches became firmly convinced, after discussing the relative merits of the mare and the stallion, that they knew with certainty which would win.

The Taylor Hotel had been full for days, and the overflow sought shelter in the wagonyards. These had pens, stalls, lean-tos, tents, and tiny unpainted one-room shacks which stood with tilted walls and flimsy roofs against the fences and in the corners. An overpowering odor of horse manure clung to the yards in spite of the biting, cleansing wind. Teams of horses stood where they had been staked with ropes in the open spaces, and wagons were shoved together to make more room. The wagonyard owners ambled about, ignoring the muck that squished above the ankles of their boots, trying to raise the prices they had quoted when their customers had first come to town.

The children of Santa Rita, since it was a Saturday, played in the streets, wandering up and down in small groups, watching new arrivals. Their parents reluctantly permitted this, having decided that at least the cowboys who had raised such a ruckus in the past would not be wearing arms. And in fact the only men carrying weapons were the two Rangers, a detachment of buffalo soldiers on loan from the fort, and the deputy, Jim Boy Irons. At each road which led into town the soldiers took all arms and gave their owners numbered tickets. Other soldiers carried the six-guns and rifles and a few shotguns to the sheriff's office, where Irons tagged them and put them on the growing pile upon the floor of the single jail cell next to his one-room office. They had already decided that if they had to arrest many people they would have to take them out to the fort, and the commander had reluctantly agreed to this after a long conversation with the Ranger captain and the deputy.

Calvin Laudermilk carried a large pitcher of beer to his table at the Concho Street Saloon. On sitting down he noticed that for the first time in memory not a single one of the girls who worked at Miss Berta's big white frame house down the street was in the place. Business would without doubt be brisk at Miss Berta's, Calvin decided. He looked about the crowded, smoky room and a great smile wreathed his face as he observed the antics of a bearded old man who waved his arms as he told some complicated story.

Severn Laycon, who cowboyed at the Trace ranch, walked from the bar with a glass of whiskey in his hand and asked if he could sit down. He introduced himself and the two began a lively conversation.

A short time later the Ranger captain, John Robert Hale, came past the swinging doors and shouldered his way to the corner where Calvin sat. He greeted Severn, whom he had met recently when he had escorted Hester Trace to her home and then said:

"Have either of you seen Tom English?"

"I'm told he no longer comes in here due to some past troubles," Calvin replied.

Hale said, "Jim Boy Irons told me that most of Tom's men arrived yesterday with his horse, Sam, so he'll be fresh and rested for the big race this afternoon. Tom came in this morning, and I need to see him."

"You have some special reason for that?"

"I'm afraid so. There are rumors all over the place about his being disabled. We tried to keep that quiet, but word got out. He needs to know about this, for in my opinion he should stay away from the town. There are too many men who would like a chance at Tom English if they thought he couldn't defend himself."

"You couldn't keep him away from that race this afternoon with a ten foot pole."

"I expect you're right." Hale poured half a glass of beer from Calvin's pitcher, then drained it. Wiping his mouth he said, "In that case, I'll be at his side until he leaves for his ranch. With all this confusion, though, it won't be easy finding him." The Ranger captain added, "I know he's here in town; I caught a glimpse of him."

Hale explained himself: He had seen Tom sitting in a buckboard which Pepe Moya was driving. Luis Batalla rode his horse alongside them. The trio came into town, turned over their guns to the soldiers, then went by the wagonyard where they stopped for a few minutes. That's when Hale lost contact with them, for they turned about and went toward the south part of town.

"Why, hell, Cap'n," Severn Laycon said, "I ran across Tom English not an hour ago. I was out that way trying to find a safe place to leave Old Sue —that's the name of my mare—and my bedroll, what with the livery stable being full. Several of us staked our horses near a stand of mesquites and left our gear there. It's not too far from the wool warehouse. I saw him come up with the two cowhands you mentioned and go into the warehouse by himself. After a spell he came out, got in the buckboard, and went right by us while we were walking to town. I hollered out to Tom, but I guess he didn't hear me. I noticed at the time that he looked mighty grim."

"Probably thinking about that race," Calvin said.

After Captain Hale left, Calvin said to Severn Laycon, "Tom offered to hire me a few days back. He wants to set up a stud farm at his lower ranch north of town, with the idea of raising purebred Percherons and Thoroughbreds and maybe some Arabians too—just for the hell of it. Naturally, there would be quarter horses and cowponies as well. He has some of his Mexican cowboys who would take care of things but he said he wanted someone like me to be in charge."

"Sounds good to me," Severn commented. "What did you say?"

"My first thought was that the offer was framed in such a way as to be flattering, and like most men I am very susceptible to flattery. This made me decide that my friend English may be more subtle than I first thought. Then I brooded about it," Calvin replied. "I finally told him that I liked the idea very much. However, I took care to explain that I would tinker around with the horses and spend about all of my time with them, but that the very idea of 'work' put my teeth on edge. He said he understood and made the suggestion that I live out there as his guest while I tinkered with the horses—and he would from time to time put money in my bank account. 'Well,' I told him, 'since you put it like that, I believe we have struck a deal.' " Calvin smiled contentedly.

"Didn't know you were an expert with horses," Severn observed.

"My God, man, I'm not. The only thing at which I'm expert is savoring life, but the tragedy is that if I keep doing that in bars it will soon kill me. So I look on this new hobby as necessary for the sake of my health."

The two sat sipping on their drinks. A runty little man began to play the piano that a freighter had recently hauled in from Abilene, Texas, a town which lay about a hundred miles off to the north. The Texas and Pacific Railroad had begun serving Abilene the year before, and a teamster named Earnest Holeman had started a steady drayage line from the depot there to Santa Rita even though he had to deadhead back with an empty wagon.

Calvin Laudermilk said, "Before I begin that tinkering I was talking to you about, I intend to bring my friend Tuck Bowlegs, who is culturally deprived, in here to listen to this man play the piano. I feel reasonably certain that Tuck has never heard such remarkable sounds, and I would enjoy hearing his insightful comments along with his pointed criticisms. Tuck, I need to point out, is a redskin, but he generally considers *us* to be the barbarians."

Severn ignored Calvin's remarks, for something had caught his attention. With a sudden movement he put his glass of whiskey down on the table with a bang. His eyes narrowed as he looked across the room and he hissed, "Damn!"

"What is it?"

"That son of a bitch Milo Studly has just walked in, Calvin, and I don't choose to drink in the same bar with him. Let's head across the street to the Lost Hope Saloon." He shoved his chair back and strode from the room without another word.

Calvin looked perplexed momentarily and then, with a slight shrug, picked up the pitcher of beer with both hands and began drinking from its side. People around him stopped talking as they watched the pale liquid gradually disappear in a long series of deep gulps. He put the pitcher down, empty now of everything except a fragile tracery of foam that etched its side, and looked up. He ignored the awed looks of the bystanders, summoned up a gargantuan belch, and stated, "Waste not, want not." With that Calvin Laudermilk, who had a flair for the dramatic, walked with dignity from the room.

By 2:30 P.M. only the bartender and Milo Studly remained in the Concho Street Saloon. The citizenry of Santa Rita and the disorderly crowd of visitors which an hour earlier had clogged its bars and streets had all gone to the fairgrounds to witness the matched race between the dark stallion, Sam, against the chestnut mare, Epiphany.

Milo Studly sat without drinking at a table at the rear of the saloon, facing the two swinging doors. His large eyes widened slightly as they swung open and a man stood at the entrance, a hand on each door, with the light behind him setting his form out in silhouette against the wintry sky.

The bartender had a broom in his hand as he swept and shoved at the broken glass and debris left from the busy day. He didn't notice the overpowering smell of stale beer and spilled whiskey as he busily whisked a cloud of dirt and dust into the air. He paused a moment, straightening his back, and then said, "I'll be blamed, if it ain't Tom English! Come in." He stood to one side as though trying to usher him toward the bar.

"Could I offer you a drink on the house?"

"Not now, thanks." English apparently was waiting for his eyes to adjust to the dimness of the saloon. He stood at the bar looking at the man who sat alone in the shadows at a back table on the other side of a flickering overhead lamp. He said absently to the bartender, "Have you heard from Joe Case, who used to work here?"

"Why, yes we have. As you may know, he moved to El Paso but he still has family in these parts and I expect he'll be coming through one of these days."

"If you see him, give him my regards."

"I sure will, Mr. English."

Tom turned away and walked to the table. He stopped before it.

Milo Studly said, "I didn't think you were going to show up. I guess you got my letter."

Tom didn't respond to his statement. "You know, you don't have to go through with this."

"You're wrong—I do have to."

Milo Studly's face had turned deathly pale and small beads of fine sweat formed on his long upper lip. "I wrote you to meet me here just before the race; I knew everyone in town would be gathered there to watch it, that they would be out of our way."

The bartender stopped sweeping and stood very still behind a post so he would not be noticed. In the stillness, he could not help overhearing every word they said. With a look of morbid fascination, like a man who goes to witness a hanging, he craned his neck so he could see around the post.

"The deputy is still in town," Tom said, "and the soldiers are all around it."

"We'll find somewhere private," Milo muttered, rising from his chair. "It's time to go get our guns—unless you're going to try to weasel out of the fight," he snarled contemptuously. "The word has spread that you got hurt, but you look fine to me." His voice hardened. "You're going to face me—it has to be your choice if you fight back or not." In a distant way he added, "In time to come, folks will pay attention when Milo Studly rides into a town. Men will stand aside when he walks by after today."

Tom said, "I unlocked the wool warehouse—you know where it is. Not a soul is there; it's empty. There will be no one to stop a showdown."

"Hold on a minute—you know the place—I don't."

"My men will be looking for me; the soldiers will be patrolling," Tom said reasonably as if explaining a suggested course of action to a child. He pointed out, "The wool warehouse is big and it's private. There's as much light there as in this saloon."

"Hell, you'll go in ahead of me and shoot the instant I open the door."

"No, I want you to go in first. It's my understanding that you're looking for a fair fight, face to face, is that the case?"

Milo's voice shook slightly. "That's right."

The bartender saw Tom's face as he turned, and a ray from the sputtering lamp swept across his eyes. They looked as cold as ice, and for an instant they seemed to flash. He heard Tom say, "There's no use talking more. Head for the deputy's office and check out your gun."

Hundreds of people lined the flagged racetrack laid out by the surveyor. Women clutched scarves around their heads and necks and bundled in their wraps against the cold. Men crammed their hats down tight and turned up their coat collars. A motley collection of conveyances, single-seated buggies, fringe-topped two-seated surreys, and dozens of flat-bed wagons had drawn up on either side of the finish line. Children and dogs ran through the crowd, unable to bear the overwhelming excitement of the occasion.

The sharp, unforgettable smell of woodsmoke filled the air, for the waiting people had set fires at more than a dozen points, and they crowded around these flames, holding their hands out, trying to warm them, as their breath caused small white clouds to form around their mouths.

At the starting point Manuelito could be seen having difficulty holding Sam in check. The stallion, which lacked several months of reaching four years of age, had never been exposed to anything like the wildness of the scene, and he pirouetted in alarm, using his hind legs like a pivot, as though he were a dressage horse. The Mexican boy caught hold of the horn of his heavy stock saddle as Sam reared.

Teddie Jakes, at the last moment, had stripped his fancy black saddle with silver conchos from his mare's back and in its place had put on a much lighter flat cavalry saddle. Scott Baker had protested, pointing out that Manuelito already carried an extra ten pounds in his saddlebags, but Teddie said with a great show of righteousness that there had been no agreement as to the types of saddles to be used. With that he handed over his gunbelt to Captain Hale, and removed his heavy coat as well. Teddie stood up slightly from his shortened stirrups and leaned forward, poised for action, putting his weight over Epiphany's shoulders. He held the reins with both hands and in his right he held as well a stiff riding crop. His short, muscular chestnut mare, Epiphany, snorted and moved about under him, rolling her eyes at the sight of the big stallion which curvetted nearby, propelling himself from his reared-up position with a thrust of his powerful hind legs.

"We can't hold 'em any longer," Lieutenant Crocker yelled to Scott Baker, who had been imploring him to wait.

"Don't begin the race without Tom English, damn it," Baker yelled back at the young lieutenant, who had been chosen to be the starter.

Luis Batalla and Pepe Moya rushed up and spoke to Baker in a torrent of Spanish, explaining that Tom had disappeared shortly after they arrived at the fairgrounds. They had looked for him in vain, and had just realized that the buckboard was missing. He had left the fairgrounds.

Shaking his head, totally confused, Scott Baker hollered at the lieutenant, "Go ahead and start the race—he's not to be found."

When Lieutenant Crocker undid the flap of his holster and withdrew his long-barreled Colt, the crowd fell silent in breathless anticipation. The two riders struggled to get their mounts faced forward at the long green ribbon held by men on either side of the track. Then the starting gun exploded.

Sam, startled out of his wits by the six-gun's crash, leaped sideways, knocking several spectators sprawling, but Teddie had tight control of Epiphany and the little mare scampered headlong down the course. Hoarse cries burst from the crowd, sounding like a raucous choir gone out of control.

Manuelito had Sam back on the track and the powerful stallion's long legs pounded as he fell swiftly into a dead run. By this time Epiphany clattered a full twenty yards ahead. A small woman in a gingham sunbonnet screeched in encouragement, "Go like a bat out of the bad place," as the mare whistled past her. She obviously favored her sex in the race.

The stallion's power hurled him in pursuit, and at the two-hundred-yard mark he had narrowed the gap to a scant ten yards and was gaining rapidly. Ahead of them a wagon sat just off the track, and a man in it, overcome by excitement, squalled out an ear-splitting "heeyah" trail-driving screech and flung his hat out before him. Sam leaped sideways, crashing through two slender flag-tipped poles which lined the way. Manuelito pulled on the reins with all his might and veered back to the course. Leaning over with his face almost buried in the flying mane, he slapped his quirt upon Sam's rump.

The stallion's head stretched out and he bolted—hoofbeats rattling faster and faster. Nearing the quarter-mile pole he pulled even with the outstretched tail of the speedy mare.

Calvin Laudermilk, who had without invitation clambered up upon the judge's stand in order to have a good view, rose to his feet, screaming along with all the other observers.

Teddie Jakes looked to his side and saw the stallion's straining head pulling up near his leg. He took his stiff riding crop and for the first time in the race began to strike Epiphany with all his strength. The mare responded, pulling ever so slightly ahead of her soaring pursuer, but then the stud began his inexorable advance again, closing steadily.

The two swept by the judge's stand in a blinding cloud of dust, seemingly in a dead heat, as the crowd went mad.

Teddie Jakes pulled up his exhausted mare but Sam had just begun his race. With Manuelito helplessly hauling back on the reins, the big stud took the bit between his teeth and seemed to fly in great rushing strides as he quickly disappeared over a small hill.

A judge stood on his chair on the stand and as the stallion moved back into sight he cried out, "He's still running hell-bent for election. That's a sight to behold." He stepped awkwardly down from his chair and huddled with the other two judges.

Calvin, standing off to one side, scanned the howling mob of men and also women who threw their hats, clubbed one another on the back, and in general acted as if they had taken total and final leave of their senses. He said to a heaving cowboy who fought through the crowd and crawled up on the stand beside him, "Stand at this vantage point by me, brother, so you will have a better view of your fellow man." The cowboy looked at him through narrowed eyes, apparently wondering if the fat man who spoke so casually upon this epic occasion had gone daft.

The judges, after a heated debate, ruled two to one that the mare, Epiphany, owned by Teddie Jakes had won by a nose. After that, in the pandemonium, Teddie started collecting his winnings, grinning from ear to ear. Amid heated demands for a rematch, he said that nothing would give him greater pleasure, but that the next race was to have a purse put up by sponsors. He explained that he owned both horses now and couldn't very well have a stake race against himself. He walked about the fairgrounds, ignoring the harsh north wind, stuffing money in his pockets.

Calvin Laudermilk labored down the steps of the judges' stand at the approach of Captain John Robert Hale. Speaking to the Ranger, Calvin remarked, "It is my opinion that the best rider, as opposed to the best horse, won this race, although that mare is plenty swift."

"Let's head for town," Hale said, his eyebrows knitting in concern. "We need to locate Tom."

As Calvin mounted his towering Percheron he said to Hale, "This is the first race that one of Tom's horses has lost. I hope that isn't an omen."

"What do you mean?"

"I hope Tom's luck hasn't finally run out," Calvin said.

Jim Boy Irons, a deputy sheriff's star pinned to his heavy jacket, stood on the porch outside his new office, blowing on his hands to try to warm them. From the distance he could hear repeated roars coming from the direction of the fairgrounds. They surged in waves as he stamped his feet impatiently on the board sidewalk, trying to get his circulation going. Sick at heart at being the only man in Santa Rita to miss the horse race, he turned to go inside to the comfort provided by his pot-bellied stove. As he did he heard hoofbeats and the rattle of steel-rimmed wheels cracking over hardened ruts in the street. The deputy squinted his eyes and saw a buckboard rounding the corner and heading directly for him. Moments later it pulled to a stop and Tom English stepped stiffly down from it.

"I can't believe my eyes," the deputy said. "Why aren't you at the fairgrounds?"

"Something has come up."

"I can't imagine *anything* that couldn't wait a few minutes," the deputy stated with emphasis. He led the way into his office and quickly closed the door behind his visitor.

"The damn cavalry abandoned me," Irons complained in a hurt tone of voice. He added, "The lieutenant took his soldiers to maintain order at the track when everyone went out there. They left me here alone to guard against thieves and looters breaking into stores during the excitement, since the town is almost deserted right now. But the very idea of *you* failing to see the big race is beyond me, Tom."

He shook his head in bewilderment before saying, "Well, I guess I can't blame you for not wanting to mingle with a crowd. With that many people around there's always the off chance of one ornery peckerwood who might try something foolish."

Jim Boy Irons hesitated. Most people avoided hinting at Tom's troubled past in front of him, and he felt he might have overstepped the bounds. He gestured with his right hand and said gruffly, "Your guns are hanging from that peg on the wall yonder."

The deputy stood first on one foot and then the other as he waited nervously for Tom English to say something. At last, unable to bear the silence an instant longer, Irons said that he had to go make his rounds—in spite of the cold. With that he left and proceeded on foot down the street, going in the direction of the hardware store with its stock of guns and ammunition. These treasures, Irons calculated, would be the bait which would attract the lawless.

Alone in the room, Tom put on his gunbelt with great difficulty, trying to ignore the stabbing pains sent from his broken right collarbone and his tightly bound left wrist. Minutes passed as he bent over, forcing his fingers to move as he secured the tie-down strings of his scabbards firmly around each leg. Then he pulled out his right six-gun and, wincing, forced it up a little more than hip high. He crossed his left arm under it as a support, then turned, looking at the wall, picking out an imaginary target, and aiming at it.

After all of these years, after so many gunfights, he knew that the best of plans had a way of going wrong. A fundamental rule was to *expect the unexpected.* Tom holstered his Colt with care as he prepared for the unforeseen. Aware of the self-deception, he told himself that his salvation in the past had been a clear head and the ability to make snap decisions. This talent, he rationalized, more than made up for his present handicaps.

Tom English whispered to himself, "Take your troubles one at a time."

Wind whistled in the stove pipe which projected through the roof, and a shutter banged against the window. He felt a prickling at the back of his neck, a warning sensation he'd had so often before, and as a sudden rush of heat swept through him, he focused with great concentration on Milo Studly.

Milo tested the doorknob at the wool warehouse and stood with his back against the wall as the door swung open. He held his six-gun in his right hand, barrel pointing up as he edged to the opening. He glanced in and quickly ducked back; then gathering his courage, he slipped through the door and closed it behind him.

Sliding along the inside wall, Milo's eyes darted about through the gloom. An oppressive odor of wool and lanolin and dust fell over him. He could hear his feet shuffling on the rough boards of the floor, and could hear the wind whining through the eaves of the metal-skinned building. Looking in the small office, he assured himself that it was empty and passed by it. He stopped suddenly, dead in his tracks, staring at something odd.

Down an aisle which led through dark stacks of huge woolbags he saw a yellow light flickering. A spurt of fear jolted in his chest and he felt an extra heartbeat as he wondered, *Has the place caught fire?* The circle of amber and yellow didn't grow as he drew closer, and he saw a burning coal oil lamp set on the floor.

Frowning, he came closer. It had been placed beside a crude wooden staircase which he would not have noticed otherwise. Milo edged up the steps and saw a loft filled with boxes of papers, rusty tools, and the cast-off items that businesses seem to generate and keep rather than throw away. Milo stepped up to the loft and walked forward carefully. The thin boards which made the floor had not been nailed to the rafters and some of them rattled slightly under his weight, but when he stood erect he found he could look down and see the front entrance clearly. Turning around he saw the back door which went out toward the loading dock he'd noticed when he had first circled the building.

Milo hurried down the steps, blew out the lamp, and then went back up to the loft. Making an effort to slow his breathing, to calm his nerves, he stood without moving, swinging his gaze from the front door to the back.

He shifted the heavy revolver momentarily to his left hand while he rubbed his right against his pant leg, drying the sweat from his palm, and then transferred the weapon back. He cocked the hammer with his thumb, hearing a double clicking noise made by the oiled metal.

Milo Studly put his left hand around his right wrist in order to brace it. Then trembling from head to foot, he said to himself, "The sonuvabitch doesn't have a chance."

CHAPTER TWENTY

Milo Studly stood in the darkness of the loft looking down at the gray light which filtered through the windows upon the musty warehouse below. He felt the most overwhelming excitement of his life—a sense that he was invisible and safe—that he had total power. He held his breath as the front door slowly opened. He raised his pistol but decided not to fire; the distance was too great. A man slipped in and disappeared behind the bags of wool. Milo began breathing rapidly and he could feel his heart racing. He shook his head to clear it, and a jolt of exhilaration rippled through him as he thought; *I'm about to kill Tom English.*

Milo crept forward, trying to keep the thin, loose boards under his feet from moving, but one of them broke under his weight with a sharp cracking sound, and he froze with horror. At the same time a sudden gust of wind caused a loose sheet on the tin roof to rattle, and then the open front door slammed shut with a crash. Milo thought, *English wouldn't have heard anything with all that noise.* Moving more carefully, testing each board gradually before putting his full weight on it, he advanced stealthily until he reached the edge where he could have a clear shot at his prey whenever English moved from his cover. Then he stood very still, almost holding his breath.

At that instant a voice from directly underneath the loft said quietly, "Were you planning to shoot me in the back?"

Milo ran across the flopping boards, which chattered against each other until he reached the head of the crude stairs. His breath made sobbing noises as he caught himself. Stifling a moan he slowly leaned out, pointing his six-gun over the edge. A pistol bullet shrilled past his ear before he heard the blast. Shrieking with fear he rushed back to the center of the loft upon the creaking, limber strips of wood. Then it happened: Milo felt himself hurled sideways at the same time that he heard the gun's heavy detonation. His fall caused loose boards to slide in the direction in which his boots skidded, leaving a gaping V-shaped space between them. Another bullet splintered through the fragile wood and the shot rang out, echoing in the warehouse's hollow metal chamber. Milo's body jerked convulsively back and forth, and blood jetted from his upper leg and from his stomach as he kicked and screamed. Howling inhumanly he flopped convulsively, and suddenly his head and shoulders and arms fell through the opening between the boards. He hung there for a frozen instant, dangling head down, mouth wide open, shrieking in agony.

He twisted his body, threshing desperately about in the attempt to escape, and then he dropped in a tumbling fall, landing heavily upon his back and shoulders upon a stack of greasy woolsacks. Milo rolled over, bug eyes popping with horror, mouth wide, and he saw a form ten feet away slowly raising his arm and pointing at him. Somehow his mind still functioned. *I know what to do,* he thought. He hadn't dropped his six-gun, for both hands held it in a death grip. Blood filled his throat, it tasted hot and slick—he felt himself choking on it—he couldn't breathe. *I have to do it now,* ran through his brain. Somehow he leveled the gun and pulled the trigger. The last thing Milo Studly ever saw was the sight of a man being blown backward by his bullet's impact. The last thing he thought was: *My God—I did it.*

The rusty hinges squeaked in protest as the front door to the wool warehouse swung open. Five men waited in the whistling wind of the late afternoon, backs flattened against the wall, standing well away from the opening.

The Ranger captain, John Robert Hale, stepped to the door and called out, "Is anyone in there?"

The loose flap on the roof rattled in the norther's force, and off toward town they heard a cow urgently announcing milking time.

Hale drew his six-gun and the other men followed suit. He stepped to the door and said loudly, "This is the law—we're coming in."

A hundred yards away two very old men stood mutely near the mesquite trees where some horses were tied. These neighbors had elected to play checkers instead of going to the horse race. They had heard and then reported the gunfire.

Hale stepped through the door and moved quickly behind a stack of woolsacks. He saw only dark outlines and shadows, for little sunlight filtered through the overcast sky on this afternoon in early winter. Shuffling noises let him know that the other Ranger, Teddie Jakes, had taken cover at his side. Behind him two sets of footsteps whispered and one set thudded as Luis Batalla and Pepe Moya along with Calvin Laudermilk entered the darkened space. Even after they fell silent, Hale seemed to hear the bell-like jingling of spur rowels.

The Ranger captain stood up and walked cautiously to the door of the office, looked in, and then said, "Light that lantern in there, Teddie, and bring it along."

Moments later they followed the wavering, outstretched circle of light up the center aisle until they reached the two bodies. Teddie held the lantern high and stopped as reflections fell upon the open eyes of Milo Studly.

Milo stared up from the woolsack where he lay spread-eagled. Blood from his stomach and leg drenched the bag beneath him, and a dreadful redness had gushed from his mouth down upon his chest.

John Robert Hale swore softly and then said, "This is Milo Studly, a no-good gunsel I told to get out of town when he tried to goad Tom into a fight a while back." Fear came into his eyes and he forced himself to turn toward the outstretched boots which could be seen not far away.

"Tom?" he called out, walking slowly toward the fallen man. He sank to one knee in the darkness beside him and turned around toward Teddie Jakes, who still stood next to Milo's body, holding the lantern above him as he looked down in fascination.

"Damn it, Teddie," Hale's strong voice boomed out, "bring me some light."

The five men crowded then about the body, looking down in confusion.

"Who in the hell is *this?*" Hale finally demanded.

Calvin Laudermilk finally said, "Well, Captain, it's Walden Doggett from Montana. He led the men who came here to kill Tom English."

Teddie Jakes put down the lantern and holstered his six-gun. Then he pushed his hat back on his head and complained, "I don't understand."

"I don't either," Hale replied.

But Luis, after speaking briefly to Pepe in Spanish, said, "I spoke to this man today." He paused reflectively before continuing.

Luis explained how he had ridden alongside the buckboard which Pepe drove with Tom English as his passenger. Tom had told them that he needed to go alone into the Concho Street Saloon around two-thirty, about half an hour before the race. He had his gold pocket watch with him, Luis mentioned, and during the trip he kept looking at it. They got to town more than an hour early, so Tom had them drive around to pass the time. They happened by the new wagon yard and, Luis related, Tom called out, "Stop here."

"We didn't know what had caught his eye," Pepe said, joining in the story. "He was staring in the wagon yard at a big hombre who wore a long duster." Pepe hesitated, then looked down at the body at his feet. "It was this man," he said, pointing.

"Tom told me to go into the wagon yard to give him a message," Luis said. "I rode my horse through the people and wagons and horses until I got up close to him. Then I said, 'Tom English wants you to know there is an empty wool warehouse about a mile to the south of here. Go down this next road and you'll see it. He said to tell you that it is as good a place as any for a fight, and at three o'clock, when everyone in town is at the horse race, you'll find one there."

Pepe said, "After that he had us bring him here. We waited outside, and when he came back he said, 'We'll see what happens now.' After that we went to town."

The five men slowly walked down the aisle and out of the warehouse. When they reached their horses Teddie Jakes said, "I still don't understand."

"It's beyond me too," Calvin stated. "Come to think of it, this man Milo Studly came in the Concho Street Saloon a short time before I left it. I was drinking with Severn Laycon, who said he wouldn't stay under the same roof with the man."

John Robert Hale mounted his horse and sat there, musing. All of a sudden he began to chuckle, making dry, husky noises, before he said, "Don't you see what happened? My God," he emphasized, "it's so simple that it never occurred to me."

The others looked dumbly at him. Pepe, who had been on foot, rode Sam, the horse which now belonged to Teddie Jakes. The big stud backed and bowed his neck, but Pepe urged him forward with a touch of his spurs until he could hear what was being said.

The captain said, "He was hurt—he couldn't use either hand, and two men waited to face him. Well," John Robert Hale remarked, "I wish he'd called on me or someone for help—but that's not his way." Hale gathered up his reins and said, "It was *a special kind of trap*—with him as the bait— for each man must have fired thinking that he shot Tom English."

CHAPTER TWENTY-ONE

"How long has it been, Tom, since those two scoundrels killed each other in the wool warehouse?" Calvin Laudermilk asked.

"I expect you know the answer as well as I do," Tom replied. "It's May now, so I'd say about four and a half years ago."

"My point," Calvin said patiently, "is that you've had no threats in all this time. And since Jim Boy Irons got Joe Y. Poteet to name him town marshal, there has not been a single incident of gunplay in Santa Rita. And yet you continue to wear those six-guns. Bearing in mind that you never have occasion to use them, I've asked myself why you don't hang them up for good? There is plenty of time for me to spend pondering such questions while I tinker around on the stud farm, and I've come up with three possible answers. First, maybe you feel you need the exercise. I've heard of men lifting iron weights to build up their strength, if you can imagine anything so foolish. Second, it could be that you have become vain as a peacock and think they make you look manly. And third, it could simply be such a habit that you've forgotten you have them on, although this strains credulity."

Calvin sat on Sully's broad back, looking down on Tom, who rode a young bay next to him. In the pasture below them they could see several hundred mares in foal. The two men had been examining two immense draught horses, Shires, which had long hair that looked like curly feathers falling over their hooves and reaching over their pasterns and fetlock joints. The big stud and mare had been shipped from England, courtesy of Joseph St. Claire, the father of Hester Trace. He had recently arrived with the horses and two steamer trunks full of presents for his widowed daughter, who would be marrying John Robert Hale in six weeks' time.

Tom finally replied, "I've never liked the idea of being crowded. Once a man starts backing down, there's no stopping."

"That's not a good answer, but I'll not press the matter further. If you wish to cling to old ways, far be it from me to attempt to dissuade you." Calvin nodded his head knowingly and stated, "You and my crazy redskin friend, Tuck Bowlegs, may not have much of a future, but you've one hell of a past."

"You're wrong there. The only thing I've ever worried about is the future."

"That is my concern too," Calvin said. "It's time to eat. Reckon supper's ready?"

When they had unsaddled, Calvin and Tom trudged together away from the corral. In the west a desert sunset covered the entire horizon with a vivid pink, and in this seeming fire a few brilliant red clouds floated. Pale lavender washed back to the east away from the spectacular display. Calvin paused, lagging behind his companion, and stared intensely at the changing sky. He thought that if an artist painted such a scene, his critics would declare that he had taken leave of his senses. Real life, Calvin decided, can often be far more colorful than earnest, plodding humans are willing to admit.

It pleased Calvin that Tom and his family were spending more time at their new house on the west bank of the Concho, a residence they called Sunny Slope. This gave Tom the opportunity to be with his horses more, and since they lived so close to Santa Rita, Sally and the children could be near their friends. Max Hall kept arguing with Tom that he should build a big house in town just as many of the ranchers were doing, but Tom preferred the country.

On reaching the side yard, Calvin heard the sounds of laughter and conversation from the young people who had come to Rebecca's party. Several gangly boys sat or stood around Tom's fifteen-year-old daughter, whose winsome, dimpled smile came and went as she talked to them. She wore a Mexican dress made of a soft, off-white material with red flowers embroidered around it in circles ranging from the wide hem up to its open neck. Rebecca stood with unconscious grace, her weight on her left foot, the right hip projecting off to one side in a rounded, thoughtless curve. She could be mistaken, he realized with a start, for a woman of twenty.

Calvin held the opinion that the world was a mighty peculiar place—what with children changing from one instant to the next into grown-ups. At least he felt he could take comfort in Ben's having the consideration to remain a child for a while longer. He observed the little boy as he sat at one side, playing with certain of his prized possessions: an old spur and some arrowheads.

Tom and Sally stood near the boy. Sally had her arm carelessly wrapped around her husband's waist, and amusement danced in her eyes as she shifted her gaze from her daughter back to her son.

Well, Calvin thought, in spite of all our mistakes it appears that life does have a way of going on. But, he reasoned, it cannot do so if we starve to death.

"When do we eat?" Calvin demanded.

ABOUT THE AUTHOR

H. B. BROOME is a longtime resident of Texas who grew up in Broome, Texas, and today lives in Arlington. He is the author of two previous Double D Westerns, *The Meanest Man in West Texas* and *Gunfighters.*